CW00405929

# Lost on Main Street

Frank Chambers

Copyright © 2017 Frank Chambers

All rights reserved.

ISBN: 978-1542744331

Copyright © 2017 by Frank Chambers All rights reserved. This book or any portion thereof may not be reproduced or used in any manner whatsoever without the express written permission of the author, except for the use of brief quotations in a book review.

# Prologue

'Where the hell?' Kevin, assistant manager of three weeks is pacing the street outside the bar talking to himself. Inside, the bar is three quarters full, good for a Wednesday, but for how much longer? 'Why this bloody night?' he asked the empty street. It is his first night left in charge and The Alert, the bar's top crowd pullers, are booked to play. Extra staff have been drafted in from the weekend shifts, including the two sisters, Kevin cannot tell apart and can't stand. The sisters who seem to know everything about the local music scene that he does not, and who are not slow in letting him know it.

'Come on,' he pleads, willing every van that approaches to pull into the space he has reserved with two chairs and a plank of wood. Kevin disliked most of the bands that

1

played in the pub but he positively hated The Alert with their smart arsed poster of General Kitchener saying 'Be Alert,' followed by 'Your country needs lerts.' Long haired layabouts were bad enough but university student long haired layabouts were just about as much as Kevin could bear. 'You better do something, it's five to eight.' One of the sisters was at his side.

'I know the bloody time.'

'I'm just saying.' Kevin waits, he knows there will be more. 'They will be drinking up and heading for the Burns Howff if there is not somebody on those boards in ten minutes.'

'Do you think I don't know that. Your blind pal is the only person not staring at the empty stage.'

'I'm just saying, that's all.' The sister turned, made her way back inside and down the stairs to the basement bar, pursued by Kevin.

'What do you suggest I do? If the band does not turn up what can I do about it?'

'I was just saying.'

'I know you were just saying, but what exactly can I do?'

Sister number two meets them at the foot of the stairs, an empty tray in her hand. 'Nobody is ordering any more. They will be off once they finish their drinks.'

'Aye, your sister has just told me that but what can I do about it?'

Sister number two has a possible solution. She hesitates for a moment before deciding to throw Kevin a life line. 'Well there are two guys that used to play in here before their band broke up. They have been in here since six o'clock.'

'And?'

'They have a guitar with them.'

'So?'

'So, we could ask them to play until the band turn up.'

Kevin did not like being bailed out of his difficulty by his nemesis but he had no ideas of his own. 'Are they any good?'

'I don't know what they would be like now, but if this crowd leaves.....' Kevin knew the unsaid words were 'the boss will do his nut.'

'OK. Ask them if they can do a half hour for us.'

Sister number two made her way through the cluster of tables stopping at a skinny kid, long hair, leather bomber jacket ( made for a kid even skinnier than himself ), flared jeans and cowboy boots. Exactly like fifty percent of the crowd.

After a short conversation, sister number two returned with the skinny kid in her wake. 'Mr McGuire. He can do a spot for you if you want.'

'Can I do my own stuff?' the kid asked. Kevin's heart sank.

'Mm. Bands in here do covers son, maybe the odd one or two of their own. You know what the punters are like if you played in here.'

'I know, but I only have an acoustic guitar and the songs we did in the band are too complicated. Anyway I don't really know that many other songs to sing, apart from my own. I only did backing vocals with the band.'

'What about your pal?'

'Oh he can't stay. He has to catch the overnight bus to London.'

Kevin exhaled loudly and closed his eyes. 'Aye OK, do your own stuff, but just till the band turns up. Say a fiver and a drink for you and your pal?'

'Fair enough.'

The skinny kid made his way to the stage while Kevin headed for the back office, thinking it's bad enough listening to the usual shite, but some kid singing his own songs, 'I don't think so.' For Kevin it was Elvis and no one else but Elvis.

# Chapter 1

It was January, it was cold, it was pouring with rain and the number 5 bus was late.

Donny had a decision to make. He could stay where he was, dry under the bus shelter on Kingspark Road, taking his chances on the number 5 eventually turning up, or he could walk the half mile, in the rain, to the Battlefield Rest where he would have the chance of catching the number 6 or the 4, as well as the 5.

Donny chose the latter. Wrong call. He was halfway between two stops when the number 5 sped past. It was not a good start to the evening. Before he reached the Battlefield Rest, a former station on the old tram routes now converted into an Italian restaurant, a number 6 passed, but with his heavy guitar case to carry, he could not run fast enough to catch it.

He reached the stop dripping wet, where he huddled with the other travellers under the inadequate modern shelter, while diners could be spied happily eating and drinking in the warmth and comfort of the capacious former tram shelter beside them. When a bus eventually did turn up, it was another number 5.

Forty minutes late, Donny descended the stairs to the basement of Blackfriars, already knowing he would be last on the list and last on the list meant playing to an audience comprising the compère, a few die-hards and those too polite to leave, before the final act had their turn.

Tuesday night was Songwriters Club open mike night and Donny was a regular. He was also a regular at similar nights scattered across the city, but the Songwriters was his favourite, despite the fact that a band played in the upstairs bar and robbed the Songwriters Club of most of it's potential audience. Nice 'n Sleazy and the Glad Café attracted a bigger crowd at their open mike nights, but it was not guaranteed that you would get on, and if you did, it was usually only the one song. Downstairs at Blackfriars, you got to do at least two.

Pushing open the heavy swing doors at the foot of the stairs was difficult enough while carrying a guitar case, to do it quietly was impossible, and faces turned disapprovingly towards Donny, as he clumsily made his entrance. It looked like a good crowd though, but irrelevant to him as most looked like participants rather than watchers. They would be out the door as soon as they had done their spot, either upstairs to watch the band, or off to catch another open mike. The Songwriters Club's original ethos of mutual support and encouragement had slipped in recent years, Donny lamented.

Already on stage was Paul, another regular and the worst culprit of all. Paul Mallden was a student at Strathclyde University, young, good looking and talented but utterly ruthless. He lived in one of the student residences round the corner on High Street and had no trouble arriving early, often first, to put his name on compère Billy's list. He would then go back to his flat returning just in time for his spot, usually when the audience was at its maximum. When he came down from the stage, he would down his complimentary pint, before disappearing into the night.

'Still raining then?' It was Colette, a rare ally of Donny's in the dog-eat-dog world of the undiscovered singer songwriter.

'Aye, just a bit.'

'I told Billy you were definitely coming tonight and that you have been on last twice recently, so he put you on after me, just before the interval.'

'Thanks, you're a pal. Can I get you a drink?'

'No I'm fine. I am sitting up the back.'

'OK. Can you take my guitar? I want to ask Billy if he can back me.'

Donny and Colette had become good friends, despite being unlikely associates. Donny was nearing forty and easy-going by nature. He earned enough from music to maintain a simple lifestyle and was generally content with his lot. Colette, on the other hand, was a high achiever, accustomed to pushing herself. She was a Doctor at the Royal Infirmary, a fine musician and singer, and still only twenty-five.

After a visit to the bar, Donny located Billy standing at the side of the stage and wandered over. 'Thanks for putting my name down, I waited forty minutes for a bus.'

'No problem mate.'

'Can you back me on one of my songs, a kind of reggae thing?'

'Sure.'

Billy, known as Billy Bongo was a legend in the the local music scene. His reputation, not surprisingly, was gained by taking his bongo drums to open mike sessions and offering his services. It was amazing how much his contribution could enhance the performance of a lone singer guitarist. He was soon much in demand for paid gigs and recording sessions, and although these days his instrument of choice was the cajon, the moniker had stuck.

'Cheers. See you later.' Donny made his way as unobtrusively as possible through the audience and slipped into a seat beside Colette, turned towards the stage and pretended to be interested in the final verse and chorus of Paul's second song.

Polite, if grudging, applause followed the last strum of the guitar and Billy is back on the stage, microphone in hand.

'Mr Paul Malldon, the best thing to come out of Liverpool since the Beatles. Put your hands together, one more time.' More polite applause and a raised arm from the Merseyside minstrel as he stepped down from the stage.

Billy does lay it on a bit thick but everyone laps it up, and they can almost believe they are really in somewhere like the Troubadour club at the height of the singer songwriter boom, with Joni Mitchell or James Taylor lurking in the shadows, checking out the new kids in town. Under Billy's spell, Donny forgets that his wet jeans feel like solid boards strapped to his legs, and that the water cascading from his hair is forming a river flowing down his neck. This was why Donny came to the Songwriters. He was relaxed and mellow in his world.

'Next up tonight, we have a great talent and a big favourite here at the Songwriters. Big hand, ladies and gentlemen. Miss Cathy Riddle.'

A dark cloud descended and enveloped Donny. He could now feel the water running down his back and the burning sensation in his legs from the sodden jeans. It was also painfully clear that he was not in the Troubadour club, and Glenn Frey would not be tapping him on the shoulder saying, I'm putting this band together and we're looking for another songwriter. No, it was most definitely a basement in Glasgow on a wet Tuesday night. Cathy Riddle had that effect on him.

Cathy had been playing the circuit almost as long as Donny, though she was about ten years his junior. She was nice enough, had a pleasant voice and could certainly play the guitar, but her songs, they were something else. To start with there was the subject matter, all female genital mutilation and victims of abuse. Gritty subject matter in a song was acceptable to Donny, but in Cathy's hands it was just so, so depressing. Then there was the music, clumsy chord progressions, leaden rhythms and monotonous melodies. It was surprising how many people needed a smoke when Cathy Riddle took to the stage. Donny did not smoke, so there was nothing else to do but grin and bear it.

When Billy had completed an introduction that Madonna would have been proud of, it was straight into the the first song, without the usual long-winded explanation of how it came to be written, which was some consolation. Eight bar introduction, simple but catchy, then into the first verse. A nice chord progression repeated twice, before ending with the hook. Verse two the same, but you could anticipate the hook coming now and you were waiting for it to arrive, longing for it even, and then into the bridge on the minor chord. It was the kind of song, some say, no one can write any more, being in that classic, timeless mode that the modern songwriter is often too self-conscious and aware of what has gone before, to make it sound natural and spontaneous. It was like something by McCartney or early Elton John, though with a distinctly contemporary feel, no rhyme was contrived and every word fitted effortlessly into the rhythm with nothing forced. Donny did not need the club rules of only original songs to tell him this was not some obscure cover sneaked in. No, material this good does not stay hidden for long, but from Cathy Riddle, that's what Donny could not understand. A fluke perhaps, the product of those nights when the stars all line up for the songwriter and the first chords you strike sound just right, then melodies fit easily on top and words just pop into your head. It was the only logical explanation, a bit of luck, a diamond among the dross.

The second song was even better, a declaration of love, sincere and moving, sung to a lilting melody over a lovely chord progression in A minor. Once again perfect. Cathy left the stage to loud applause and warm congratulations from her fellow songwriters.

'Glad I'm not up next.' Colette spoke for the entire room, apart from the poor sod who was up next.

Billy was back at the mike. 'Cathy Riddle, ladies and gentlemen.' The compère encouraged the audience to keep the applause going by raising both arms, palms facing upward. 'That was tremendous, absolutely tremendous. One more time. Miss Cathy Riddle.' Billy's outstretched arm lead everyone's eye to Cathy, who had returned to her seat, looking a bit embarrassed at all the acclaim.

The night progressed surprisingly well after that. Billy announced that Cathy would do another song before the end of the night, which meant the crowd all stayed. Everyone was desperate to see if Cathy could pull it off for a third time, or would she revert to her usual material. It was difficult to gauge what her peers were hoping for but she was very popular all of a sudden. Even Paul Malldon stayed on, and was the first to move in on the Club's new celebrity. If Cathy's star was on the rise then he would latch on to it, if he could. At the end of the night, others had followed Paul's lead and a small crowd congregated around Cathy's table. Colette and Donny headed for the stairs.

'Time for one before we head?' Donny asked.

'Why not. I'm on nights for the rest of the week.'

The pair entered the upstairs bar where the Shivering Sheiks were announcing their final number, 'Its All In The Game', and that they would be joined on stage by a guest singer. The crowd had already thinned out a bit, so there was some space at the bar.

'Pint of Best and a Lime and Soda.'

'Well, what did you think?' Colette asked.

Donny sucked in air then let it out slowly, his cheeks bulging. 'Well I did not expect her to do it a third time, that's for sure. I must admit that was three very good songs. No idea where they came from, but three very good songs.'

'Maybe she is just getting better'.

Donny tilted his head and stared at Colette, his eyes open wide. 'All of a sudden after ten years. I doubt it.'

The pair spotted an empty table and, once the drinks

arrived, took a seat as the Sheiks struck their final chord.

'Do you know that was written by a Vice President of America?'

'What was?'

'The song the band just played, the tune was written by Charles Dawes, who was Vice President in the nineteen-twenties. Someone else added the lyrics in the fifties. He is also a Nobel Prize winner.'

'How do you know all this stuff?'

'Well while you were filling your head with irregular bowel movements, I was filling mine with music trivia.'

'Very funny, Donny. Now back to Ms Riddle. Perhaps she has been working with someone, plenty of songwriters work as a team.'

'There is nothing of Cathy in those songs, nothing whatsoever. The question is, is she simply lying when she says they are her songs, or has the real writer given them to Cathy to pass off as her own. If the latter is the case the question is why?'

'Perhaps they thought that they didn't have the right image to attract the record companies, so they let someone else perform the songs. You are always saying that it's the writer that makes all the money.'

'Good point but why choose Cathy Riddle? She's not exactly Beyonce is she?'

'That's a bit cruel. Anyway why are you so annoyed about Cathy's songs? Sounds like green cheese to me.'

'I'm not annoyed and I'm not jealous. I'm just curious, that's all.'

'It would be interesting to see if she has any more right enough. We might find out next week.'

'If she comes back, that is.'

After they downed their drinks, Colette gave Donny a lift back to his flat on the South Side before she headed home to the West End. Nothing more was said about the Songwriters Club's new star. Colette had a good gig coming up on Saturday night, and she filled Donny in with all the details during the fifteen minute drive.

Cathy however was the only thing on Donny's mind as he climbed the stairs and turned the key in the door of his top floor flat.

# Chapter 2

Inside the flat Donny put the kettle on, then opened his guitar case and placed his guitar on its stand, before putting the case away in a cupboard. It was good to have it near at hand, so he could pick it up, whenever the notion struck.

Donny liked his flat and liked living in Mount Florida. It was not as trendy as the West End or the Merchant City. Not even trendy for the South Side where most of the biz was centred on Shawlands about a mile away. For Donny however it had music credentials, and that was important to him.

His bedroom window overlooked the house on Carmunnock Road where Alan McGee, founder of Creation records and the man who discovered Oasis, was brought up. Primal Scream's front man Bobby Gillespie was raised just round the corner. The pub across the road once featured a house band consisting three former members of The Sensational Alex Harvey Band plus Dan McCafferty of Nazareth, both Scottish supergroups of the seventies. Then there was Hampden Park, home of Scottish football, but also a major concert venue which was just along the road. Donny had paid to see Bruce Springsteen, U2, Oasis and The Red Hot Chilli Peppers, and for free he had watched The Rolling Stones, The Eagles and many others through the west tunnel, a secret viewing point, known only to local music fans. Donny had also found out that folk classic and contender for Glasgow's national anthem, The Jeely Piece Song, had been penned nearby, when local writer Adam McNaughton viewed the new high rise flats in Castlemilk from his window.

Yes, the area had a musical heritage and Donny liked to suck in that air, though he had long since given up on emulating any of these local heroes. He was a good musician and had a strong voice but, as a performer, he was just not memorable, and he knew it. There was nothing to set him apart from the crowd, nothing new or original, and of course he was now well past the age where he could launch a career as a pop star. His love was music nevertheless and it did provide his livelihood. He played guitar and sang in a wedding/function band which was mostly just Saturday nights and he taught guitar during the week. There was also the occasional gig, playing covers in pubs. At least he could say he was a professional musician, which suited him fine. No early rises, no clock to watch and no one to answer to.

Donny did still have ambition though, a burning ambition in fact, one that consumed most of his waking hours and one that cost him the few relationships he'd had. That ambition was to pen a classic song, preferably also a hit, but foremost a classic, one that would stand the test of time. To further this ambition Donny had embarked on a course of study, equal to any masters degree. He had amassed a collection of books on the subject that filled the shelves in his living room, The Art of Songwriting, Ideas for Songwriting, Songwriters on Songwriting, The Secrets of the Beatles, The Songwriters Handbook, Beating Writers Block, Unlocking the Mystery of Songs, The Songwriters guide to Collaboration. The list went on and on. There were rhyming dictionaries and books on popular phrases and quotations. Books like How Music Works, Understanding the Language of Music and many others on music theory. Then there were the biographies, everything from Life by Keith Richard to Irving Berlin and Woody Guthrie, shelf after shelf, a dozen on Dylan alone. Added to these were the audio and video material, documentaries recorded from TV, interviews recorded from the radio, anything that might provide a clue to the secret of songwriting. All these resources were studied intently in a quest to uncover that elusive magic formula needed to construct a great song.

On top of this there were the numerous songwriting courses and workshops he had attended. Week long residential marathons where very earnest but mostly talentless posh kids would scribble away, either alone or in revolving collaborations, by day, then perform their creations in the evening to a collection of nodding heads too well brought up to offer any meaningful or constructive criticism.

When not actually in the process of writing songs, Donny passed his days recording demos when he could have taken on more students, and evenings were devoted to trying out new material at open mike sessions when he could have been chasing down more paid gigs. Songwriting was his passion, the one subject he knew more about than almost anybody else, which was why he could not get Cathy Riddle out of his head.

He made himself a cup of tea and checked his emails to see if any of the demos he had sent off recently had generated any interest. They had not.

When Donny headed to bed he couldn't sleep, for he knew something, that in all likelihood, no one else in the city's music community could know. Cathy Riddle played no part in the writing of those songs. She simply did not possess the skills, or know how, to produce work of such quality. Donny understood the evolutionary process a songwriter goes through en route to penning that perfect song. He also knew Cathy. Her songs had not improved, musically or lyrically in all the time she had been coming to the Songwriters club. There was absolutely no chance she had worked out the elusive formula in the past four months, for that was the last time he had seen her perform and that was most definitely the old Cathy. What was really keeping him awake though was the knowledge that somewhere in the city, there might be an undiscovered talent, someone flying under the radar, someone better than himself he freely admitted, but who was it, and why oh why were they hiding behind Cathy Riddle.

Donny woke late on Wednesday morning. There was only one text message on his phone. It was from Colette and simply said 'give me a call when you wake up'. He went through to the kitchen and put the kettle on to boil then scrolled down his contacts for Colette's number.

'Hi, it's Donny. You OK?' Colette sounded breathless.

'Yeah I'm fine. I'm in the park. Been for a run.'

'You got time to talk?'

'Yeah I was about to stop anyway.' Colette had completed five laps of a circuit within Kelvingrove Park, about six kilometres in total, something she did regularly, mornings if she was working the day shift, late afternoon when she was on nights.

'You said to phone.'

'Thought I would do a bit of research for you. It turned out to be dead easy, its all on her Facebook page.'

Donny didn't really do Facebook. He knew the need for self promotion in his line of work but also realised that with his infrequent posts, detailing his modest successes, he was in fact advertising to the world his lack of progress. ' What did you find out?'

'You can check for yourself but basically everything seems to have changed for Cathy, since two months ago. She has put up a video of herself at the Butterfly and Pig doing one of the songs she did last night. It has been viewed nine hundred and sixty four times and there are loads of comments. There is also a mention of a session on Celtic Music Radio, it was two weeks ago, but you can still listen to it on the internet. I haven't tried that yet. Seems she has been to some other open mikes , again loads of favourable comments. Things like, 'loved your songs' and 'hope you will be back next week,' but everything started two months ago. Before that, nothing.'

'OK thanks, I'll check it out. Bye.'

The kettle had come to the boil but Donny ignored it, he had a better idea. He would quickly get washed and dressed, then take his laptop to Arturo's, a coffee shop and deli, adjacent to Hampden Park. There he could take advantage of its WIFI and the invigorating powers of its coffee.

There was indeed plenty of information to be found on Cathy's Facebook page. Donny could work out she had done seven or eight open mike sessions, had a demo played on BBC Radio Scotland and played that live session come interview on Celtic Music Radio. Each had generated favourable comments. There was also mention of a gig in the upstairs room of The Vale, a pub next to Queen Street station. Donny remembered this occasional music venue well. He had played at one of these nights, five pounds at the door with each of the three or four acts getting a cut. Everyone entering was asked who they had come to see, and that artist received two pounds out of the five. Colette and her friend Tom had come along to lend some support and Donny had paid them in. It was a good night, two bands and two singer songwriters and the place was packed. After Donny had done his spot, sandwiched between the two bands, the promoter tapped him on the shoulder then dropped eight pound coins into his hands, an overall loss of two pounds. He wondered if Cathy would fare any better.

Another coffee was ordered, headphones connected to the laptop, then Cathy Riddle Celtic music radio was typed into Google.

Cathy had played the same three songs she did the night before plus one other, equally as good. In between songs she was asked the usual questions about what motivated her to write and the meaning of the lyrics. Cathy was vague in her reply but songwriters generally are, especially the good ones, they either don't want to reveal their secrets or they fear that if they analyse things too much, it might break the spell and their powers will vanish. When compared to the hundreds of interviews Donny had listened to, he had to admit Cathy's answers sounded much the same. There was also the dreaded question on how the career was going. This question always made Donny cringe any time some local hopeful got time on the radio. Upcoming gigs in minor venues were made to sound like a world tour and the meagre air play granted to their self produced CD was equated to cracking the daytime playlist on Radio 1.

Cathy in fact came across rather well, stating straight away that she did not have any gigs planned at the moment, and cleverly said that Celtic Music Radio was the first station to pick up on the demos she had sent out. This last comment perked up the presenter no end, and she took the opportunity to confirm the station's policy of promoting local talent, followed by a dig at the big boys for missing an opportunity. That section of the program was then wound up with gushing praise and an appeal to any promoters listening, to take note. 'Cathy Riddle, can't wait to see her live in concert and remember you heard her first here on Celtic Music Radio 95FM.' It was then straight into some fiddle tune, as Donny clicked the cross on the top corner of the screen.

Frustratingly, the interview gave no clues to the identity of the writer nor did further scrutiny of her Facebook page. The fact that Ms Riddle was pulling off the deception with ease only heightened Donny's curiosity.

There were no other avenues for Donny to explore, so he wasted half an hour surfing the football forums on the internet, finding mostly transfer speculation and abuse, or banter to put a positive spin on it, between rival fans. It was then back to his flat to tidy up, for this was a working day with four students due for lessons.

When Donny first placed an advert offering guitar lessons in the local newspaper he expected to be contacted by parents eager to give their offspring another of those opportunities that they themselves did not get. It turned out that those who contacted him were mostly adults, ages with himself and some considerably older. People in fact who did not get the opportunity when they were younger, but now had the time and the money to remedy the situation. They included two school teachers, a nurse, an accountant, a civil engineer, a couple of stay-at-home mums, a north sea oil worker and a number of early retirees. There was also a handful of older secondary school pupils and university students. Some liked to come as a group with a bottle of wine, where the lesson played second fiddle to the socialising. Most would linger long after their time was up to chat and all had become friends.

Every couple of months, Donny would host a music night for his students and his musician friends in the back room of a bar on King Street. Donny was a good host and organized proceedings, so that everyone felt comfortable. The chords to some well known standards would be distributed in advance, so those less confident could practice. The evening would kick off with Donny or one of the experienced musicians doing a couple of songs and the rest joining in, when they were ready. Everyone loved these nights. For the musicians, it was like a gig with a particularly appreciative audience and for the beginners, a taste of what it is like to be a performer. Everybody got to know each other and Donny became the epicentre of an expanding social network of like minded-people.

First up today was Kenny, the North Sea oil worker, who

was completely different to any of Donny's other pupils. He worked two weeks on the rigs, followed by two weeks off. He would come twice each week when at home, and practice what he learned during any free time that he got back on the rigs. The truth was that Kenny was now just as good as Donny on the guitar but he liked coming for lessons. None of his friends were into music and the time he spent at Donny's was the only chance he got to play with another musician or to talk about music.

Kenny made good money on the rigs and had bought himself a vintage Gibson 330 electric guitar to supplement the Yamaha acoustic he had started on. The Gibson was an object of beauty and Kenny had confided in Donny that it cost him three thousand pounds from a guitar shop in the Trongate. Despite twenty years experience, the teacher had no idea that guitars existed at such a price, apart from very rare models, or one previously owned by someone famous. Donny was not at all sure if his pupil was telling the truth, so much so that he made a special trip to the city centre music store to check out Kenny's claim. To Donny's amazement it was true. There were numerous guitars costing that price and higher on display in locked cabinets, and an assistant confirmed that they had no trouble selling them, many to people in the oil industry.

Kenny always came in the afternoon, evenings were for his mates. Five-a-sides then the pub, Ibrox to see Rangers then the pub, or just the pub. Donny doubted any of Kenny's mates knew he had learned the guitar. That was a different compartment of his life, like his work or his wife and daughter. It was hard keeping up with Kenny who was really past the stage where someone still took lessons, but

Kenny did not have the time or the inclination to organise his own continuing development. Donny would scour the internet for tabs of guitar parts or learn them himself straight from the record, before teaching Kenny

The door bell rang at ten minutes to two. Donny knew it would be Kenny, he was always early.

*'Aw right?'*

'Hi Kenny, come in. How are you doing?'

*Don't ask. Went straight tae the Horse Shoe Bar fae the station yesterday. Ah had already tanned six cans on the train doon fae Aberdeen so ah had a bit o' a heid oan me when ah woke up this mornin'.'*

'You OK for your lesson?'

*'Aye, nae danger. Nipped intae the Clockwork fur a reviver afore ah came up.'*

'Is that your Yamaha you've brought?'

*'Aye, ma heid's no' up tae the electric the day.'*

This scuppered Donny's plans somewhat. He had learned all the lead parts in 'The Sultans of Swing' for Kenny but you can't really bend the strings enough on an acoustic.

'We could do a bit of Django Reinhardt.'

*'Whit?'*

'Its gypsy guitar style.'

*'Sure. Ah'll gee it a go.'*

Django Reinhardt was Donny's standby for his better pupils if he had failed to prepare in advance or if he still had some time left at the end of a lesson. The gypsy guitarist only had three working fingers on his left hand after suffering burns in an accident so had to develop his own unique style. It was all about feel and rhythm and was great fun to play. Donny put Reinhardt's version of Sweet

Georgia Brown on the CD player for Kenny to listen to, then looked out his well thumbed tab sheets before passing a very pleasant hour. It was Kenny that noticed the time.

*'That's jist aboot three.'*

'Oh right. Do you want to work on this or go back to the Dire Straits next time?'

*'Up tae you.'* That was the thing with Kenny he always left it up to Donny. He did not want to think too much. That was what he paid a teacher for.

'Better go back to the Sultans then.' Best keep Django in reserve was what Donny was thinking.

*'Nae bother. See ye in Friday then?'*

'Sure Kenny.'

Once Kenny had paid up, Donny saw his pupil to the door. There was time to check his emails and make a cup of tea before the next lesson, two sixth year pupils from Kingspark Secondary, who came together straight from school.

The final pupil of the day was Diane, a social worker who was due at seven thirty. However she phoned to cancel at half five, rearranging to come the next day. Cancellations were an occupational hazard and a source of frustration, but Diane had freed up the evening for Donny, and he was secretly pleased.

# Chapter 3

Seven months previously.

Stuart stared at the last of the five A4 size pages prepared for his perusal. The only sound in the room was the gentle hum of the air conditioning unit as it efficiently countered the August heatwave outside. On the opposite side of a clutter free desk, his accountant sat with his hands clasped and his mind on his next appointment, as his client tried to digest the information in front of him. The summary showed that in the last accounting period, royalties for Stuart's early work had slowed to a trickle. Even 'Over The Castle Wall', he was shocked to read, brought in less than five thousand dollars, the lowest since it was a number one record in nineteen seventy-nine. Everything, including co-writes, production and artist royalties amounted to one hundred and fifty two thousand dollars and thirty two cents. Fees for production and session work added another ninety three thousand. More than enough for most people Stuart realised and enough for himself at one time, but not now. It did not even cover his office expenses. From his inside pocket, he removed the most recent statements for his business and personal bank accounts, and passed them to the man opposite who appraised the documents keenly, making the occasional note. It was not a comfortable experience for the client.

'Income quarter of a million, expenditure one and a quarter million. Result misery, as Mr Micawber might say.' The accountant stared blankly at Stuart, he did not laugh at the joke.

Stuart had in his working life performed on, written or produced over one hundred hit records and, although some royalties were still coming in, they were now no longer sufficient to cover current commitments. The meeting ended with polite small talk and a limp handshake.

The news was a bit of a blow certainly but not entirely unexpected. Royalties had fallen every year for the past ten and in recent years other earnings from music had began to dry up. Stuart had not said anything to his wife, he did not know how. Despite his foreboding that this year the news would be particularly bad, he still said nothing. He and Heidi had been together for twenty years and money had never been a problem. Back then royalties were never less than a million and Stuart was still earning double that annually, as a producer and musician. Economise was not a word in his or Heidi's vocabulary. Now money worries were keeping him awake at night. It was not knowing how Heidi might react that terrified him. Then there were the kids to consider. They had only known good times, how could he take that away from them.

Stuart left the building and crossed Hollywood Boulevard, heading for the parking lot, noticing the Capital Records tower in the distance. It reminded him that what he needed was another hit, if that was the appropriate term these days. Easier said than done. He remembered the early days working in London when, if he saw someone dressed in an outlandish style he had never seen before, he would always talk to them and try to find out what music they were listening to. On occasion, he had even followed them to discover if there was some hip new club he hadn't heard about. It could have been the start of the next shift in musical tastes. That's how it was done back then, find out what the kids wanted, then give it to them quick, before somebody else did. But that was then, he had no intention of chasing the latest fad these days, he would not know where to begin. There were a few irons still in the fire, he reassured himself. Some long shots perhaps but desperate times required desperate measures.

Stuart was tired, and once back in the car, he closed his eyes for a few moments. He hardly slept the night before, anticipating an awkward encounter with the accountant. It really is true, he was beginning to realize, that people are embarrassed to meet you, when you are down in this town. Tonight, sleep would be even harder to come by. He could take a pill of course, that was once his answer to most things but not any more. Heidi had embraced all things Californian, which meant Stuart had too. This meant healthy eating, plenty of exercise in the outdoors, moderate amounts of alcohol, wine excepted, and a predisposition for natural remedies. A book Stuart decided would be his natural remedy for insomnia, it was what always worked for him as a teenager back in Glasgow where he would read in bed till he eventually fell asleep. It worked then, why not now. There was a book store on Sunset just a mile from the house, he would call in on the way home.

Pleased that he had made a decision Stuart opened his

eyes, started the engine and then exited the parking lot.

Ten minutes later Stuart's beautifully restored sixty-nine Mercedes convertible turned into the car park of Tower Records, the book shop was just across the road. Inside the shop he spotted a table with a sign saying New Releases. Stuart went over and started picking up books at random to check out the reviews on the back cover. If it did not have a review he put it back. One particular title caught his eye. 'The Morelli Murders'. It was the name Morelli that attracted him. Morelli's Ice Cream was one of his earliest memories. The shop sat at the bottom of the tenement that he lived in as a child. Stuart picked up the book, there were no reviews but he started to read it anyway. At the end of the second page he decided to buy.

. . . . .

It was past nine on Thursday morning before Colette returned home from her night shift at the Royal Infirmary. It was easy to find a parking place, which was the one advantage to working nights. Colette manoeuvred her Land Rover into a double space beneath her front windows. The station wagon conversion was not the most suitable car for the crowded streets of Glasgow's West End, where a resident's permit did not guarantee that any spaces would be big enough to accommodate the seven seater. The vehicle was even less suited to the car parks at the Royal Infirmary, but it was not purchased with the city in mind. Eleven thousand pounds for a vehicle entering its thirteenth year with more than one hundred thousand miles on the clock would seem like madness to most urbanites, but

Colette was not a typical city dweller. Much as she loved living in the city, she also liked the outdoor life. Wild camping in the Cairngorms, mountain biking in the woods outside Peebles or walking the hills of Argyleshire where her family owned a cottage, five hundred metres up a steep dirt track, high above Loch Craignish. It was during these weekend pursuits that the Land Rover proved its worth. Replacement front seats, an upgraded heater and a new stereo system, complete with iPod connection, ensured none of the motoring comforts were sacrificed.

Colette was exhausted as she climbed the stairs to her first floor apartment which overlooked Kelvingrove Park with views to Glasgow University in the west and Park Terrace, sitting high above the rising slopes of the park to the north. It was the junior doctor believed an excellent place to live, a quiet and peaceful retreat yet within easy reach of all the restaurants, bar and shops that the West End had to offer.

Once inside, Colette headed straight for the bedroom. It had been a hectic night in the Coronary Care Unit with two emergency admissions, one of which had to be taken down for surgery at 4.30am and had not returned to the ward, before the end of the shift. Before getting into bed Colette checked her texts and emails. There was nothing that couldn't wait.

The previous afternoon, Colette had listened to Cathy's radio session. Though she did not possess Donny's obsession, writing songs and performing them remained her principle activity outside of work and she had come to appreciate just how difficult it was to compose a great song.

Having studied Cathy's broadcast, Colette had no hesitation in concluding that she had heard some very good songs, perhaps even great songs. She also agreed with Donny that it was extremely unlikely that Cathy was the writer, at least not on her own. Colette had sent a text to her friend telling him she was now every bit as curious as he was.

For Colette, there was a number of advantageous possibilities in unmasking the mystery writer. First she could suggest a co-write, see if some of that magic might rub off on her own songs. Second was the chance to ask him or her to write something exclusively for herself. Thirdly, the writer might be persuaded to grant permission for Colette to record the songs already out there. Donny had explained the copyright laws and she knew the writer retained the right to nominate, who released the first commercially available rendition of a song. Once released, anyone could cover it of course, as long as they paid the royalties to the writer, but the first person to record a song was always accorded the status of the original artist.

Yes, finding the mystery writer, Colette realised, could be very much to her advantage. It would be exactly the same for Donny of course but Colette knew her friend would never have thought of that, which perfectly illustrated the quality that endeared him to her so much, but also the one that frustrated her the most.

Colette emerged from her bedroom at few minutes past past four with daylight already fading. She had been noticing that the long winter nights were receding as she did her regular circuit of the park in the mornings and was able to at least catch a glimmer of daylight, when she finished the day shift at the start of the week. This afternoon however looked bleak, a heavy sky threatened snow and when she viewed the park from her sitting room window, it was devoid of people. Even the ever resilient dog walkers were conspicuous by their absence. It would not put Colette off however, her daily run was a ritual that was missed only under exceptional circumstances.

It was almost twenty hours since she had eaten anything substantial, so Colette went into the kitchen to pour some fruit juice and microwave a bowl of porridge, a proper meal would be prepared after her run. While she ate she checked her iPhone.

There were three messages to deal with, one from her mother inviting her for dinner on Sunday, one from Donny saying to get in touch when she got the chance and one from the drummer of rhythm and blues band, the Dexies, confirming the pick up time for Saturday's gig, though on this occasion they would be billed as Heart of Glass, a Blondie tribute act, fronted by Colette.

The idea of doing the tribute thing occurred to her after she had heard at work that a young psychiatrist from Edinburgh was doing a Debbie Harry act, and had even been featured on TV. As a tribute act was already a case of plagiarism, Colette had no qualms about copying her idea. As it turned out, there were nearly as many Blondie tributes as Elvis impersonators, but a call to an agent confirmed there was still plenty of work to go round, as long as you looked the part, he added. Colette did look the part. A blonde wig, some black eye make-up and a short black and white striped dress and she was transformed. The songs were easy for her to sing, and Debbie Harry's mannerisms, simple to mimic. All she needed was a band.

An ad was placed on Gumtree for musicians and Alec, drummer and organiser of the Dexies, responded saying he had a full band ready to go. They would back her on tribute nights while continuing to do their own thing the rest of the time. It seemed the ideal solution, so Colette agreed to meet up. The guys in Dexies she observed could easily pass for the musicians in Blondie, but that would be as the members of Blondie might look today not as they looked in their seventies heyday. Alec however pointed out that everyone would be looking at her. The agent had suggested as much, so Colette agreed to join the guys, reducing the average age of the band by eight years in the process.

A text would suffice for Alec and the same for her mother, but she decided to call Donny.

'Hi Donny. It's me. Anything to report?' Donny had not been letting the grass grow under his feet.

'I have transcribed the lyrics to the four songs so I can examine them for clues. I put the titles Cathy had used into Google, to see if anything came up. It didn't. Nor has alternative titles or quotes from the lyrics, so I think we can eliminate the possibility of the songs being stolen from some obscure source.'

'But that's just the lyrics, there is also the melody. Cathy could have taken that from another song.'

'True, but how can I search for a tune if I don't have a title.'

'I have an app on my iphone.'

'How do you mean?'

'You just play a section of a song and it comes up with its name.'

'No. That only works for commercial recordings.'

'Still worth a try.'

'You would be wasting your time. Anyway, Cathy has been busy in the past twenty-four hours. According to her Facebook, she has declined a gig at the Vale. There has been some further radio play for her demo, seems like just local stuff from the comments. However, the most interesting thing is Cathy has announced she will be appearing on the Danny Kyle stage at Celtic Connections.'

Celtic Connections is Glasgow's midwinter festival of Scottish traditional music and anything, no matter how loosely, connected to it. Hence the name. The Danny Kyle stage is a program of free concerts, billed as a showcase for emerging talent. It is always well attended and can be a great launching pad for an artist, because of the publicity it can generate. Spots are much coveted but difficult to get and it has been known for musicians from as far away as North America to travel at their own expense, to perform for twenty minutes, unpaid, so they can put 'appeared at Celtic Connection' on the CV, such is the international reputation of the festival.

'When is she on?'

'Tonight. I am just about to leave. Do you want to meet me?'

'I can't. I need to get some practice in for that gig on Saturday. I'll call you later to hear how it went.'

It was Cathy rather than Saturday's gig that was on Colette's mind as she ran her usual circuit of the park as darkness descended. The tribute nights were great fun and the best paid work she got as a musician, but it was only a couple of gigs a month and would never lead to anything better. Hooking up with a really good songwriter, on the other hand, could be the passport to that elusive recording contract. The problem was someone seemed to have got in there first and had at least a two month start. She would never say it out loud but Colette shared Donny's opinion that Cathy Riddle was an unlikely choice by someone as the vehicle in which to deliver their creations to the world. She was not the greatest singer around, not the prettiest, not the youngest and she lacked stage presence. Cathy's recent successes were down to the quality of the songs alone, Colette reasoned, not anything else. However, a buzz was certainly building, a momentum that could soon be unstoppable. Time was short if this fledgeling phenomenon was to be halted. The question for Colette was how?

# Chapter 4

Three months previously

Geordie stared with disdain at the envelope in the young man's hand, widened his eyes slightly, and nodded almost imperceptibly. It was enough to indicate that the bearer should place the envelope on the table. No words were spoken. The young man did as was intimated, turned and left the room. Geordie knew the small package would contain exactly five hundred pounds, there was no need to check. With a dismissive wave of the hand, someone picked up the envelope and took it away. The paltry sum embarrassed Geordie as did its origins. Since this particular revenue stream had opened up, he had collected six thousand pounds. It would all go to charity he had decided, for he neither needed the money, nor wanted it. There was an irony here because that's where it had come from in the first place.

Begging in the street was an unregulated industry and one that was expanding fast in the city. Little surprise then that somebody would step in, where the authorities feared to tread. It was not Geordie that had assumed that role but he now felt it necessary to intervene. If left unencumbered by tax or regulation, these entrepreneurs in this new sector would grow and grow and would soon have the resources to consider expansion into the more established areas of the black economy, his areas. Geordie decreed that a fifty percent levy on the top earners was appropriate. Top earners were at liberty to recoup their losses, by setting the tariff for those further down the chain.

Interventions like this, Geordie knew, were a necessary part of maintaining the status quo in the fragile structure of which he occupied a pre-eminent position. Similar action had to be taken with the very lucrative employment market for illegal emigrants, for example. There was always something new coming along and you had to be vigilant, though it was not always possible to clip the wings of these new entrants to the market quickly enough, unfortunately.

Even within his own camp however, there was some disquiet about moving in on street begging. His associates understood the reasons why it had to be done but it still felt wrong. Geordie was keen to show his troops, as well as anybody else taking an interest, that it was not about the money, it was just business. To this end he had taken a table for ten at a boxing bout to be staged in a city centre hotel. The event was in aid of a hostel for the homeless, facing closure. He would not go to the event himself but he would send some of his team and all of the six thousand pounds. It was the ideal opportunity to redirect the money to where it should have gone in the first place. If the public used its common sense instead of taking the easy option, men like him would not need to step forward to sort out the mess. That was how Geordie saw things. His boys would no doubt return with the customary haul of signed footballs and old firm team shirts from the ubiquitous charity auction. Such items were always useful as gifts to keep people sweet and more effective than money for securing casual favours. So not a complete write down for the six thousand pounds.

Business concluded for the day, Geordie rose from his chair put on his coat and prepared to leave. In the room next door a team of girls were cold calling the elderly with the promise of loft and cavity wall insulation that would come with a fifty percent government grant. The fact that the cost would be double the price you could get from any local company, was not mentioned of course. As the completely innocent girls (Geordie always used naïve young girls for this purpose) further enticed the gullible with the promise of a lifetime guarantee, and the assurance that the company were fully registered with all the relevant trade organisations, they had no idea they would soon be out of a job. So too, would be the man the girls all assumed owned the company, the man that drove a new white BMW four wheel drive and called them all pet. No, the government scheme is coming to an end and the inland revenue, the VAT man and a multitude of others will be pressing for long overdue payments. It was time to move on.

Geordie left the building unnoticed by any of the workers and made his way to a four year old dark blue Volvo. He will not be back. The bank accounts were already empty and a misogynistic former brickies labourer will be left alone to face the music, for Geordie's name appears nowhere on any company documents. There would be one more man in the city with good reason to hate him,

Geordie accepted. One more name on a very long list.

. . . . .

Donny decided he would use the train to get him to the city centre. Three commuter lines passed through Mount Florida station, so you never waited long for a train, and they could get you into town in twelve minutes which was just as well, as he was running late. He had two lessons that afternoon and both lingered, leaving him little time to study the lyrics of Cathy's songs. Only one showed any promise, being about a place rather than about feelings or relationships. It was titled 'Main Street' and had a few specific references that he could research when he got back.

It was almost five before Donny left Central Station and made his way to the top of Buchanan Street. It was five past before he began to climb the steps that lead to the Glasgow Royal Concert Hall. Inside the building, he could hear the hum of voices coming through the doors of the exhibition hall opposite. As usual the place was full, three hundred canny Glaswegians and tourists taking advantage of the free entertainment. The Danny Kyle stage attracted an older crowd than other events at the festival due to its early start and, unusual for any gig in Glasgow, there was no queue to get a drink. Someone was on stage introducing the first act. It was not Cathy, so Donny headed for the bar and ordered a pint. When the five pound note he held in his hand did not cover the cost he understood the lack of said queue.

Donny spied an empty seat, took his valuable drink and settled down to enjoy the evening, viewing the stage over a sea of grey and bald heads. Two young lads were first up and one of them leaned into the mike.

'My name is Ross and this is Cameron and together we are, Ross and Cameron'. Despite the uninspiring stage name they were amazingly good, one on fiddle, the other on guitar, playing a blend of traditional influenced tunes and jazz. A sort of Gaelic Stephane Grappelli and Django Reinhardt. Just the thing to get the crowd warmed up, they vacated the stage to rapturous applause. Next up was a Skiffle group, comprising guitar, double bass, washboard and harmonica and again the standard was high. They were seasoned pros about double the age of the first pair and kept the audience engaged with their quirky style and fine musicianship, particularly from the harmonica player. They also finished their set to enthusiastic cheering.

A short interlude followed as the stage was prepared for the next act which looked like an amplified band, not the usual thing for the Danny Kyle stage. Donny thought he recognised someone supervising the equipment being set up on stage. He thought it was Steven Mackay whom he had worked with briefly when they were both teenagers. Steven was only eighteen when he was given the responsibility of directing the music for an amateur production of Hair at the Village Theatre in East Kilbride. Donny had picked up a week's work, playing guitar. Steven was the youngest musician in the assembled orchestra but totally on top of the task. When he finished his studies at the RSAMD, he headed straight for London, first to play piano in west-end shows but soon progressing to musical director, both in the west-end and with touring productions and was now very much in demand, as well as being hugely respected. Donny knew he would often return to Glasgow between engagements, he also knew Steven did not under any circumstances work for free. So what was he doing here on the open stage?

When the rest of the band appeared, Donny recognized another face, Jake Copeland, who, when not working, which was not often, propped up the bar in Blackfriars. Like Steven he was a veteran of the touring circuit and a seriously good guitar player, accustomed to playing with the best. Even more intriguing. Whatever was coming up was certain to be good. Donny indulged himself with a moment of schadenfreude, as he imagined the solitary figure of Cathy with only her guitar to provide backing, following this. The stage lights were still off, and the compère was waiting at the side for the signal that the band were ready, before stepping forward to make the introduction.

'Ladies and gentlemen we have something a wee bit special for you tonight. I want you to give a big Celtic Connections welcome to someone you will undoubtedly be hearing a lot more of in the future. Miss Kate Rydelle.'

Donny's mouth fell open as he spoke to himself in silent, stunned disbelief. 'Miss fucking Kate fucking Rydelle. You must be fucking joking.' It was no joke however and a stunning redhead that bore a vague resemblance to Cathy Riddle stepped into the spotlight. Gone were the dowdy clothes and Doc Martin boots, replaced by an elegant red dress and five inch heels. The unkempt wild curly hair had been tamed by a very stylish cut and it was clear now that she had lost weight.

The band had already started playing, immediately falling into the groove, keeping things tight till Kate, for it was apparent that Cathy was now dead, confidently picked up her acoustic guitar and pulled the strap over her head. With a smile of acknowledgement to the band she stepped forward to the mike and straight into the first song with the boys right on the beat.

It was again the song she started with two nights before. It was impressive then but with professional backing, it was raised to another level. Jake and the bass player were adding backing vocals and harmonies and Steven's piano arrangement added further layers of interest. Kate was demanding the full attention of the room and every head, with the exception of Donny, was focused on the stage.

Donny was scanning the crowd for those that looked a bit out of place, for he now realised what was going on. It's not easy for an unknown artist to assemble an appreciative, engaged audience of three hundred people and that is what you would want if someone important, someone you wanted to impress, was coming to see you perform. If Donny was correct there would be some movers and shakers, as they say, with us tonight. He spotted a few candidates then decided to return to the bar. It was worth the cost of the overpriced beer, to gain a better vantage point and there they were, sitting together, a group of more than a dozen, some taking notes. Donny knew they would all be rivals in the search for new talent, but there was no point in hiding. In the music business everybody knows everybody.

Kate progressed through the same songs she had performed at the Songwriters which Donny now realised was simply a rehearsal, and the band lent a faultless backing. Between the third and fourth song she thanked everyone for such a great reception and introduced the band, sounding every inch the consummate professional. At the end many were on their feet clapping loudly. The compère signalled that an encore was permissible and the band launched into a song Donny had not heard before but once again a triumph. When Kate eventually left the stage she was guided to a door marked 'No Exit' which she passed through, followed by the music execs, including some Donny had failed to spot.

Donny retook his seat and sat through the final two acts but he could have been staring at the wall, for all the attention he was giving them. He was in a state of shock, never before had he witnessed such a rapid, such a spectacular, such a complete transformation. Suspicions as to the authenticity of her songs seemed churlish now, for surely what he had witnessed was the birth of a star. Donny could already hear himself reciting at some future gathering that he had known Kate Rydelle before she was famous, and that he had been present at what would surely become part of Celtic Connections folklore.


As Donny headed back down Buchanan Street, he felt foolish about the last two days and did not have the heart to contact Colette and explain he had started her on a wild goose chase. Instead it was Colette who contacted him.

'What do you make of that then?' Donny forgot that the gig had been broadcast live on local radio.

'Well you heard it, she was completely brilliant.'

'Yes because the songs were brilliant.'

'It wasn't just the songs.'

'No, that was a fantastic band too. No wonder Cathy or should I say Kate sounded good.'

'No Colette, you had to have seen it, a complete transformation. You would not have recognised her, new look, confident, oh and there were about twenty industry people, record company types, publishers perhaps and music press. It was a showcase gig. I must admit I would never have believed she was capable of it, if I hadn't seen it with my own two eyes'.

'What is it they say? It all starts with a song.'

'That's true but tonight was the whole package.'

'On the back of someone else's talent.'

'Listen Colette I know it was me that put that thought in your head, but after tonight? You just had to have been there'.

'What are you saying, she wrote those songs herself?'

'I'm sorry. I'm thinking that maybe I was wrong. If she can transform herself so completely in three months maybe she learned how to write great songs in that time too.'

'What if she was working with the band?'

'Not the type to sit back and let someone else take all the credit.'

'Well that's that then.'

'Sorry.'

Colette had ended the call without another word, which was not like her. Donny thought about calling her back, but what would he say.

He was nearly back at Central Station but he did not fancy going back home just yet, so he changed direction and headed for Blackfriars.

Over in the West End Colette was angry with Donny. He had convinced her about his mystery writer theory, now he had suddenly changed his mind. Colette however had not changed her mind. The problem was, without Donny's knowledge, she did not know what she could do about it.

Whatever she did do would have to wait till tomorrow however. Her shift started in thirty minutes.

# Chapter 5

Donny was hoping Jake would have returned to his berth at the Blackfriars bar after his brief set at Celtic Connections. Donny was very interested in finding out the inside story on Cathy's progress.

Unfortunately there was no sign of Jake so he had to make do with one of the guitarist's drinking cronies.

'I saw your pal up the Concert Hall,' Donny remarked.

*'Awe Aye.'*

'Great wee set backing Cathy Riddle. She plays downstairs here on Tuesday nights sometimes.'

*'Right.'*

'You didn't go up to see the gig yourself then?'

*'Naw.'*

'Did you know that Jake was playing?'

*'Naw.'*

Donny could see he was getting nowhere. 'Well you can tell Jake when you see him I really enjoyed it.'

*'Aye nae bother.'*

Donny ordered a pint and took a seat against the wall opposite. After half an hour there was still no sign of Jake. He downed the dregs of his pint and stood up to leave when he noticed Colin Burns had come though the door and was heading in his direction. Colin was the one person in the Songwriters Club that had always supported Cathy.

'Hi Donny. I saw you up at Cathy's gig. Pretty good eh.'

'Yeah, very impressive. That was some band she had behind her'.

'It certainly was. She has been rehearsing with Jake on and off over the past month, whenever he was available. It was him that put the band together.'

'The band was put together just for today?'

'No. I think the plan was to stage a showcase gig sometime next month on a Sunday night when all the boys would be available. You know the kind of thing, invite the record companies and that. She has been doing loads of open mikes and things trying to build up a following.'

'So I heard.'

'Then she got the chance of tonight's gig with an audience already in place. Too good a chance to miss. Jake managed to get the guys together for a rehearsal last night and again this afternoon, it was only a few songs and you know what they are like, it would have been dead easy.'

'Yeah, I played with the keyboard player ages ago, he is some musician. She did well getting him in the band.'

'Suppose so.'

'That's a great bunch of songs she has now.'

'Yeah I know.' Colin was brimming with satisfaction now that his faith had proved to be justified.

Donny tried to pump Colin for more information but he didn't know that much. Cathy had told him she had been sitting on the songs for some time but wanted to wait till they sounded just right, before she let anyone hear them. Colin knew Cathy had made some demos but he did not know where she recorded them, or who the musicians were.

Nor did he have any idea where the money came from. He did however know that the spot on the Danny Kyle stage was offered after the session on Celtic Music Radio. That was the extent of Colin's knowledge, so the pair could only guess at how Cathy had managed to make such rapid progress, and what her future strategy might be.

A couple of hours of speculation later and still no sign of Jake, Donny made his way home, none the wiser as to how such a metamorphosis was accomplished nor how it was financed, for as far he knew, Cathy only worked part time in a children's nursery earning just enough to cover the cost of the room, she rented in Partick and keep herself fed and clothed.

When Donny awoke next morning, his head was sore and his throat was dry. He now regretted his trip to Blackfriars the night before, for he learned little he could not have worked out for himself. Colin seemed to confirm that Cathy had written the songs by herself, so the only mystery, if there was one, was where the money came from. It could have been her own savings of course or she could be maxing on her credit card, which was the simplest explanation. Donny was growing weary of the whole thing. Good luck to Kate Rydelle. It was time he got back to his own life.

Kenny was due in the afternoon, so Donny looked out his notes on Sultans of Swing.

The Dire Straits classic is much admired by aspiring guitarists, despite being nearly forty years old and despite the band that produced it, falling out of fashion. The recording has a unique guitar sound that can only be produced on a Fender Stratocaster and Donny possessed such an instrument. This would give him the edge over Kenny's 330. Donny was feeling the strain of maintaining teacher superiority over his pupil.

By the time Kenny arrived, he had practised all the guitar parts and had meticulously set the controls on his Fender Twin Reverb amp. Kenny would use the small Roland Cube practice amp.

'How are you doing Kenny? Good, you brought your electric today.'

*'Aye, thought ah better get ma money's worth oot o' it.'*

' Do you want a coffee or a cup of tea?'

*'Nah, yur aw right. Wull ah plug in here?'* Kenny indicated the little Roland.

'Yeah Kenny.'

Kenny opened the case and removed his instrument. A nineteen sixties vintage Gibson ES 330 in cherry red. It was indeed a thing of beauty with its arched top and double f holes.

Kenny plugged in his guitar and the lesson began. As usual the pupil picked things up fast. Donny had learned most of the solos by finding tutorials on youtube and felt a little guilty that Kenny didn't realise this.

'You can find this all on the internet you know.'

*'Ah canny be arsed wae aw that. Easier if you jist show me.'*

'Sure no problem. Listen we will stop there for a bit. I'll put the kettle on.'

Donny went through to the kitchen and returned five minutes later with two cups of tea and a caramel wafer each.

*'Whit ur ye writin' aboot Brigton fur?'* Kenny had a sheet

containing Cathy's lyrics to 'Main Street' in his hand.

'What do you mean?'

*'Sorry ah saw it lyin' oan the table. Is it wan o' yur songs?'*

'No, it's by a friend of mine.'

*'Ur they fae Brigton?'*

'No, She's from up north somewhere. Why?'

*'The song's aboot Main Street o' Brigton.'*

'I don't think it is about anywhere in particular Kenny, Main Street just gives it an Americana feel, that's all.'

*'Um telling ye, it's aboot Brigton.'* There was a hint of irritation in Kenny's voice.'

'Are you talking about Bridgeton in the east end? How could it be about there?'

*'Cause it's aboot Main Street o' Brigton.'*

'There's a street in Bridgeton called Main Street'.

*'Aye.'*

'That's a bit odd is it not? Main Street should be in the city centre.'

*'Well it's ca'ed Main Street, an it's in Brigton, an that's whit this song's aboot.'*

'How do you know?'

*'Look.'* Kenny pointed to one of the lines. 'Drivin' down Main Street. The cross was left behind us we were going to the dogs'. *'Main Street runs fae Brigton Cross tae Shawfield Stadium, ye know, the dug racin'.'*

'You think the song's about that.'

*'That's whit Ah'm saying. There's anither bit aboot walking on the green. That wid be Glesca Green jist five minutes away.'* Donny took the sheet from Kenny's hand. *'It's a bit oot o' date mind ye. Ye cannny drive fae the Cross any mair. The street wis blocked aff aboot thirty years ago. Tae git ontae Main Street fae the Cross ye need*

*tae go doon James Street first.'*

Donny realised where Kenny was talking about. Road realignments meant it didn't really lead to anywhere. He had driven past it many times but had no idea it was called Main Street. 'Was it once a proper main street, you know with lots of shops and things?'

*'Aye, ah think so. Ma da talked aboot it. Ah think it wis a busy place afore the redevelopments. So aye, a proper main street. Kin ye no jist ask yur pal?'*

'I will do Kenny. Next time I see her. We better get back to work.'

Twenty minutes later, Donny was closing the door behind his pupil. He headed back into the living room and picked up the sheet containing the lyrics to 'Main Street'. There was something he remembered from the day before, a line that said 'You took me all the way to Paradise'. Donny had thought it was just referencing the old Billy Fury song 'Half Way to Paradise' but now realised it was talking about Celtic Park. Paradise was what the Celtic fans called their home ground which was only half a mile along London Road from Bridgeton Cross. Funny that Kenny did not mention that one.

So there seemed to Donny no doubt that the song was about Bridgeton. It sounded so personal when Cathy had sung it but how could that be, she had no connection with the place and it appeared to be set in a time, before she was even born. He picked up his phone.

'Sorry, did I wake you up? We're back in business. Kate Rydelle is a fraud!'

# Chapter 6

1971

**Triangles will be similar if the ratio of their corresponding sides are equal or if the triangles are equiangular.**

In the second back row of the fourth year class, in a seat by the window, Daniel Quick 4B conscientiously copied down what was written on the blackboard at the front of the room but he was not taking any of it in. The same could have been said for any one of the previous six lessons that day. His mind was elsewhere. Not even the sound of rain lashing against glass, or the rattling of the ancient sashes, a few inches from his head, could draw his attention. Safely stored inside the zipped pocket of his blazer was without doubt his most cherished possession. Perhaps it was foolish to bring the precious piece of paper to school but there were too many of his fellow pupils who had questioned whether he really did possess such a prized item that Dan felt it necessary to prove them wrong and today was the last opportunity to do so. The item in question was a much coveted ticket to see the Who live in concert. It would take place at Greens Playhouse that very night. It would be his first ever gig.

Purchasing the ticket was no mean feat, requiring a dedication fans of other forms of entertainment could never match. Forty-eight hours before the sale began, a queue had formed outside an electrical goods store on Sauchiehall Street that acted as agent for the venue. Those that knew the ropes brought sleeping bags and thermos flasks. The majority, Dan included, were to discover that the night time temperature is significantly lower than that of the daytime even in summer. Anyone that lacked the dedication to endure a minimum of twelve hours on the pavements, well-prepared or otherwise, would be disappointed as supply was outstripped by demand. Such was the degree of interest that an extra date was hastily added to the tour which would see the group return to the city, three weeks later. However that first show, the one on twenty-first of October nineteen seventy-one was where everyone wanted to be.

At the front of the class the teacher had drawn diagrams to supplement his definition and had started to work through some examples on the board. Dan duly copied everything into his jotter. None of it made any sense. The next step he knew would be a series of questions fired at random to a dozen or so pupils round the class to test who had been paying attention and who had not. Dan could only hope to be spared that particular ordeal today.

The rest of the class were soon dutifully forming fractions to represent the scale factor, multiplying by the numerator, dividing by the denominator then expressing the result as a decimal to an accuracy of three significant figures, accomplished only with the aid of pencil and paper.

In the second back row by the window however, thoughts were not on geometry, but only on set lists. Would it be the early mod anthems, the sixties hits, the masterpiece that was 'Tommy' or as he hoped, tracks from the brilliant new album with its futuristic electronic intros and pounding guitar chords. Music had taken over Dan's life in the past year. The two pounds, including tips, earned each week from a paper round, matched the cost of an album and most weeks that's where the money went. Each new purchase would be played from beginning to end, both sides then returned to side one, track one and enjoyed all over again. Favourite tracks would then be repeated over and over.

Things were changing fast for all the young people in the room that day whether their focus was on exam grades or rock concerts but for others, outside their teenage world, that day would bring a tragic change. As the O level maths class packed away their books and jotters at end of the penultimate period of the day, a gas explosion ripped apart a line of shops in one of the cities outer suburbs. Shop workers, customers, pedestrians and passengers on a passing bus would take the full force of the blast. The Clarkston disaster would claim the lives of twenty-one and injure one hundred.

.  .  .  .  .

Donny watched from his window as the black Land Rover pulled into the only available space on the street below. He had already put his coat on but had decided to avoid the cold by waiting inside till Colette arrived. He hurried down the stairs and climbed into the four wheel drive waiting with its engine running.

'I've only got an hour before I am due at the hospital.'

'Plenty of time. You can drop me in town, when we're finished.'

'Where to then?'

Donny had not told Colette anything about his discovery, preferring to show her instead and was enjoying keeping her in suspense. 'Bridgeton. I'll give you directions.'

Colette performed a u-turn using the entrance to the Clockwork car park to gain sufficient width and headed back the way she had come, along Cathcart Road. To Donny's amazement Colette knew how to get to Shawfield dog track. Once there, he gave directions.

'Go past the stadium and cross the bridge, we will be turning left at the lights.'

Once through the lights Donny gave the instruction to take a sharp right.

'OK, pull over, we're here.'

The street was deserted, no cars moving and no one walking on the pavement. The houses on each side of the road were new, replacing the old sandstone tenements. The area had a suburban or small town feel despite being only a mile from the city centre.

'You know the song 'Main Street' that Cathy sang.'

'Yes.'

'Well this is it. This is the Main Street in the song.'

'Are you joking?'

'No, it was one of my students that spotted the references in the lyrics. This street is actually called Main Street. At one time it was a busy place full of shops and pubs and everything, before the old tenements were pulled down. It was the centre of a densely populated area, but that was more than forty years ago.'

'Are you sure? You are saying the song is about this street?'

'No doubt about it.' Donny took out a copy of the words and line by line explained everything that Kenny had told him, plus the things he had worked out by himself.

'But Cathy comes from up north.'

'Exactly.'

'What! Do you think someone from around here wrote it?'

'Perhaps. The thing is, I'm not sure Cathy knows where the song is set. I mean, I've lived in Glasgow all my life and I didn't know the name of this street.'

'And whoever did write it, didn't tell her?'

'Or they don't know Cathy has been singing it.'

'You mean Cathy has taken someone else's song? She would never expect to get away with that.'

'I'm not so sure Colette'

'Well would she? The person who wrote it is bound to find out wouldn't they?'

'You think?'

'Of course they would. How could they not?'

'You're a Johnny Cash fan, aren't you?'

'Yes.'

'Take out your iphone. Go to youtube and put in 'Crescent City Blues' then play it.'

Colette did as she was asked. 'It's just like 'Folsom Prison Blues.'

'Except it was written years before Johnny Cash penned

his song.'

'Even the words are almost the same.'

'That's my point. Johnny Cash had been playing his version for fourteen years, before the original writer heard it on the radio. Fourteen years. It is probably his best known song, a number one in the country charts, he sang it on TV, it was played on the radio thousands and thousands of times yet it took fourteen years for someone to come forward. That guy, I think his name was Jenkins, had made records himself, he was in the music business yet he never realized.'

'That's amazing Donny.'

'I could go on all night. George Harrison's 'My Sweet Lord' for example. That's a rip off of the Chiffons 'He's So Fine.'

'Hold on Donny. Everybody has heard that one. The songs are similar but I don't think they are the same song and besides, I don't think someone like George Harrison would be so stupid.'

'Sure! Listen to Jody Miller's version of 'He's So Fine' and tell me it is two different songs. It is done in Harrison's style with acoustic guitars and a pedal steel. The point is artists steal song ideas or even complete songs all the time, so it is not so far fetched to believe Cathy has taken someone else's song, perhaps changing it a bit, new title for example and the writer knows nothing about it.'

'But if it became a hit they would sue.'

'If you can prove it and can afford the lawyers.'

'OK Donny, why do you think the writer doesn't know Cathy is performing their songs?'

'Well, lets just stick to this song. First, if you listen to the lyrics it's all 'we were ' and 'I was', it's all very personal but it can't have been written for Cathy.'

'Why can't it have been written for Cathy?'

'Because it is out of date. You can't drive from the Cross to the dogs any more. The road is no entry at the Cross and at the other end, a new road cuts it off from the dog track completely. And as you can see it is no longer a main street, is it?'

'You think she doesn't realise this is the Main Street in the song.'

'She probably thought the same as me, that it was no place in particular, just about Small Town USA. That's the kind of image it paints. Besides, Cathy would have said something if she knew it was about old Bridgeton.'

'And the real writer?'

'The song is written in the present, it's not about looking back. I think it was actually written when this was the main street. Its got that classic quality and could easily have been written forty years ago.'

'But why would someone sit on such a good song all these years?'

'I have absolutely no idea. That's what we need to find out.'

The pair sat suggesting possible scenarios but neither could think of anything credible. They eventually relapsed into quiet contemplation. It was Donny who broke the silence. 'We better leave it there for now. If you drive along the length of the street you can drop me at Bridgeton Station, it's at the Cross. I'll show you how to get back to the city centre from there.'

Colette started the engine and checked for other vehicles

before pulling out. There were none. 'Where are you off to?'

'Partick. There is someone there I think can help us. I'll let you know how I get on.'

Bridgeton Station was deserted. Donny felt a bit vulnerable standing alone on the platform and was relieved to see that the electronic board indicated that the next train was due in three minutes. When the train arrived, it was full with people heading into town for a night out. The line ran underground through the city centre emerging into the open again at the Exhibition Centre. Partick was the next station after that.

Donny exited Partick Station and headed east on Dumbarton Road, looking into every pub on the way. In the fifth pub he tried, he found what he was looking for.

'Hello Derek. How are you doing?'

'Donny! What are you doing over here?'

'I'm heading for the train, thought I would pop in for a pint. I was up seeing Colette but she had to leave for the night shift.'

'You heard about Cathy?' Derek asked.

'No! Heard what?'

'She has a few record companies interested in signing her.'

'That's great Derek. She was down at the Songwriters this week, had some new songs. They were very good.'

'You mean a lot better than the old shite?'

'Well I wouldn't say that.'

'No?' Derek raised his eyebrows.

'Well the old ones were a bit depressing, I suppose.' Donny was choosing his words carefully. Derek had a room in the same flat as Cathy and they had also been a couple for a while. He would accompany her to open mike nights but Derek was not much into music and found such nights a waste of time. When faced with the choice of music, or Derek, Cathy chose music.

'I felt like slitting my throat sometimes, listening to those songs.' Derek reminisced.

'When did she change over to the new stuff?'

'A few months ago, I think. I would see her in her room with this old reel to reel tape recorder. She bought it and a bunch of tapes down the Barras for forty quid.'

'A reel to reel, eh. Bit retro. Probably trying to get that classic sound. Has she got a mixing desk?'

'You mean with all the knobs and faders and things?'

'Aye.'

'Don't think so, she just sits with her guitar and puts headphones on.'

'Well whatever she is doing it's working.'

Derek did not come up with anything else so when Donny finished his pint, he headed back to Partick Station. It was only three stops to Central where he could change to the Mount Florida line.

Derek had given Donny something to think about though. Nobody used reel to reel recorders any more, at least not one that can be picked up for forty quid. Technology had simply moved on. Forty pounds could buy software for your computer that would digitally record, add effects, edit and master a track with ease. To do the same thing with an analogue reel to reel would require numerous other pieces of equipment.

It wasn't the information that Cathy had bought an old

tape recorder that Donny deemed important, it was the fact that it came with 'a bunch of tapes'. If Cathy was not recording with the machine, what was she listening to and who had made those recordings.

# Chapter 7

It was Sunday before Donny and Colette could meet up.

Saturday was usually a busy time for Donny, typically five or six lessons spread over morning and afternoon followed by a wedding or function gig with the band in the evening.

January was not however a good month for weddings and functions but Donny did have a booking, backing a singer at a Burns Supper, though the eighty pound fee was less than a quarter of what he picked up for the average wedding gig.

Colette had fared much better, two hundred pounds for her share of a sixty minute set, headlining a tribute night in an Ayrshire hotel. Other acts included a twelve stone Meat Loaf and a balding Marc Bolan, all cheered on by an audience mostly too young to remember the original acts in their heyday.

Donny had sent a text to Colette on Saturday afternoon saying he had some information but she did not wake up till 5.15 and was due to be picked up at six, leaving only enough time to do a few quick circuits of the park, shower and get something to eat. Colette had to call Donny from the van, and with all the guys there, did not like to ask too many questions but agreed to meet up on Sunday morning, to follow up on his lead.

Colette was on her second coffee when Donny turned up twenty minutes late. Burns Suppers always involved whisky and too much whisky did not agree with Donny, so it was with some considerable effort that he forced himself out of bed for the eleven o'clock rendezvous.

'You made it then.' There was a hint of disapproval in Colette's voice. She had already completed six laps of Kelvingrove park that morning.

'Sorry, you know what it's like.'

'No.'

'Come on. It was a Burns Supper, drinking whisky is compulsory.'

'Is it?'

'Well anyway, sorry I'm late. How was the gig?'

'It was good, but never mind that. Tell me what you found out.'

'OK. I went looking for Cathy's old boyfriend last night, you know Derek, he used to come with her to open mike nights.'

'Yeah I remember him.'

'Well he told me she bought an old reel to reel tape machine and a box of old tapes to go along with it, down at the Barras market. The trouble is you need a bunch of other stuff to record anything worthwhile on it and according to Derek, she only has the recorder. He said she sits in her room with headphones plugged into the machine with her guitar in her arms.'

'I don't get it.'

'She is not able to record anything.'

'Sorry, I must be missing something.'

'I think she is listening to, and learning, whatever is on

those tapes. That's where the songs came from. Well, that's my theory anyway.'

'Right. That would make sense, I suppose. So what's the plan?'

'We go along to the Barras and try to find out who sold the tapes and hopefully find out who the original owner was.'

'Good idea. Do you want to go now or do you want to get a coffee first?'

'Better get a coffee first.'

With a coffee and a bagel inside him, Donny felt ready to face Glasgow's flea market. A couple of minutes after leaving the coffee shop, they were crossing High Street where the stylish Merchant City meets the grittier East End. The market was a further two hundred yards along the Gallowgate.

The four city blocks that form the Barras are not for the faint-hearted and the visitor must see beyond its dilapidated state and its purveyors of smuggled cigarettes and pirate DVDs, to appreciate its charms. The real appeal is the stalls selling the contents of house clearances, where among the rubbish there is the opportunity to find something unique, or at least very rare, a Star Wars figure in original box, an Elvis record on the Sun label or simply a replacement part for some treasured but broken household fixture.

It was however, the stalls specialising in electrical equipment and musical equipment that Donny and Colette were interested in today. Donny approached the first one he saw.

'Do you ever get any reel to reel recorders?'

*'Naw mate, nae demand fur it these days.'*

This was typical of the response from other stall holders but eventually they approached someone, who was more helpful.

'Have you tried Black Bob?'

'Don't think so. Where's his stall?'

'He's on the top floor across the road.' The vendor pointed to the entrance of the building across the street. 'He fixes old record decks and things.'

'Thanks, I'll give him a try.' Donny and Colette made their way out of the large shed they were in and crossed the road.

'Did you hear what he said?'

'Heard what Colette?'

'Black Bob. He called the man Black Bob.'

'Yeah I heard. Some guys just talk like that. Especially the old ones.'

'Well I don't like it.'

'You'll hear a lot of things down here you won't like. Sorry.'

At the top of four flights of stairs they found a sign saying Hi-Fi Sales and Repairs. A young lad sat behind a counter.

'I was looking for Bob.' Donny said.

'He's no' here.'

'It's my friend. She bought a reel to reel a few months ago.'

'We don't do refunds.' The voice came from behind Donny and had a West Indian accent.

Colette took over. 'Our friend bought a reel to reel recorder somewhere round here. She is very happy with it. I was wondering if she bought it from you and if you had any more?'

'Only had the one. It was a while back, four or five months, don't remember who bought it. I got it from another stall holder. Not much call for them these days.'

'Can you tell us which stallholder?'

'Don't remember.' Bob turned away indicating that this was his last word on the subject.

'OK, thanks for your time,' Donny said, before he and Colette turned and made for the stairs.

'You can give your friend this.' Donny and Colette turned back to see Bob hold up a five inch reel of tape. 'Came across it the other day it must have fell out the box your friend bought. It is no use to me.'

Colette took it from Bob's hand. 'Thanks I'll pass it on.'

Donny and Colette hurried down the stairs without saying a word. Once back on the street, Colette broke the silence.

'Do you think it is from the same writer?'

'Don't know but there's a good chance.'

Colette looked at the paper label stuck on to the middle of the tape spool.

'What does it say?' Donny asked.

The tape appeared to contain two songs. 'The Die is Cast' and 'This River Don't Flow.' There was also a date. 1975.

'Could be the same era as 'Main Street.' Colette observed.

'Maybe, I don't recognise those titles though. We'll need to listen to it somehow.'

'Eric at Bankside Studios has a reel to reel. Will I call him and see if he's free or do you want to look for the stall holder that gave it to Bob?'

'Not sure I believed him but even if he is telling the truth we would need to ask every stall holder not just the ones selling electrical equipment. Why don't we see what is on the tape?'

Colette scrolled her contacts and hit Eric's number. When Eric answered, he told her he was doing some editing on someone's track he had recorded the day before but she could still come round and he would set up the tape.

'We can go round now if we want.'

'Great.'

Colette's car was back in the Merchant City so they retraced their steps back to Albion Street before heading east once more.

Bankside Studios are housed in a former school building on the banks of the Clyde only about a half mile from Main Street Bridgeton. Colette pulled into the empty car park and sent a text to Eric who came down from the top floor studio to open the locked door to the building.

'How are you doing? Come in.'

Eric led the way back upstairs and into the studio. 'What's on the tape?'

'We don't know' Donny explained. 'We think it could be by someone that Cathy Riddle has been ripping off.'

'Oh right.'

Colette explained their suspicions and brought Eric up to date on what they had discovered so far.

'I'll put the tape on then. Do you want me to record it and burn a CD at the same time?'

'That would be a big help.' Donny answered.

Eric attached the reel to his machine, feeding the tape round the mechanism, over the record/playback heads and onto an empty reel.

'OK, that's us ready.'

The tape had thirty minutes of material consisting six versions of the the song 'The Die is Cast' each version a little different, the writer experimenting with alternative timings and rhythms. 'This River Don't Flow' turned out to be an instrumental, comprising acoustic and electric guitars.

All three listened with only the occasional comment until the tape ran out. The singer was male and sounded young. Eric was the first to speak.

'Was that any help to you?'

Donny and Colette looked at each other, disappointment showing on their faces.

'Well it was not what I had hoped for.' Donny conceded. 'It would have been good to have heard one of the songs Cathy has been singing or at least hear something I recognized. That song is not even that good.'

'At least we know it is a man we are looking for.' Colette added.

'I suppose that's something. Assuming it is the same person on Cathy's tapes.' Donny reasoned.

'He was using a reel and a cassette recorder.' Eric explained. 'It was a pretty crude way to record but without really expensive gear, its about the best you could do back then. That's why the sound quality of the backing is so poor on the instrumental. The lead guitar sounds good though.'

'Yeah I think it's a Gibson 330. One of my pupils has one, sounds just like the guitar on the tape.'

'A 330! Impressive. Wouldn't have thought there would have been too many of them around here in the seventies? Unless you were doing well'

'Maybe we could look for Glasgow guitarists playing one of those guitars in the seventies,' Colette suggested. 'We could ask in music shops.'

'Don't know if there is any still open from that time,' Eric said. 'McCormacks would have been your best bet but they closed five years ago. You could try Southern Music on Cathcart Road, they might have been on the go in the seventies.'

'Yeah I know it. It's just down the road from me.'

'Do you want me to drive over there now?' Colette offered.

'I don't think they open on a Sunday, I'll walk down tomorrow.'

Eric had to get back to work so Donny and Colette took their CDs and headed back to the Land Rover.

'Do you fancy something to eat? My treat.' Colette offered. 'We can go over what we have found out so far.'

'Sure. What do you have in mind?'

'There is a new tapas place near me. I've got a voucher I haven't used yet, three tapas with bread and a glass of wine each, we can choose six different dishes and share.'

'Sounds good to me.'

On the drive over to the West End they listened to the CD Eric had made for them, but failed to find any new clues. Donny had told Colette he would make his own way home so they drove to her flat, parked the car and walked from there. That way, Colette could have her glass of wine.

The tapas place was quiet which was unusual for any eatery in the West End at lunch time on a Sunday. On the plus side, it was possible to get a seat by the window.

'I'll get us a drink. What do you want?'

'Just a bottle of water.'

Donny wandered over to the bar and considered the choice of beers but there was no sign of someone to serve him. When someone did appear, he picked a cider for himself and the girl started to pour. A tiny, tiny stream of liquid emerged from the pump. Slowly, very slowly, it started to fill the glass.

'Sorry, the air needs changing but I don't know how to do it,' the girl explained.

Ten minutes later Donny returned with a bottle of water and a three-quarters full pint of cider.

'What kept you?'

'There was only a dribble coming out of the cider pump. Had to tell her to stop and give me what she had or I could have been there all day. Oh and the pimientos and albondigas are off the menu.'

'They only have seven dishes on the menu. Sorry, this was a bad choice.'

'I'm sure I can find three things I like.'

'I thought I would check Cathy's facebook while I was waiting. Guess what?'

'I don't know. What?'

'Its been taken down.'

'Has it now?'

'And that's not all. I did a search for Kate Rydelle and found a brand new facebook page linked to a very slick web site and of course no reference to Cathy Riddle.'

'She's certainly moving fast, I'll give her that,' Donny conceded. 'Lets go over what we have discovered so far.'

'We know Cathy has been learning songs from some old tapes.'

'And those tapes were made by a musician, a very good one at that.'

'You mean because of the guitar playing' Colette asked.'

'Yeah it was pretty good, don't you think.'

'I agree. Looks like he was trying to perfect that first song, so also a songwriter.'

'I think it's a safe bet that he is the source of Cathy's new material but we still have no idea who he is. We also have nothing to prove that Cathy is not the writer.'

'Unless she starts singing 'The Die is Cast.'

'That's true, there could have been a version on one of the other tapes but it still wouldn't prove Cathy did not write it.'

'But the tape has a date remember, nineteen seventy-five.'

'She could say it is a new recording on an old tape. I think we need to track down whoever recorded that tape, back in seventy-five.'

'We could play the tape to people who were around back then, see if anyone recognises it. They would need to be about sixty years old by now.'

'Some of my guitar pupils are that age. I could start with them. There is also a lot of guys that age that listen to the bands down the Scotia Bar, we could try there too.'

'The guys in the tribute band are not far off that age I could ask them.'

'There is still the guitar remember. We might track him down that way.'

The girl from behind the bar came over to take the food order. Two portions of patatas bravas and one each of what was left on the menu. When it arrived it was minus the promised portion of bread and Pinot Grigio replaced the Spanish White, Colette had asked for.

With the amount of competition in that part of town, they both agreed that the tapas bar's days were numbered. Donny gave it six months, Colette gave it three.

# Chapter 8

1980

The face of Britain's first female Prime Minister was on the cover of most of the newspapers stacked neatly on the low shelf. The next day would mark the first anniversary of her coming to power. A girl picked up one of the papers, studied the picture for a moment and read a few lines, before returning it to the shelf. Maybe it will be good to have a women in charge she had said at the time of the election, her reasoning being it could hardly be any worse. She was wrong, things could and did get worse, at least for her. She took down a magazine from a higher shelf and flicked though the pages, then selected another, then another. They were all returned to their original position. The girl eventually purchased ten Embassy Tipped and a Milky Bar, before awkwardly manoeuvring a pram out of the small shop. Outside she lit up before braking off a piece of the white chocolate for the child. She looked up and down the street, then pushed the pram slowly westward along London Road towards Bridgeton Cross.

From a dairy she bought a half pint of milk, from the bakers a small loaf and from a corner shop a copy of the newspaper she had looked at in the first shop. She checked her watch, half past eleven, the Post Office, her next destination, would be full but that suited her fine.

When she arrived the Post Office was indeed full of customers. The pram was left outside and the girl waited for fifteen minutes in a queue, the child in her arms. When it was her turn to be served, she bought two stamps. Back outside, she pushed the pram as far as the last shop on the south side of Main Street then crossed over and walked on the north side back towards the cross. If there was a shop window worth looking at she did so, lingering for as long as she could without looking suspicious. Back at the cross she stopped at the corner of James Street to attend to the child in her pram. The child was quite happy playing with her toys but the mother made a show of comforting her, addressing her by name in a voice a little louder than was necessary. While pretending to pick up something from the ground, the girl glanced up at a window on the opposite side of the street. She could not see anybody but that did not mean that nobody had seen her. Eventually she turned the pram back towards London Road

It had taken twenty minutes pushing the pram to reach Bridgeton and it would be longer going home, as it was slightly uphill. She had managed to spin out the buying of a handful of items she could just as easily have done without for two and a half hours but she would be back next Saturday to do it all again. After all she had done the same thing every week for nearly a year, winter and summer, rain or shine.

.  .  .  .  .

Monday morning was another lie-in for Donny. After the tapas bar the day before, he had made his way home for two afternoon lessons then went out to an open mike session in Shawlands in the evening. No one in the pub knew about Cathy's change of name or change of fortune and he was glad to put her out of his mind for a while and concentrate on his own songs. He tried out the reggae influenced song he had sung at the Songwriters Club which got a good reaction from the audience. Not wanting to push his luck he chose a cover for his second song, Jake Bugg's 'Trouble Town'. Donny's rendition met with general approval and was followed by generous applause.

Once back home, the itch returned and he was on the laptop for a proper look at Kate Rydelle's new web site.

The site was very professional with pictures of Cathy, all taken since her transformation. Her biography was all true as far as Donny could tell but it was what it failed to say that mattered. No mention of her age for instance nor when her songs were written. There was a video of Thursday night's gig but the caption simply stated Celtic Connection Festival and did not reveal it was one of the free events. Without telling any lies, the site projected the image of a talented young lady well on her way to a successful career in the music industry.

Cathy was still on Donny's mind as he made his breakfast the next morning. There was no need to hurry, his task for the day was simply to visit Southern Music, a mile down Cathcart Road towards the city centre and it would not be open till after lunch.

Donny knew the shop well and always went there for strings, plectrums and guitar leads. He had also bought two guitars and an amplifier from the shop over the years. The proprietor Chic had been there all that time so it seemed a good place to ask about someone playing a Gibson 330 back in the seventies.

Donny left the flat at one o'clock. It was cold but dry so he decided to walk and set off along Kingspark Road and then onto Cathcart Road. As he neared the music shop, the shutters were just being raised.

'Hi Chic. There's something you might be able to help me with. Have you got a minute?'

'Sure. Come in.'

Donny followed Chic inside and wound his way between amplifiers stacked on top of each other and the array of guitars resting on their stands to reach the counter.

'I'm trying to find someone who played a Gibson 330 in the mid seventies, wondered if you might know someone.'

'Bit before my time, the seventies.'

'He could have used the 330 after that. May have sold it at some point.'

'I've bought a few to sell on over the years. Do you know the model or the colour?'

'Afraid not.'

'Not sure I can help then. You could ask Big George who does the repairs for me, it's more his era. He might know someone. Do you want his number?'

'That would be great.'

Donny called the repair man straight away. He told George that he had come across an old tape and wanted to track down the person that recorded it. George said he would listen to the recording if he brought it to his house and gave an address in the Gorbals.

Donny thanked Chic and left the shop, turning right and heading once more towards the city centre. It was a further mile walk to the address in the Gorbals.

When Donny found the address, he pressed the flat number on the door entry system. Once George released the lock, he made his way to the second floor maisonette flat. George was waiting at the open door and it was clear why he was called Big George, he stood five feet four inches tall but must have been over twenty stone in weight.

'You found it OK?'

'No problem.'

George gestured for Donny to come in and led the way to the living room. The room was clean with some nice items of furniture but every available space was taken up with amplifiers stacked on top of each other and rows of guitars, at least thirty, leaning against each other in makeshift racks. The room looked like a condensed version of Chic's shop.

'Some collection of gear you've got, are they all for repair?'

'No these are mine. The ones for repair are in the workshop.' George nodded towards the kitchen.

'Do you sell them?'

'No point, they are going up in value faster than any interest I would get on the money at the bank.'

'Fair point.' Eccentrics were common enough in music circles but this was beyond anything Donny had come across before. The best option he decided was to pretend it was all perfectly normal. 'You got a Gibson 330?'

'Two.' George raised his eyes to the ceiling. 'Upstairs, I keep the valuable ones there. Let's hear this tape of yours then.'

'It's been copied on to a CD. It was originally recorded

on a reel to reel. It had a date, nineteen seventy-five on it and I recognized the sound of a 330. A friend plays one and it feeds back if he is not careful, the same thing happens on this recording.'

'Aye, it's the hollow body that's the cause.'

'I was thinking that a 330 may have been pretty rare in Glasgow back then, so maybe it belonged to a successful musician, someone well known.'

'Because of the cost you mean?'

'That's what I thought.'

'Not sure I agree with you. There was plenty of work for musicians at that time, in social clubs and dance halls and the like. My band played every night of the week back then.'

George put the CD on an impressive Hi Fi system and sat back on a strategically placed recliner chair to listen.

'And you want to track down this guy?' George was clearly unimpressed with what he was hearing.

'He is trying to perfect an original song. There is a lot of different versions.'

'Maybe try the next version then.' George used the remote control to quickly listen to a section of each version of the song.

'Sorry don't recognise it.'

'The next one is an instrumental.'

George was more impressed with this track and listened in silence all the way to the end.

'That was better.'

'Did you recognise it?'

'Naw.'

'Well, thanks for listening.'

'What about the Casino?'

'Sorry?'

'A Casino, it could be an Epephone Casino. It's very like a 330, difficult to tell them apart. All the Beatles had them in the sixties. Lennon plays one at the Apple rooftop concert.

'I thought that was a Gibson.'

'No, a Casino. The guitar riff on 'Ticket to Ride' that was played on a Casino, which was McCartney by the way not Harrison. If the recordings are from back in the seventies I'd say it is more likely to be a Casino than the 330.'

'And back in the seventies, do you remember anyone playing one? He may have come from Bridgeton.'

'Too busy playing with my own band. Didn't get the chance to see other bands that much.'

Donny thanked George for his time and left.


The Gorbals area sits just over the river from the city centre and Donny headed in that direction once more, his destination, the Scotia Bar. He was in need of a pint even if there was no one to ask about the tape and he could catch the number 5 across from the pub which would take him all the way home.

As expected the bar was fairly quiet. Donny ordered a lager and an all day breakfast then took a seat against the wall, opposite the bar. The Scotia is one of the oldest pubs in Glasgow and has changed little in the past hundred years with lots of nooks and crannies for drinkers to hide in. The walls are adorned with pictures of old Glasgow and photographs featuring customers and staff, past and present.

Donny looked around hoping to see someone he knew

or at least someone to strike up a conversation, but without success. He started to study the pictures on the wall just for something to do and spotted something he had never heard of before Big George had enlightened him, not half an hour since. A photograph of a band performing in the Scotia featured a guitarist playing an Epiphone Casino. It was true, it looked very much like the Gibson but with the word Epiphone on the headstock.

The barman signalled his all day breakfast was ready and Donny went over to the bar to collect it.

'That picture of a band over there, do you know who they are?'

'The Briggait Blues Band. They play in here on a Wednesday night.'

Donny recognised the name, he had been in a few times to listen to them but the bands played in the far corner and the strange shape of the pub meant he never got a good look at them but he had it in his head that the guitarist played a Les Paul.

'I'm interested in the guitar he's playing. You wouldn't have a contact number would you, so I could ask him about it.'

'Why don't you ask Doc.' The barman nodded towards the end of the bar.

'Doc?'

'John Dougherty, he plays harmonica in the band. That's him with the hat.'

'Thanks I will.'

The harmonica player did not look like he was going anywhere soon. Doc could wait till the all day breakfast was consumed.

Ten minutes later Donny returned the empty plate to the bar before approaching Doc.

'Hi. I've seen you play a few times on Wednesday nights. Great band.'

'Cheers.'

'I was looking at the photo on the wall over there, the guitarist has a semi acoustic. Did he not play a Les Paul?'

'Aye he did. Only got that one a few months ago.'

'It's an old Epiphone Casino, pretty rare.'

'Is it? I don't know much about guitars. I know he got it on Gumtree, some arsehole over in Bridgeton.'

'Bridgeton!' Donny tried hard to conceal his excitement

'Aye. He was there about four times before they agreed a price. That's what Mikey told me anyway'

'Mikey, is that the guitarist?'

'Michael Rooney, aye.'

'Can you give me his number?'

'He'll no' sell it.'

'I don't want to buy it. I want to contact the person that sold it.'

Donny could see Doc was getting a bit suspicious so he tried to reassure him.

'I have an old recording of someone playing one of those guitars and I have been trying to track him down. As I said, it is a pretty rare instrument and Bridgeton would fit.'

'Sorry I don't like giving out anybody's number.'

'I could come back on Wednesday and ask him in person but I don't want to wait that long.'

Doc thought for a moment. 'We're rehearsing tonight. Always end up in here afterwards.'

'Thanks, I'll pop in later.'

Donny delighted at his good fortune returned to his seat to consider this new piece of information. If what Doc said was true the guitar was put up for sale round about the same time the old reel to reel turned up at the Barras. Bridgeton is just along the road from the market. It was too much of a coincidence they had to be connected. Donny downed the remains of his pint and left the pub.

He was feeling rather pleased with himself as he sat upstairs on the number 5 back to Mount Florida, and was looking forward to telling Colette. He would call her once she finished work.

There was no answer to her phone at five thirty so Donny left a message saying he may have tracked down the guitar. It was seven before Colette got back to him.

'Hi. I just got off, its been a long day. You found the guitarist?'

'No, just the guitar or at least I may have'

Donny filled her in on the day's events.

Colette asked, 'Do you want to go down to the Scotia tonight and meet this guy?'

'That's what I was thinking but he won't be there till late and I know you are up early, so I was going to go down by myself after my lessons.'

'Not on your life. I want to be there. What time?'

'Say ten?'

'OK ten. See you then.'


Donny arrived back at the pub at five past ten. There was no sign of the band. He knew Colette would be another five minutes or so, not wanting to be first to arrive. A pint and a soda water with ice was ordered at the bar and before the barmaid had finished pouring, the band entered by the far away door. Doc noticed Donny straight away and nudged one of the group and nodded towards Donny who recognised the face. The guitarist made his way across to the bar.

'Is it you that's interested in the Casino?'

'Well the previous owner anyway.'

'Shifty wee prick. What do you want him for?'

Donny briefly told Mikey about the tapes without going into detail and without mentioning Cathy, explaining that he was trying to track down the writer because he liked the songs.

'It'll no' be him. I doubt that he could even spell guitar never mind play one.'

'How did he come by the guitar?'

'God knows. You wouldn't believe a word he said so I didn't ask. He was trying to make out he knew what he was talking about, but he didn't know what he had. The strings were tarnished and rusty and way out of tune but apart from that it was in pristine condition. If I hadn't instantly disliked him, I would have told him to put it on ebay. He would have got offers from all over the country.'

Colette arrived and was introduced to Mikey, then Donny handed her the soda water.

'Do you want a drink Mikey?'

'Nah you're OK. The boys will have got me one in already.'

'Do you mind if we sit down a minute and you can tell us what you know?'

All three sat down at the same table where Donny had enjoyed his all day breakfast earlier in the day.

'If the seller was shifty were you not afraid the guitar was stolen?' Donny asked.

'He had the original receipt from McCormacks and it was for the same address we were sitting in.'

Colette sat up in her seat. ' Did it have a name on it?'

'Daniel Quick. Twenty-first of June nineteen seventy-five.

'And the address?'

'Number 7 Main Street Bridgeton.'

# Chapter 9

On leaving the Scotia, Colette with Donny in the passenger seat drove straight to Bridgeton to have a look.

Number 7 Main Street was a handsome blonde sandstone tenement that had thankfully been spared from redevelopment, and sat just off the cross which still retained nearly all of its fine buildings. They both realised it was opposite the spot where Colette had parked on Friday night when she dropped Donny off. Number seven had a door entry system with names attached, but none of them said Quick. Directory enquires did not have a telephone number for that name at that address and even google came up with nothing.

It was a bit late for chapping on doors so it was decided that Donny would arrive early the next morning, wait for someone to leave the building, then ask if there was anyone named Quick living there.

To get to Bridgeton from Mount Florida by public transport meant a train into town then another out to the east end and it transpired that it could not be done in the thirty-five minutes promised by the timetable. The upshot being it was past eight thirty before Donny reached Main Street and it appeared any residents of number seven heading to work had already left, leaving Donny with nothing else to do but admire the buildings around the cross, as he waited for someone to emerge from the common close.

Five wide streets converged here and at one time each of them was lined with tall tenement buildings, stretching into the distance, the canyons between a hive of activity. Shops, places of business, places of work, places of leisure all competing for space in what was at one time part of one of the most densely populated cities in the world. To keep warm, Donny wandered around the cross admiring some fine architecture. The large Victorian shelter and band stand particularly caught his eye. It sat in the middle of the cross and had been beautifully restored with new paving laid around it. After checking that out Donny went over to the imposing Olympia Theatre building which had also been recently redeveloped. Originally a theatre then a cinema, the building was Grade 2 listed and he was interested in finding out what it was now used for. Turning to check, he saw someone leave number seven and enter the convenience store on the corner. Donny hurried back and waited outside the shop. When the man, who looked to be in his late sixties, left the shop he headed back towards number 7. Donny approached him as he neared the entrance.

'Excuse me. Can you tell me if there is someone called Quick living here?'

'That would be Agnes you're talking about.'

'Could be.'

'Who died last August.'

'Oh I'm sorry to hear that.'

'Aye. She was nearly ninety mind you. Lived opposite

me.'

'Is there any family that still lives here?'

'Nah. It was just herself. Her man Jack died fifteen years ago.'

'It is actually a Daniel Quick I am looking for.'

'Daniel! It's Daniel you're looking for?'

'I think he is a musician.'

'Sorry son, but Daniel got knocked down on the London Road, must be more than thirty years ago. Did ye' not know?'

'No I didn't.' Donny was looking confused.

'You OK son? You're looking a bit pale.'

'I'm fine thanks.'

'Well you don't look fine. You look as if you have had a shock. It's a cup of strong tea you're needing. Come up, I'd be putting the kettle on anyway.'

'Thanks, a cup of tea would be very welcome.'

'Well in you come. My name's Tam by the way.'

'Donny.'

Tam lead the way through the close and upstairs to his flat. Once inside, the kettle was put on to boil and Donny explained that he had heard some songs recently, that may have been written by Daniel.

'Is that a fact? I never met the boy, the accident was before I moved in.'

'When was that Tam?'

'Nineteen eighty.'

'And Daniel died before that?'

'Aye, here it's longer than I thought. Must have been about seventy-eight.'

'What happened?'

'Coming back from his work I believe. He worked at Graham's, the plumbers merchants. They used to be the other side of London Road. I was told there was a bus at the stop by the old railway station. Daniel tried to cross in front of the bus as a lorry was overtaking. He was only twenty-two.'

'Is there any family that I could talk to about Daniel?'

'No' really. There was only his sister Marie. She went on the bingo trip to Blackpool twenty odd years ago, met a bloke in a pub and never came back. Left her man and her fifteen year old son. The boy is also called Daniel by the way.'

'Are they still about, Daniel and his father?'

'If they're no' in the jail.'

'Do they live around here?'

'I think so, but I couldn't tell you where. He was at the funeral, Daniel that is, not the father. Marie came up to arrange things. They didn't sit together. I remember that.'

There seemed no point in hiding the facts from Tam, so he told him about the tape machine and the guitar that once belonged to Daniel.

'I didn't know anything about the music son. Agnes never said, nor Jack for that matter when he was alive like. I do know that Agnes kept all his stuff though. Never threw a thing out when he died. Marie and her mother would fight about it. Daniel was the favourite, I suppose.'

'Yet she named her son after him?'

'That would be Agnes's idea.' Tam got up and put three tea bags in a pot and poured in the boiled water.

'It must have been hard,' Donny remarked. 'A constant reminder of the brother she always resented.'

'I suppose so.'

There was little else that Tam could tell but Donny was happy to stay and chat about when Main Street buzzed with activity, and just about everything a person needed to get by could be found within a hundred yards. They both lamented that the planners got their way, destroying a community and a unique way of life in the process.

It was past eleven before Donny left and made his way back to Kingspark Road. He was a bit deflated as he sat in the near empty train. 'What had he discovered?' he asked himself. His answer was, not much. The date on the tape matched the time of Daniel's accident and the guitar matched the sound on the tape but there was nothing to indicate he was a songwriter and, apart from his address, nothing to suggest that Daniel made the recordings Cathy was listening to.

Donny had asked Tam if he had any idea how to contact the sister but he didn't. He wasn't even sure she was still in Blackpool. It seemed likely that the nephew found his uncle's guitar in his grandmother's house after her death and sold it before Marie returned. Tam didn't know the nephew's surname and was sure none of the other neighbours would either.

The review of the evidence was doing Donny's head in so he decided to give it a rest, and promised himself he would return to his own songwriting for the rest of the day. The early evening would be given over to lessons and later on there was the Songwriters open mike.

There were no problems with buses this week and Donny reached Blackfriars in plenty time for the nine o'clock start. He had a quick look in the upstairs bar first, looking for Jake, but there was no sign of the guitarist. The noise wafting up the stairs from the basement indicated that there was a good crowd in tonight. Donny had expected it, but was still taken aback when he pushed though the heavy doors. Every seat was taken and people were standing against the walls. It was three deep at the bar. There was more than three times the usual number in the room.

'Good crowd!' It was Billy Bongo holding an open note book displaying a very long list. 'Its only one song tonight.'

'What?'

'Sorry.' There was a take it or leave it look on Billy's face.

'OK, put me down.'

'It will need to be late on I've got twenty names already.'

'You're joking?'

'Sorry.'

'Put Colette on after me then. She has to work late.'

'Can't do that tonight, there's too many wanting to put their names down.'

'The Cathy effect?' Donny suggested

'No doubt about that.'

'She'll not be down tonight.'

'She said she might be down.'

'That was Cathy. Have you heard from Kate?'

'No,' Billy admitted. 'I tried to phone her but got no answer'

'Why am I not surprised?'

There was a group of regulars huddled round a table near the stage, looking well put out. Donny squeezed through the throng to join them. 'Good news travels fast.'

'Hi Donny.' It was Evelyn, another of the good guys and

a journeyman like himself. 'Every chancer in the city is here. They think the record companies will be in, or the press.'

'And are they?'

'Not that I can see.' She offered to share her seat so Donny put his guitar case at the back of the stage before accepting her offer.

The first four performers were complete strangers. Two were not bad but all tried too hard to impress. Even Paul Malldon had lost his usual swagger. When it was his turn he put too much emotion into a song that did not require it. When the interval arrived it was a relief. The only person to buck the trend had been Gordon Hutcheson the club's longest serving member. His forte is comic folk songs in the style of Matt McGinn and he supplied some much needed light relief with a song about mobile phone use in public spaces called 'That's me on the train.'

When Donny saw Colette come through the door he rose from his meagre perch and made his way over to meet her.

'Well I didn't expect this.'

'Don't get too excited. Billy wouldn't put your name down. You probably won't get on.'

'Nice one! I just passed him on the stairs and he didn't let on.'

'Sorry I did try but he had a list as long as your arm. I'm not sure I'll get on myself.'

'I'm going to try anyway. Can you get me a bottle of water?'

Colette went in search of Billy while Donny headed to the bar which had thankfully calmed down a bit, purchasing a pint of Amstel and an outrageously expensive plastic bottle of water.

Colette returned looking annoyed.

'Any luck?'

'Nope. List already too full.' Donny quickly changed the subject.

'Don't you want to know how I got on this morning?'

'Of course, that's more important.'

Donny broke the news that their only lead had died in nineteen seventy-eight and relayed everything Tam was able to tell him. The information added to Colette's gloom.

'He doesn't sound like someone who has written some great songs, does he?'

'No he does not.' Donny conceded. 'But he must be connected to our man.'

'Or woman?'

'Or woman, but I think we are looking for a man if it's connected to Daniel. It's Glasgow in nineteen seventy-eight we're talking about, remember.'

'Mm.' Colette knew he was right but she was still peeved that he had a spot on the busiest night in the club's history and she didn't.

'Are the Odd Couple performing tonight?'

'Donny and Colette turned to find Pat Cullen, blogger and freelance journalist. Pat covered the local music scene in his blog and had a good reputation for spotting up and coming talent. He also reviewed gigs and demos for the evening paper.

Donny was first to respond. 'Hello Pat.' How are you doing?'

'Not so bad. Yourself?'

'Aye fine.'

'And you Colette?'

'Good thanks. Are you down hoping to see Cathy or should I say Kate?'

'No, I didn't expect her to be here but I knew there would be a good crowd in. Thought it would be worth my while.'

'Seen anything you like so far?' Donny asked.

'What do you think?'

'Last week was better.' Colette chipped in.

'So I heard. I missed the whole Cathy phenomenon. Didn't see it coming. I feel a bit of a dick.'

'You didn't see the Celtic Connections thing then?'

'On Thursday night you mean.'

'Aye.'

'No. I had an invitation too. It was sent to the paper unfortunately and they are none too pleased I passed it up. I went to see an American band at King Tuts instead, supposed to be big in New York. They were shite.'

'What do you make of Cathy's sudden change of fortune?' Donny enquired.

'Not you as well. People have been nipping my ear all night. Get over it. Cathy has got it together now, her old stuff is history.'

'But is it all her work?' Colette posed.

'Outside of this room nobody cares. Of course she is getting help. I heard the line-up of that band that's backing her. Someone's paying. Will they get their money back? I don't know.'

'It's not the promotion that's bothering me.' Donny stated. 'Good luck to her with that. It's the songs themselves. Did Cathy write them?' Colette tapped Donny's ankle with her foot, warning him not to give too much away.

'I don't know how much is Cathy and how much is her co-writer but she is the face the public will see. It's not unusual, as Tom Jones might say. You know that.'

Donny was puzzled. ' Wait a minute. What do you mean her co-writer?'

'W. McSwiggen.'

It was Colette's turn to be nonplussed. 'W. McSwiggen. Who's that?'

'Cathy's co-writer. The paper has a promotional CD. Very professional, pressed, not burned on a computer, placed in one of those fancy cardboard jobs. Anyway I noticed its got copyright reserved to K. Rydelle and W. McSwiggen printed on it.'


Donny never did get to sing. Billy's one song rule was systematically undermined by the seven minute anthem and the three minute introduction. Donny gave up hope after the third performer of the second half. He and Colette made for the bar across the street for a chance to talk.

Pat had been unable to supply any information on who W McSwiggen was and most irritating to Donny and Colette, he didn't seem to care.

'Any ideas Donny?'

'On McSwiggen?'

'What else?'

'Never heard of him.'

'Do you think he is the one on the tapes? On the tapes Cathy has that is.'

'I don't know. Did she track him down after hearing the

songs on the tape? That would make sense. If the songs were written in the seventies he will probably be over sixty by now and quite happy to stay in the background. A bit like Martin Quittenton.'

'And he is?'

'Co-wrote Maggie May and You Wear It Well, with Rod Stewart. Rod's first two number one hits.'

'I didn't know that. I just assumed Rod Stewart wrote them himself.'

'Most people do, and that's the point, but Quittenton's name is there on the record and he picks up half the writing royalties without any of the hassle. McSwiggen could do the same.'

'But at least Rod wrote half the song. Cathy has done nothing.'

'Still a good deal. Cathy discovers the songs, recognises the quality and goes out there and makes them work. He had the songs all these years and did nothing with them.'

'That's another thing, why has he never done anything before now?'

'Good point but if the songs do come from the same period as our tape then you have to remember that type of music was well out of fashion by then. It was all Punk followed by New Wave then into the eighties, it was New Romantics. With no internet to contend with, the record companies called the shots and being out of fashion meant being down and out. He probably gave up.

'But Donny, that goes against everything you have always said. A good song is a good song, no matter what style it was written in.'

'Well it's the only thing I can think of.'

There was a sense of anti-climax on the drive back to the South Side. It looked like there had been no mystery to solve after all. For Donny, no skullduggery to uncover and for Colette, the chance of collaborating with a master songwriter had gone. Few words passed between them, each believing that the other blamed them for a pointless wild goose chase and a wasted week. When Donny climbed down from the Land Rover, there was no arrangement to keep in touch, only that they would see each other at next week's open mike.

# Chapter 10

Six months previously

Cathy picked up the old dark blue school notebook and stared once again at the front cover. Written in blue ballpoint pen and scored through with two lines in black were the words O level History (Alternative) 1972. It had come into her possession as part of a job lot, a battered suitcase without its lid containing a tape recorder, assorted tapes, a pile of papers and notebooks picked up at a stall in the Barras market.

Cathy had visited the stall, flicking through a cardboard box of twelve inch vinyl, when another stall holder came up and deposited the case on the floor beside her.

'Think you can shift this Bob?'

'What is it?'

'Music stuff, from a house clearance.' Bob leaned over his stall to have a look, noticing a reel to reel recorder.

'Does it work?'

'Don't know, its been under a bed since the owner died forty years ago.'

'Leave it there and I'll have a look. How much are you looking for?'

'I thought fifty.'

'Fifty! I'll be lucky to get that myself and that could take weeks. I'll give you twenty, if it sells.'

'Deal.'

Cathy had been listening to the conversation with interest, a reel to reel recorder might be good to use for home demos she thought. She had read that tape produced a warmer sound than digital. She bent over to have a closer look. Sticking out of the heap of loose papers was the sheet music to Ride a White Swan by T Rex. When Cathy had examined further, there were at least twenty copies of sheet music, all from the early seventies. The other papers were hand-written lyrics and chords to songs whose titles she didn't recognize.

'How much for the whole box?' Cathy asked.

'Sixty for the lot.'

'I don't know if the tape machine works and the rest is just rubbish. I'll give you thirty and I'll get it out of your way. That's ten pounds profit for two minutes work.

The stall holder smiled, he had not noticed that Cathy had been listening to his conversation. 'Forty.'

'Deal.'

The journal in her hand was part of a set of three, each one fashioned from the unused pages of school notebooks.

She flipped open the hard cardboard cover and looked inside. The first dozen or so pages had been neatly cut out, leaving long narrow stubs connected to the binding. At the top of the first of the remaining pages, written in block capitals were the words, 'MUSICAL NOTES  22 August 1975.' The first entry was, 'passed the audition for the Willie Stewart Band (YA BEAUTY!!!) Thirty songs to learn for a week on Tuesday. Only know four of them. HELP!'

Cathy had read these words many times. She had read everything from cover to cover in each of the three volumes twice, and the final two months entries many more times than that. She identified with and understood the writer better than anyone she knew or had ever known. If there is such a thing as a soulmate, something she had previously doubted, then surely she had found one in the pages of an old journal that smelled of damp. Cathy felt an attachment to the writer, she connected with him, wished she had been born into the same era as him, wished she had known him. The writing style was simple, natural, unforced, and Cathy would read her favourite passages for the sheer pleasure of it. The life of a semi-pro musician with a mundane day job was made exciting, even glamorous, within those pages. Appreciative fans when the band played, admiring girls when they stopped and lock-ins in pubs at the end of the night. The cast of characters were vivid in Cathy's imagination. The stars of the soap opera were band members Willie, Dennis, Ronny, the writer and Bobby, the roadie who ferried the band to and from gigs in the works van that a trusting employer allowed him to take home at night. Cathy laughed out loud reading the account of the night the band were on the Loch Lomand road, on their way to a gig at the RAF base at Machrihanish. Bobby's boss on a weekend break with his wife and family overtook the van, put on his hazard lights and indicated that Bobby should stop. In the writers own words

*'If you can keep your head when all*

about you are losing their's, then you'll be a roadie my son.'

Bobby told everyone in the back to keep their heads down, don't make a sound and don't move. Only Willie was visible in the front seat. Bobby jumps out quick and meets his boss as far away from the van as possible.

Boss. 'What the fuck is this then?'

Willie. 'I was going camping. We usually go in my mate's car.' indicates Willie who gives a wave, suppresses a laugh and flicks the remains of a joint into the long grass at the side of the road.'We usually go in his car but it wouldn't start and we couldn't work out what was wrong.'

Boss. 'I trusted you, ya cunt.'

Wife. 'Alasdair! Will you mind your language, the children can hear you.'

Boss. 'No fucking wonder.'

Wife. 'Alasdair!'

Boss to Bobby. 'See what you've done?'

Bobby. 'It is just this once, its never happened before. I tried to phone the office, thought I would catch you, but there was no answer.'

Boss. 'Do you think my head buttons up the fucking back?'

Wife. 'Alasdair!' Louder this time.

Everyone in the back of the van gets the giggles and the van starts to shudder. Willie pretends it is caused by him and starts moving about in the front seat. Looks like he needs to pee.

Bobby. 'I'm really sorry. I'll put in the petrol.'

Boss. 'Damn right you will.' No response from the wife this time, damn must be an acceptable word for the children to hear.

Bobby. 'I'm really sorry.'

Boss. 'You're not even insured if it's outside work. Do you know that? What if you have an accident? What then?'

Bobby. 'No, it's ok. My own insurance covers me for driving any vehicle. I'm not that daft.' Bobby does not own a car. 'Look I'll turn round right now and go back if you say so but we're nearly there. What do you say?'

Long pause

Boss. 'Where are you going anyway? The anger has gone out of his voice.

Bobby. 'Arrochar, it's only another five miles.'

Boss. 'Arrochar! That's where my caravan is.'

Ronny can't hold it in and lets out a grunt. Willie pretends to sneeze and tells us under his breath that Bobby's boss is looking at the van. Bobby stays calm. Dennis whispers his leg has gone to sleep and he will need to move it. Willie does his I need to pee routine.

Bobby. 'You're going to Arrochar too, that's brilliant. I'll stand you a pint if you *are in the pub, we all will.' Boss does not pick up on the slip.*

*Boss. 'I'll hold you to that. Remember this is the last time.'*

*Bobby. 'It won't happen again.' Bobby jumps back into the van. 'Wanker.'*

Ten minutes later a brown and tan Ford Granada turns into the camping and caravan park while a blue Transit van, wheel arches scraping the tyres, passes straight on.

In addition to the band members, the journals had a strong supporting cast including the likes of agents, promoters and venue owners, all of them described in the most unflattering of terms. Adding further colour were the plethora of extras, mentioned once, then never again. Then there were the guest stars who would suddenly appear, stay for a few entries, then disappear just as quick, like the sound engineer with the tattoo on his arm, that was so badly done that he always had a large sticking plaster covering it. Cathy knew the names or nicknames of many of these people, but the one name Cathy did not know was the that of the writer himself. In the three years covered in the journal, he had not recorded his own name once. She also knew little of the writer's personal life for the journal only related to his music, from performing on stage to practising alone in his bedroom, from the cover versions he struggled to master to his own compositions that the band showed no interest in hearing.

Cathy picked up the third of the set of three notebooks and turned to the final page of writing though there was little need, she knew every word by heart. Cathy read the final two entries anyway. Could it really be true? It was hard to believe but what if it was true?

Cathy knew what she had to do but had been putting it off. After a further minute of hesitation she turned to her laptop, an email had already been written. Cathy read it through one more time, attached the audio file already prepared and pressed the send button. Turning back to the notebook, on impulse Cathy tore out the final two pages of writing and placed them in the pocket of her jeans.

.   .   .   .   .

Neither Colette nor Donny slept well on Tuesday night. Each had the feeling that a unique opportunity had been snatched away from them. When it had been assumed that Cathy had in effect stolen someone else's work, there were many possibilities for both Donny and Colette. All that had to be done was track down the writer who, overcome with gratitude, would be only too willing to share their genius with them. Irritatingly, it now looked like everything was above board after all and the partnership of Rydelle and McSwiggen was not only working, but working fast.

For Colette, she had lost the chance to team up with a writer that would supply the finesse she knew was lacking in her own compositions, if they could have been persuaded to collaborate as a co writer. It would have been someone who had in fact already produced the goods and could have delivered excellent material right into her hands now, if she was able to entice them to do so. At the age of twenty-five, time was already running out she realized, so for Colette a swift assent to the higher echelons of the music world, without the customary period of poverty and struggle, was the only option. She would never consider giving up a medical career she had worked so hard to achieve any other way. The events of the past week had allowed her to acknowledge an ambition that was kept suppressed in her subconscious but now aroused, it couldn't be ignored.

With Donny it was the chance to learn that was now lost, and learn first hand from someone who had cracked the formula he had strived so hard to find. Someone that could have supplied the answers, he had long been searching for. Someone, perhaps, who could be persuaded to review Donny's own songs, providing that genuine authoritative criticism so hard to come by. He knew no amount of books, documentaries or courses could deliver what some time spent with the genuine article could. The last seven days had heightened his ambitions and the thought of losing that sense of opportunity was depressing.

Colette's subconscious mind must have been working overtime because when she woke at six thirty, she knew she had only one card left to play if her new found aspirations were ever to be realized. She would need to gain access to McSwiggen, whoever he was. She would contact Cathy direct. It would be awkward of course, as they had never been friends, and never really had much to say to each other in the past, but Colette had confidence, she would think of something to say. If she could not have McSwiggen to herself, sharing with Cathy would have to do. Implementing this plan would take place after her shift, allowing her subconscious mind a whole day to come up with a workable strategy.

Donny woke at ten also in a surprisingly optimistic mood. If there was no foul play and everything was above board why not just ask Cathy for access to her co-writer. He was not after all wanting anything other than some advice. He was not trying to steal her collaborator, just learn from him. That was decided, he would contact Cathy and see if she could arrange a meeting between him and her co-writer. A very reasonable request surely, from one songwriter to another. Before that however, there was a long overdue trip to the supermarket, followed by a full afternoon of lessons. Don't just charge in however, give yourself time to think about the best way to ask the question, Donny told himself.


At 7.15pm Colette left her flat to make her way to Stewartville Street in Partick, a distance of about a mile. She had found Cathy's address in the Songwriters Club newsletter. The newsletter also contained a phone number but it was too easy to make excuses on the phone or say, I'll get back to you, or simply say no.

Colette had decided to travel on foot. The weather was not too cold and was dry but more importantly, the long walk out past Kelvingrove Museum and across the river Kelvin into Partick, would give her more time to think what she would say to Cathy, for her subconscious mind had failed her and despite thinking about it all afternoon, she really had no ideas. By the time she turned off Dumbarton Road into Stewartville Street, Colette was not at all confident her, not thought out, plan would be successful, but what other options did she have.

The entrance to the close was unlocked so Colette was able to walk straight in and make her way up the stairs towards flat 2/2.

'Looking for someone?' It was Donny making his way down the stairs.

Colette was uncharacteristically flustered. 'What are you doing here?'

'Same as you, I expect, but she's gone. Her flatmate said she left on Friday night without a word to anyone.'

'Did the flatmate tell you anything else?'

'Only that Derek is in the Lismore and that he might know more.'

'Are you heading there now?'

'Might as well.'

'I'll come too.'

Donny and Colette made their way back down Stewarville Street towards Dumbarton Road.

'Billy Connolly lived in this street when he was a child,' Donny remarked.

'Did he? Do you know what number?'

'No. I just remember reading it somewhere.'

It only took five minutes to reach the pub, all varnished wood and original fittings. Derek was indeed present as they had been told.

'Hello Derek'

'Donny! Don't they have any decent pubs in the South Side?'

'To tell you the truth we were looking for Cathy. I was up at the flat and your flatmate told me you were in here.'

'Aye, it was on Friday that she left. When I got in from the pub her room door was open and all her stuff was gone.'

'Have you any idea where she went?'

'No. She never said anything to me about moving out.'

Derek was the only person that could help despite his apparent lack of knowledge, so Donny decided to get a round in and they all took a seat in the corner near the door. Colette unusually, took a half of cider reasoning that it looked a bit more sociable than her usual soda water. Derek asked for a malt that Donny couldn't pronounce. He got him a Glen Grant instead.

'I checked out Cathy after I talked to you. She has made amazing progress, Derek.'

'That's what I was telling you. She told Eileigh, the other girl in the flat, she hopes to get a deal soon.'

'Did you know she has changed her name?'

'No. What to?'

'Kate Rydelle.'

'No way.'

Colette was getting impatient with Donny's beating about the bush and decided to interject. 'Do you know her co-writer, W McSwiggen?'

'Will McSwiggen?' Derek looked puzzled.

'I suppose so I didn't know what the W stood for.'

'That's the landlord's son. What makes you think he is Cathy's co-writer?'

'His name is on a promo demo sent to the papers.'

'Well there must be some mistake. I can assure you, Will

McSwiggen is not the songwriting type and besides, Cathy hates him.'

'What do you mean?' Donny asked.

'He is a bit of an arse, you know, always hanging about trying to chat up the girls when he collects the rent, which has to be cash of course, and never a receipt.'

'You shouldn't put up with that,' Colette advised.

'Aye sure. His father is Geordie McSwiggen. You heard of him?'

'No.'

'Well lets just say it's his way or the highway. It's a good flat and the rent's not too high which suits me. As long as you don't cross him, you're fine.'

'What is he? Some sort of gangster? Donny asked.

'You could say that.'

'What do you mean?'

'On the surface he's legit, owns pubs, has a bunch of flats and other stuff that he rents out, but who knows. He also has a garage up Springburn direction. Will is the idiot son. He collects the rent and runs the errands. Any problems, Geordie sorts it out. If anything were to happen to Geordie, Will wouldn't last five minutes.'

'Has this Will got anything to do with the music business?' Colette asked

'You might say that. He runs club nights up the town for posh kids. You know, hires a pub or a big room, gets in a DJ playing dance stuff. He charges a fortune at the door but I suspect he makes most of his money dealing.'

'Drugs?' Colette checked.

'What else? The venues usually chase him after the first night and he has to find somewhere else.'

Colette looked at Donny. 'Doesn't sound like a songwriter does it?'

'No it does not.' Donny agreed.

'I can one hundred percent guarantee it.' Derek chucked in. 'I don't know why Cathy would get mixed up with him, as I said she hates him.'

Donny emerged from the Lismore at ten thirty satisfied that he had extracted every useful piece of information Derek possessed. Colette had left an hour earlier. Donny had learned that Cathy was from Oban and had come down to Glasgow originally to work in a call centre, operated by a car insurance company. She had two brothers and two sisters, all older than her. One brother lived in Glasgow, one sister in Dundee and the other two still lived in Oban, as do her parents. In the flat, Derek occupied the former living room for which he paid the largest rent, and the two girls had a bedroom each. They shared the bathroom and the tiny kitchen. Technically this made the flat a house of multiple occupancy, requiring a licence, but the McSwiggen's didn't bother with details like that. Derek explained that she had given up her current job in the children's nursery two months back to concentrate on music, ignoring all advice from himself and Eileigh. Derek had never seen McSwiggen and Cathy together apart from rent days and could only suggest that he had put up the money in exchange for a cut of any future earnings, a theory shared by Colette. Donny was not so sure, pointing out that writers' royalties were usually the biggest part of an artist's income, earning money even after they are dead. Cathy would know this and not sign away her rights lightly.

The fact that the rights probably belonged to someone else in the first place did complicate things of course, but that could not be discussed with Derek.

Out on the street Donny couldn't help noticing the contrasting fortunes of Partick and Bridgeton. Both had been neighbourhoods of tightly packed tenement buildings but for some reason Partick had largely been spared the planner's attention in the sixties and seventies and was now adapting well to the modern age. There were no vacant premises, as far as Donny could see, on the area's main thoroughfare and the street was busy with people even at that hour. Houses, that were too small for the large families of the past, were now spacious airy apartments for one or two people. Partick, it seemed to Donny, had been allowed to evolve and reinvent itself, whereas Bridgeton did not get the chance.

Colette had been pleased with the night's revelations. The jaws of defeat had stalled and victory was once again a possibility. The source of Cathy's success was still out there somewhere, certainly being exploited if McSwiggen was involved, and possibly unaware that it was happening. Donny too was once again curious. He thought it was unlikely that Daniel Quick was that writer, from what he had learned in Bridgeton the day before and the fact that the song on the tape was pretty poor. Daniel must be connected in some way, Donny was certain of that, but in what way?

It was not yet eleven as Donny stood on the platform of Kelvinhall underground station, time yet for one more port of call before the night was over.

Donny could hear that the The Briggait Blues Band had already started their final set as he approached the Scotia Bar. Inside was less than half-full, Wednesday was not the best night for a pub gig. Donny ordered a pint at the bar then made his way round the odd shape to take a seat a few feet in front of the band. Mikey gave a smile of recognition, seeming to understand that Donny had returned with more questions to ask. The guitarist was playing the Epiphone Casino through a Marshall amp and four by twelve cabinet, and the combination was producing a very pleasant sound to Donny's ears. Blues was not his favourite style of music but the band were all fine players and the half hour till the end of their set passed quickly.

'Did you forget to ask something?' Mikey inquired, while removing his guitar and placing it against his amp.

'Maybe. I found out that Daniel Quick died in nineteen seventy-eight. His mother kept all his stuff and she only died herself a few months ago.'

'Right. That would explain why the guitar is in such good nick.'

'Yeah, probably hadn't been played for nearly forty years. The guy that sold it to you was his nephew I think.'

'Did you find out what you wanted anyway?'

'Afraid not.'

'Thought so. Did you talk to the dick that sold it to me?'

'No. That was his grannie's house you were in. His name is also Daniel, but not Quick. I don't know his second name but I don't think he will be able to help.'

'What was it you wanted to know again?'

'I've got this old tape and wanted to track down the people on it. I'm pretty sure it is Daniel playing your guitar, but I don't know if he was also the singer or the writer. I was wondering if there was anything else you knew that might help. Did anything else come with the guitar?'

'No, just the guitar.'

'And the original receipt.' Donny prompted

'Aye, and the receipt.'

'But nothing else?'

'It says Willie Stewart Band on the case. Is that any help?'

'The Willie Stewart Band?' Donny was searching his pockets for a pen.

'Aye. Do you want to see it?' Mikey retrieved the case from behind the amplifiers and passed it to Donny. 'Look.' Mikey pointed to two strips of thin plastic with raised lettering stating 'Daniel Quick Willie Stewart Band'. 'Ever heard of them?'

Donny shook his head. 'Have you?'

'If it was nineteen seventy-eight it was eleven years before I was born.'

'Good point.'

'Some of these guys might know.' Mikey nodded towards some of the older drinkers at the bar. 'Anyone heard of a band from the seventies called the Willie Stewart Band?'

'No. but you can book them for next Wednesday,' retorted one of the group. The rest shouted, 'good idea.'

'Aye very good. Seriously anybody heard of them, or a guitarist called Daniel Quick?' The older drinkers shook their heads. One of the barmen repeated the questions to the far side of the bar but nobody that side had heard of them either. 'It was worth a try.'

'Thanks.'

'You could try on Friday night, it will be a lot busier then.'

'Might do that. Listen, I never said. I really enjoyed your set. That's a great sound you're getting from your guitar.'

A ten minute discussion on the merits of the single coiled pick-up compared to that of the humbucker ensued, which would have lasted longer had Donny not remembered that a number 75 passed down Stockwell Street at ten minutes past twelve. January was not a time to stand around at bus stops, if it could be avoided.

# Chapter 11

Six and a half months previously.

Stuart could not believe he had never thought of it before. All those nights lying in bed worrying where the next hit might come from, and all that time the answer was a mere ten feet above his head. Nat Quilby was the man to thank for the answer to all his problems and it had only cost him twelve dollars. If it wasn't for the fact that Mr Quilby died in nineteen ninety-seven Stuart would have tracked him down to express his gratitude in person.

It was the book, the one he bought on the way back from the accountants. The paperback that sat on the table marked new releases. The Morreli Murders by Nat Quilby. Stuart had picked it up intending only to read the first paragraph. He liked it, read some more and decided to buy. It served its purpose well. The story diverted his mind from his troubles and exhaustion eventually brought sleep as he had hoped. It had taken two weeks to read the book to the end.

Stuart was eating breakfast the morning after finishing the book, wondering what he would read next, the book sat on the table beside him. Perhaps he might buy another book by Nat Quilby he thought. He looked inside the cover to see if there was any information and was amazed to notice that the book had first been published in nineteen seventy-five and re-printed this year. He had never suspected that the story was not new.

That was the eureka moment. The book had looked like any of the other books on the New Releases table. Stuart was happy to pick it up. And when he did, he liked it and bought it. Surely I could do the same thing with music, Stuart thought. In the attic was either the master or a copy of every recording he had ever been involved with, including all the pre digital stuff from the nineties backwards, his most prolific period. A bowl of muesli and natural yoghurt was pushed to one side then Stuart took the stairs to the top of the house, two at a time.

The attic was one big room running the whole length of the house, with the staircase entering in the middle. It was exclusively used for storing recording tapes and discs, everything from his first sessions with punk bands in nineteen seventy-seven. It was not the hits he was interested in, they could remain carefully stored in their custom-made, locked flight cases, for they were already out there, familiar to three generations. It was all the other songs, the ones that never made it into the record stores or on to the radio, that's what excited him, and there was plenty of it, boxes and boxes full. Stuart knew there were many fine songs that were never included on the albums for which they were intended. Good tracks rejected for the flimsiest of reasons, too long, too short, too different from the rest of the album. He could even remember tracks rejected because they were considered too commercial and the band feared it would harm their credibility and alienate their fans.

It was all coming back to Stuart as he opened boxes, finding names he had long stopped thinking about. He was finding what he remembered as good original songs by professional songwriters that were suddenly ditched by the artist in favour of something inferior, written by themselves, so that the artist could get all the royalties. Some of these songs found a new home where they were appreciated, many did not.

There were more boxes than he thought, recordings Stuart had completely forgotten about. He decided to be systematic and take the boxes one at a time out to his home studio above the garage. He picked the oldest box and headed downstairs.

The TEAK reel to reel recorder was switched on for the first time in ten years and one of the ten inch spools loaded. As the tape spun round at fifteen inches per second Stuart was re-acquainted with work he had long forgotten. Early takes, featuring only acoustic guitar or piano, revealed songs in their primitive state, only on later takes did the production values of the time date the music. This is what he was looking for, raw material, pure and unfashioned, ready to be recalibrated for the present market. He had forgotten how much the recording process could change a song, making it unrecognisable from the songwriters original demo, in some cases.

The frenzy of activity taking place in the studio was reminiscent of old times and Heidi happily attended to the kids, leaving Stuart in peace to get on with it. She was blissfully unaware of the desperate nature of the endeavour.

Over the course of the next two weeks, many gems were

uncovered. A lot of material, even though they had been released, never got proper promotion from the record company and therefore sank without trace, leaving further seams of gold unknown to the music listening public. Stuart was also finding some well-produced tracks that had been pulled at the last minute because the public's tastes had suddenly changed. Stuart understood this and perhaps he had even been party to the decision, no artist (or producer) wants to be tagged as old hat but these were excellent pieces of music and now available for reincarnation.

Stuart's head was buzzing with competing ideas and he had started listening to the demos he received every day via email, searching for the right voice. Pop music was no longer fashion driven, at least not in the way it was in the past, the internet had seen to that. So just as with the book, if the music was new to the listener, if it was packaged like new, would anyone care that it had been created twenty years earlier or thirty or forty. It would be new to them and that's what would count. It just had to be presented to the music buying public in the most palatable way. That was the secret, always had been.

.     .     .     .     .

Needless to say the internet had never heard of the Willie Stewart band when Donny asked on his return from the Scotia. Now as he ate a bowl of porridge for breakfast he tried every combination of Willie Stewart, Daniel Quick, music, songs, guitars and Bridgeton that he could think of, but still came up with nothing. If Willie Stewart was still alive, he was no longer involved in the music business. Six of Donny's guitar pupils were of an age to remember local bands of the seventies and a text was sent to five of them. Colin, who did not do texts, was phoned instead. None of them could help. Colette could ask the guys in her tribute band and if that failed, the Scotia on a Friday night was still worth a try but for now Donny was out of ideas. He boiled the kettle for a cup of tea and turned the TV on. Big George! The name just popped into his head. Donny picked up his phone and started scrolling down his call register.

'Hello George, it's Donny McNeil here. I came down to see you last Friday.'

'About the old tape.'

'That's right.'

'I take it you haven't found him yet.'

'Well actually I think I did but he died in nineteen seventy-eight.'

'Nae luck.'

'I've got a name for him though and the band he played with and I thought you might know something about them.'

'Cause it's my era you're thinking. Don't rub it in. OK what's the name?'

'Daniel Quick.'

'Doesn't ring a bell.'

'I think he played in a band called the Willie Stewart Band.'

'Scotland's most successful record producer?'

'Who?'

'Willie Stewart.'

'I've never heard of him.'

'Oh I think you have.' George was enjoying this.

'No. Definitely never heard of him.'

'Over The Castle Wall?'

'Stuart Williamson?'

'The very same.'

'Stuart Williamson is Willie Stewart?' Donny was astonished.

'Changed his name when he went down to London.'

'Did you know him?'

'Not really. We used to play all the same gigs, the Burns Howff, the Ship, the Amphora. I saw the band play a few times. They just played covers like the rest of us back then but they were class, Steely Dan, Santana, Van Morrison, all note perfect with cracking vocals and harmonies. They were some band.'

'But they never got anywhere?'

'No they didn't. That is the music industry's loss. I don't know why they broke up but Willie headed for London and the rest as they say......'

'Do you know of anyone else that was in the band?'

'Ronny Gibson who played on 'Over The Castle Wall.' He is the owner of Big Beat.'

'The drum shop in town?'

'Aye. He set it up with the money he made in the Baggies. I think he followed Willie down to London but got fed up with the music scene and came back up the road and opened the shop.'

'Thanks George, that's been a big help.'

'No problem.'

So Willie changed his name and so had Cathy, Donny thought to himself. Coincidence? He knew all about Stuart Williamson. He penned and produced 'Over The Castle

Wall' for one hit wonders, the Baggies. It was a huge record just before the wheels came off the punk bandwagon. Few people realise Williamson is Scottish due to the low profile he has kept throughout his career. After the success of that first hit, he became the go to guy for producing guitar based pop and the hits just kept on coming. Donny knew however that Williamson did not write any of them, apart from the Baggie's solitary success. He moved to America in the mid-eighties when synthesisers were taking over the UK charts and continued successfully over there. Donny was not sure if he was still working or indeed if he was still alive.

Wikipedia confirmed he was still alive but not if he was still working. He had writing credits for some tracks in the noughties though. Hits seemed to be non-existent these days but he had been working with some credible artists fairly recently. Apart from lists of tracks he had produced, there was scant information about Stuart Williamson on the internet.

Donny sent a text to Colette. 'Think I have found something. Call when you get the chance.' He did not expect to hear back until after her shift, which would give him some time to think things over.

Was Stuart Williamson behind Cathy's pitch for stardom? It was a possibility. Was he and Cathy in some way connected, related even? If so, why offer help now and not years before? It seemed unlikely that he was the writer. 'Over The Castle Wall' was a huge hit but as a song it was rubbish, in Donny's opinion, though excellently produced. If Williamson was capable of writing songs of the quality Cathy was now singing, surely he would have recorded them by now. Then there was McSwiggen. Is he connected to Williamson? Donny wondered.

Donny decided a visit to Arturo's was required to get the grey cells working at full capacity. He would continue his research into Stuart Williamson there. More pressing however was the need to prepare for Kenny's last lesson, before he went back on the rigs. It was becoming less and less cost effective, continuing to teach Kenny, as every lesson required time to source new guitar parts. Kenny would happily pay more but Donny did not want to give the game away that the teacher was struggling to keep ahead of the pupil, deciding instead to treat preparations as part of his own continuing professional development.

Once outside his flat, Donny changed his mind about Arturo's. The temperature was barely above freezing but the sky was clear, a perfect day for a walk. Donny set off along Battlefield Road, his destination, Langside Library. The music section was small but well stocked with books on Scottish artists. Donny had learned much from its shelves over the years. There was one book in particular that he had taken out more than once, a chronicle of pop music in the city.

Ten minutes later Donny was crossing Sinclair Drive and climbing the steps to Langside Library. Once inside he made straight for the far corner. Luckily the book he was after had not been taken out. He took it down from the shelf and flicked through its pages for the entry on Stuart Williamson. He had read it before but could not remember the details. It soon became apparent why, there was no detail. No mention of Willie Stewart nor anything about his life before leaving for London. The only piece of information that he did not already know was that Williamson was born in Rutherglen, which was next door to Bridgeton.

There was nothing else on the shelves that yielded any information on Stuart Williamson. Donny suspected that would be the case but he had gone through the motions anyway. What did disappoint him more however, was the lack of anything that would give him ideas on what to do with Kenny, who was due in less than three hours.

Donny left the library to make his way back home. He turned the corner onto Battlefield Road in time to see a city centre bound bus pull into the stop. On impulse Donny ran to catch it.

Big Beat was an impressive operation, a double fronted shop on Trongate, crammed full of every form of percussion instrument, with plenty of staff on hand to sell them. One of the assistants approached Donny as he entered the emporium.

'Is there anything I can help you with sir?'

'I'm not buying. Sorry.' The assistant looked a little worried. 'I was hoping to have a word with Ronny Gibson. Is he in?'

'Can you tell me what it is about?'

'Its about his old band, The Willie Stewart Band.'

'I'll go and ask. What name will I say?'

'He won't know me but my name is Donny McNeil.' The assistant disappeared down a flight of stairs at the back of the shop. Donny had a look at the drum kits.

'Is there anything I can help you with?'

'It's OK I'm getting attended to.' A dispirited salesman returned to behind the counter. The first assistant returned followed by a bald-headed man, dressed completely in black. The assistant pointed towards Donny.

'You wanted to see me?'

'Hello. Are you Ronny Gibson?'

'Aye. Alan says you wanted to ask about the Willie Stewart Band.'

'That's right.'

'Well you are the first to come into the shop and ask that. What do you want to know?'

'I came across an old reel to reel tape that I think was recorded by Daniel Quick.'

'Wee Dan. I've no' heard that name for thirty years. Dan is dead. Did you know that? He got knocked down by a bus.'

'Yeah I knew. It was a lorry actually, he had ran in front of a bus.'

'Was it? I was living in London at the time. Poor guy.'

'I just found out that Stuart Williamson played in the band with you and Dan.'

'You're not the first to come into the shop asking about him.'

'I didn't think I would be. The thing is, these tapes I've got. I wanted to know who wrote the songs.'

'Did they sound like someone else? Like something that had been done before.'

'No.'

'It wouldn't be the Willie Stewart Band then?'

'How do you mean?'

'We were destined to failure in the songwriting

department from the very start but didn't realise it.'

'How's that?'

'Me and Willie that is. We had been in bands since we were fifteen. We learned hundreds of songs. By the time we were eighteen we could play Stones and Beatles stuff, and all the other bands at the time, as good as they could themselves. The trouble was when we tried to write our own material, in our twenties, they always sounded like someone else, and worse than that, like someone who was already out of date.'

'Why did Stuart change his name?'

'You mean why did Willie change his name? The record companies all knew Willie, at least by name, we had been sending demo tapes to them for years. When punk came along Willie thought he could jump on the band wagon even though he hated the stuff. He didn't think they would take him seriously if he suddenly turned up playing punk, so he simply changed his name and they were none the wiser. Willie went down to London in the summer of seventy-seven. I didn't fancy it. I worked in the tax office and only worked with the band at night. Willie only had the band.'

'What about the other guys?'

'Willie didn't ask them. He knew they wouldn't fit in. Dan was a right hippy, though he was still in primary school when all that flower power stuff was happening, he still had really long hair and said 'man' at the end of every sentence. Dennis, the base player, was the oldest in the band and was married with a kid.'

'Could you not have kept going without Willie?'

'The Willie Stewart band without Willie, eh? Like the Sensational Alex Harvey Band without Alex?'

'Suppose so.'

'Willie was the singer and shared lead guitar with Dan. He was too hard to replace. I got a job in a club band and just worked weekends.'

'And the other two?'

'Don't know. Once a band splits up you go your separate ways, you know how it is. I never saw Dan again, sadly. I have met up with Dennis but that was not until years later.'

Donny knew exactly what he meant, you may spend every night of the week with the band playing gigs or rehearsing, then the band splits and you never see some of them again. 'Did Dan or Dennis do any writing do you know?'

'Well, not Dennis. Dan might have, but he never wrote anything for the band. Why do you ask?'

'One of the songs I heard was about Bridgeton.'

'Aye, Dan came from Bridgeton right enough, but as I said, he never showed anything to the band.'


Ronny was quite happy to talk so Donny kept asking questions.

'How did you come to join the Baggies if you didn't go down to London with Willie?'

'I went down about six months after Willie. He had been answering ads in the musicians wanted columns of the Melody Maker before going down and ended up joining one of the bands. I think Willie was the only one that could actually play but they had the contacts. They were all living in a squat at first. Anyway they got a deal and went into the studio to record their first single. It was awful. When the rest of the band left the studio, Willie stayed, overdubbing and rerecording the other guys' parts. When the band heard it they hated it and insisted that the original version be released. Oh, and they sacked Willie. It flopped of course. The label dropped the band and offered Willie a job sorting out some of the other bands on the label. That's when he got me down. I thought this is probably my last chance to do something in music, so I gave up the tax job and headed south. Hardly anyone could play their instruments properly. Me and Willie would show them what to do or, more often than not, play it for them. Willie was arranging the songs, doing overdubs on guitar and adding backing vocals, eventually taking over as producer.'

'How did the Baggies come about?'

'That was more than a year later. Punk was dying and the label with it. It was the final throw of the dice. The Baggies were from Birmingham, had been signed for two years but had only released one single that only just made the top one hundred. Only the singer was left in London, the rest had all returned home. Willie came up with the song after seeing the Skids on Top of the Pops, it's the same idea as 'Into The Valley'. Willie said it is about a gang from where he lived in Rutherglen fighting with a gang from Castlemilk, which was the other side of a big wall.'

'The song is about Glasgow then, I didn't know that.'

'Well the Baggies were from Birmingham so it seemed best not to confuse the record buying public. None of the band played on the record but the label got them back to do all the promotion. I appeared in the video and on Top of the Pops with the old drummer miming backing vocals and playing tambourine. We never did any live gigs.'

'So who actually played on the record?'

'Just me, Willie and the singer, Gorden Cottle. Willie spent weeks on it. We went back and started from scratch four times. There was endless takes for the vocals and overdubs. We all knew it was our last chance.'

'And it worked.'

'Yeah it did.'

By the time Donny left Big Beat, the sun had already dipped behind the buildings on the south side of Trongate, casting long cold shadows over the street. It had been a fascinating conversation. Ronny had lost contact with Willie after returning to Glasgow and knew nothing of what his old mate was doing now but Donny was more than happy to listen and learn from someone who had actually been there and done it. He also had a number for Dennis, the Willie Stewart band's bass player. Donny was pleased with the days work and wondering what to do now, when he suddenly remembered.

'Shit! Kenny!'

# Chapter 12

There was a little over an hour of daylight left. Just enough time to drive home, change and complete five or six circuits of the park, before it got dark. That would still leave sufficient time to shower and make it to Café Go Go for five thirty. Colette turned the key in the ignition, pulled out of her parking space at the Royal Infirmary's multi-storey car park and headed for the exit.

She had read Donny's text but knew he would be busy with lessons for the next four or five hours, so did not reply. When she did reply, she told herself she wanted to have some news of her own. The previous night, she had checked out the Kate Rydelle website and facebook page. Cathy was sill attracting interest and gathering lots of fans but there was no new information, nothing to say she had left the city for example, and no mention of W. McSwiggen. A further search of the internet did find McSwiggen, Geordie that is. There were some newspaper articles on court cases, including one of attempted murder, that had either collapsed or failed to secure a conviction when witnesses failed to turn up or they had changed their story in court. Sometimes Geordie was the accused, sometimes he had been called as a witness. The only reference to Will was in providing an alibi for his father on an assault charge, five years ago. Colette would need to know exactly what she was dealing with, if she was to step on the McSwiggen's toes.

Crawford Cunningham picked a goats cheese and caramelised onion panini from the chilled cabinet and took it to the counter where he handed it over to be prepared. He added an Americano to the order and asked for some cold milk on the side. The cafe was busy but he spotted a couple of empty tables at the back. He selected the table furthest away. It was a pleasant surprise to hear from the girl that had lived next door to him from age five until she went off to University in Dundee, eight years ago. Since then, they had met only occasionally, the two year difference in their ages meant they were moving in different circles any time Colette returned home during the holidays. Crawford would have agreed to meet up for any reason but the fact that it was to pick his brain on his specialist subject was most intriguing. Criminology attracted more suspicion than interest in the neat suburban streets where they had grown up. Why don't you study Law, he was often advised. His masters degree, passed with distinction, did not get the same level of praise others received for ordinary degrees, in more conventional subjects. Embarking on a Ph.D. did nothing to enhance his standing. Crawford knew that former school friends found him a bit weird and he had learned to keep his field of study quiet.

The panini, nicely toasted and served with some salad, arrived at the same time as Colette. Crawford rose quickly to greet his friend sending the knife and fork, wrapped in a paper napkin, to the floor in the process.

'It's good to see you Colette. Can I get you something?'

'It's OK, I ordered a coffee at the counter. Good to see you, Crawford. How are things?' Colette took the seat opposite her childhood friend.

'Fine.'

'Has your mum accepted your choice of career yet?'

'No. She's still embarrassed by it. Still wants me to do Accountancy and work with my dad. I don't think she will ever get over it.'

'How are things going anyway? A Ph.D? Pretty impressive!'

'Well I'm not there yet, but it's going fine.'

'What is it you are researching anyway?' Colette already knew the answer.

'The effects of the Proceeds of Crime Act.'

'And is it effective?'

'It's early days. You know what they say, every time you improve the mouse trap, the mice get smarter.'

'Good point.'

Colette's coffee arrived and Crawford offered to share his panini which she declined.

'You said on the phone that I might be able to help you. Something to do with my course?'

'Do you know anything about someone called Will McSwiggen and his father Geordie McSwiggen?'

'Yeah I know about Geordie. I know you better stay well out of his way.'

'What about Will?'

'Don't know much about him. He was brought up by his mother. Geordie keeps him out of the business, the crime side that is. Second generation crime lords, it doesn't usually work. They are rarely as hard or as cunning as their fathers, they never needed to be. What's this all about Colette?' Crawford sounded concerned.

'A singer acquaintance of mine has teamed up with Will. He is down as her co-writer but I don't think he has anything to do with the writing.'

'Songwriting? That's a new one but you never know. They are always looking for ways to invest the money they make from crime or find ways to disguise where the money comes from. What's your friends name?'

Colette told him most of what had happened over the past week. Crawford listened with interest then asked the one question Colette knew would be coming.

'What is it you're hoping to achieve exactly?'

'Well that depends on what I find out.'

'Do you think your friend is being coerced?'

'She is not a friend exactly and no, I don't think she is being forced. She is doing pretty well out of it actually.'

'If the McSwiggins are involved I can assure you, if she is doing well, they will be doing better. Do you want to warn her about what she is getting into? If you do, you will need to be careful.'

'At the moment I can't contact her anyway. She has changed her phone by the look of things and moved out of her flat. Oh I didn't say, the flat is owned by Geordie McSwiggen.'

'Looks like she knows what she is getting involved in. I think you should leave well alone.' Crawford put his hand on Colette's arm.

Colette smiled. 'Don't worry I'm not going to do anything stupid. I agree Cathy is not an innocent in all this but I would still like to find out how you go from being a no hoper to the verge of stardom in three months.'

'So you can copy her?' Crawford had a knowing look on his face.'

'Well something like that. You would need to be involved in music to appreciate that things like that just don't happen. I would still like to know everything there is about the McSwiggens. All I know about Geordie is that he has never been convicted.'

'Oh he has been convicted. He did time for armed robbery, when he was only seventeen.'

'I googled him earlier, there was nothing about that, just a load of newspaper articles about trials that had collapsed.'

'Pre-internet times. It was a jewellers shop in Paisley. Four of them went in wielding hammers. The owner put up a struggle and got badly hurt, Geordie drove the getaway car. They got away with a substantial amount, I can't remember the exact value but it was big news at the time, from what I've read.'

'How did they get caught?'

'One of the gang, someone called Malcolm Oliver, kept one of the rings and gave it to his girlfriend who couldn't help showing it off. Someone shopped her and the gang were all arrested within a week of the robbery.'

'They must have been furious with her. Did they hurt her?'

'The girl was left alone as far as I know. It was Oliver that carried the can. He should never have kept anything. The rest of the haul was well gone, probably down south, abroad perhaps.'

'What happened to him?'

'Who knows? He disappeared the day he was released. Maybe he just knew it was best to get out of Glasgow, maybe his remains will turn up some day.' Colette winced.

'And after Geordie was released?'

'He was a lot more careful who he worked with.'

'Did he go back to armed robbery?'

'No. Things had changed by the time he got out. There was a heroin epidemic in the city. Nobody was doing armed robbery. It was all about supplying smack. That, and cannabis.'

'And that's what Geordie turned to?'

'It took him a while but he eventually took over most of the city centre. When others got into wars over territory, he kept out of it. They didn't see he was getting bigger all the time. Nor did the police for that matter.'

'Why did the police not notice?'

'If a criminal makes some money he tries to disguise where it comes from, otherwise the police will be on to them. So they start a legitimate business and channel the money through that. Could be a hairdressers or a tanning salon, anything that deals in cash. That way it appears that the source of the wealth is the business. Put the family or just some false names on the payroll. If you saw the books, it looks like a thriving business with a big turnover but if you ever visited it would be devoid of both customers and employees. They would need to pay some tax but a bent accountant would keep that to a minimum. A small price to pay for clean money to flaunt.'

'And is that what Geordie did?'

'Oh he was smarter than that. He started the business first. He may even have been going straight but the temptation of easy money was too great.'

'Would that be the garage?'

'Yeah, how did you know that?'

'Cathy's flatmate mentioned that he owned a garage.'

'Its not far from Stewart Street police station, just the other side of the motorway. Officers had been using it virtually from the day it opened, unaware that a drug operation was growing under their noses. Everything at the garage was more or less above board, as it is today in fact, but drugs have to be moved which was the weak link in the suppliers operation. Geordie spotted an opportunity. The police you see kept tags on the cars of known criminals. If they saw a car they recognised, they would follow it and see where it went. It might lead to someone they didn't know about. They might of course have reason to stop and search the car. This made it very precarious for the suppliers to get the drugs to the dealers, who in turn sold them on to the users.'

'Couldn't they take the bus, or walk?'

'Not likely Colette. Go to meet some dealer on foot with a couple of thousand pounds worth of heroin in your pockets, then make your way back with the money. I don't think so.'

'Sorry, just a thought.'

'Anyway that's how Geordie got into the business. He would provide a car when a supplier had to move some drugs. The car would only be used once, then go back on the forecourt to be sold. Lots of different gangs used Geordie. Soon he was running taxis and ice cream vans, vehicles that could go into the schemes without attracting attention, at least for a while. Geordie became an integral part of their operation. The gangs, that worked with Geordie, didn't get caught. But the ones that didn't?'

'Because the police recognized their cars.'

'That, or because someone tipped them off.'

'Geordie?'

'Nobody knows for sure. What I do know is that the number of serious players shrunk to about six by the end of the eighties and the police think four of them were connected to Geordie. He was doing a bit of supplying himself by this time, which was tolerated by the other gangs because he kept it in the city centre. Every gang had their own territory you see, but nobody had control over the city centre. When ecstasy came along he was in the right place at the right time. By the time the others had cottoned on, Geordie had the market sewn up. A fait accompli. When the police eventually twigged, Geordie was operating way behind the front line and could not be implemented in any activities. That was more than twenty years ago, he is even more insulated now.'

'And he still has the garage.'

'And it still serves the same purpose, a never-ending supply of cars for him and his associates, making police surveillance near impossible. People arrive in one car and leave in another.'

'Is he still involved in drugs?'

'There is still money to be made supplying drugs so that would be a yes. To tell you the truth, I don't know everything that he is involved in these days. There is plenty of suspicions but no proof but I recommend that you stay well out of his way.'

'Is there anything you can tell me about Will?'

'As I said, not much. Like is often the case with criminals, the son is brought up in an entirely different environment from the father. He simply can't hack it in Geordie's world. The police will still be watching him, trying to find a way to get to the father. Geordie will know that of course, so Will will be kept well out of it.'

'I was told that Will does a bit of dealing himself at club nights he runs in town.'

'If that is true, he must be mad. It would be a good arrest for an ambitious cop and it would be embarrassing for Geordie, which is not a good thing to happen.'

'Perhaps Will is striking out on his own? Maybe that is what his entry into the music business is all about.'

'Could be, I suppose. The son showing the old man that he is able to stand on his own two feet. That might make an interesting subject for research.'

# Chapter 13

1971

The guitar came flying though the air. Dan watched as if it were all in slow motion. It rose in a shallow arc, reached its zenith, then fell, slowly at first before picking up speed. The neck had separated from the body, the result of the instrument being repeatedly smashed against the floor. The two parts stayed connected, thanks only to the strings.

Dan was quick to react. Judging the trajectory perfectly, he leapt from his seat, dashed thirty feet forward to coincide with the guitar as it landed. He was quick but others were quicker. A dozen teenage boys tugged and pulled at the broken instrument. Within seconds there were fifty. Dan immediately formed an alliance and for a few moments it looked like they may triumph by working together, but a new partnership had joined the affray, older, stronger and by some margin, more determined. The battle was soon lost and Dan returned to his seat. 'At least I can say I touched Pete Townshend's guitar,' he told his companions.

A memorable rock concert had reached its conclusion. As an exhausted band departed the stage and elated fans shouted for more, Dan watched two of the men who had wrestled the guitar from the grip of the young fans, climb the stairs at the side of the stage and disappear behind the banks of amplifiers.

The house lights came up and the manager, immaculately dressed in evening suit and bow tie, pleaded with the crowd to leave. Only when roadies started to dismantle the equipment on stage, did Dan and his friends concede that the staff were telling the truth after all, when they said the band had already left the building.

Out on Renfield Street, the wind and rain had not let up. Dan did up the buttons on his brown cord Levi Jacket in an effort to keep out the cold. It was not too late for the bus but the three friends were in no hurry to return home. They were still in a state of euphoria and the walk back to Bridgeton would afford them more time to relive the experience. For the friends, it was the antics of Keith Moon and Pete Townshend, kicking over drum kits and smashing guitars respectively that they recalled with most enthusiasm. That, and the reaction of the audience. For Dan, it was the music. He took it all in, mesmerized at the number of bass notes John Entwistle could cram into a single bar, amazed by the way Keith seemed to follow the vocals of Roger Daltrey only returning to conventional timing for the instrumental passages. He alone realized the synthesizer intro on 'Baba O'Riley' and 'Wont Get Fooled Again' must have been on tape and was the only one to have studied the way Pete played both rhythm and lead at the same time.

Conversation was only interrupted when the trio stopped at Glasgow Cross to buy chips. From inside the cafe, Dan watched a news vendor take delivery of the next day's early editions. Once the string holding the bundles together had been cut, the vendor began to shout out the headlines on the front pages. Dan had put the explosion out of his head. He left the cafe and bought a copy to take home. His father drove a bus on the route passing the scene of the disaster. His mother had heard the news on the radio that a bus was hit by the blast and Dan had found her in a state of hysteria when he got home from school. He took her to Mrs Kennedy next door to ask if they could use her phone. The bus garage could not confirm what bus was involved in the blast or if the driver was injured. An anxious hour passed before his father had phoned the neighbour's house to say he was OK. His bus had been stopped by police a mile from the scene and the passengers asked to disembark and continue their journey on foot. All the police would say was that there had been an incident at Clarkston Toll. It was not until Dan's father had returned to the city centre, that he found out what had happened.

. . . . .

Donny was hurriedly trying to heat up a can of tomato soup when he received a text.

'Also got some news. Call when you get a chance.'

Donny called straight away.

'Hi Colette. I've got ten minutes before my next lesson. You will never guess who was in the same band as Daniel Quick.'

'Who?'

'Stuart Williamson.'

'Who's that?

'What. You have never heard of Stuart Williamson?'

'No. Should I?'

'You have heard of 'Over The Castle Wall,' surely.'

'Over over over the castle wall.' Colette sung in a passable Birmingham accent, just like the record. 'That was this guy Williamson?'

'He wrote and produced it. I can't believe you have never heard of him, he's a famous record producer and he comes from Glasgow.'

'Sorry. Do you think he is the person on Cathy's tapes?'

'I don't think it is as simple as that Colette. Although he was a top producer, as a songwriter he was something of a one hit wonder. But there has got to be some kind of a connection. Don't you think?'

'Too much of a coincidence otherwise, but why all the secrecy?'

'I don't know. Listen I am trying to grab something to eat before the next lesson. Do you fancy the open mike at the Butterfly and Pig tonight? I can tell you everything I have found out.'

'Sounds good. What time?'

'Say about nine?'

'See you there.'

'Oh sorry, what was it you found out?'

'I'll tell you tonight.'

'OK, see you later.'

Donny turned the heat off the saucepan and buttered some slices of crusty bread. It would keep him going till after his last two lessons.

It had been a trying afternoon for Donny. He got back to Kingspark Road just as Kenny emerged from the

Clockwork. Guitar case in hand, he was standing on the opposite side of the road from the flat, waiting for a gap in the traffic. If Donny had not ran the last forty metres, Kenny would have reached the entrance before him.

'Hi Kenny. You're early.'

*'Meetin' some o' the boys for a game o' fives efter. Thought ah'd better be sharp.'*

Donny opened the door and they made their way up to the flat. 'How did you get on with the Sultans of Swing?'

*'It's been a heavy week. Didnae get the chance tae practice.'*

The tension that had been building in Donny's head all day disappeared in an instant. 'Oh, that's too bad. We can go over it again and see how we get on.'

*'Nah yur aw right. Ah'll dae it next week when ah'm back on the rigs. Ah've got a CD ah want you tae listen tae. Ye heard o' Joe Satriani?'*

The tension returned with a vengeance. 'Joe Satriani, that's a bit advanced but we can give it a go.' Donny meant advanced for himself, never mind Kenny.

By the time Kenny left an hour later, Donny was shattered. His attempts at copying the great man's technique were hopelessly inadequate and he had to eventually throw in the towel. 'This is a bit difficult. Best to leave it with me and I will work it out for next time.' By this Donny meant scour youtube for instruction videos.

*'Aye, nae bother,'* shrugged Kenny

Between Kenny's lesson and the soup break Donny had two pupils. First was Grant, a retired Chemistry teacher who had mastered all the chords but could not change from one to another fast enough to remain in time. Donny had suggested using a capo on the third fret, making chords easier to form, but it made little difference. It appeared that the problem was Grant could not focus on two tasks at the same time.

After Grant was Lynn, who worked in the Job Centre on Battlefield Road. Lynn refused to play any chords that hurt her fingers, though she had at long last agreed to cut her finger nails. Here, the capo trick was working a treat. If only Lynn would stick to playing the guitar and not insist on singing, the teacher would be happy.

Donny poured the soup into a bowl and sat at the table to eat and check his emails. There were two rejections for songs he had submitted to management companies, each with a variation on the familiar phrase, not suitable for any of our artists at this moment. There was nothing from the production company making the film set in Edinburgh, which Donny interpreted as good news, the way things have been going lately. Matthew, the drummer in the function band had sent a date for a wedding reception at a hotel in Troon on the first Saturday in August and also confirmed the pick up time for Saturday's gig. Donny logged onto facebook where he was now one of three thousand friends of Kate Rydelle. There were no posts from Cathy about moving home and nothing about McSwiggen. There was however news that 'Main Street' was record of the week on a radio station in Ireland, despite the fact that it was not available for sale. This brought a wry smile to Donny's face. Two years previously, his band had been asked to back a young country singer on three dates over a weekend, on the Emerald Isle. The band, the singer and her manager all travelled together in the same van with the manager at the wheel. When they arrived on the Friday afternoon, the manager headed straight for a local radio station. Once he found the place he took one of the singer's CDs and slipped two fifty euro notes into the case then got out of the van, crossed the road and entered the building. Five minutes later, he was back in the drivers seat, performed a quick three point turn and headed for the venue. The radio station was barely out of sight when the title track of the album was on air with the singer being described as a great new talent from Scotland.

# Chapter 14

Two and a half months previously

When does a career criminal retire? How does he retire? These were the questions on Geordie's mind as he drove home. It was a problem that had been on his mind for some time, mainly because he knew it would soon be on many people's minds, both inside and outside his tight circle of associates, and as always he liked to stay one step ahead. He was fifty-eight years old and with no family member as natural successor, it was only natural that people would start thinking about the future. Criminality in Glasgow was not like the Mafia, there was no tradition to follow, no recognised set of rules or a code of practice for such a situation. It was all much more anarchic than that. Geordie knew he had made many enemies over the years and that number was continuing to grow. It was only a matter of time before the disgruntled and disaffected realized that critical mass had already been reached. All that was necessary was that they band together and he could easily be ousted. Luckily, most were too stupid to add up the numbers.

He had at least made up his mind on who would take over. It would be a single person and not shared or divided amongst his lieutenants, as may have been expected, creating further acrimony, no doubt. Will that decision be accepted? Geordie was not certain, but better one strong man in control. One strong man with reason to be grateful, in case assistance was ever needed in the future.

Geordie knew he could never completely retire, he would always need to maintain some contacts, for he accepted that he would be watching his back for the rest of his life. The legitimate and semi-legitimate businesses he would keep for himself, of course.

To even mention that he was thinking of getting out could set off a dangerous chain of events. The lives of his team, even more so than his own, depended on the illusion of power, for they were more exposed. If any of his rivals were to detect weakness and make a play for his operations, they would start by picking off his team one by one until the rest either changed sides or fled. Weakness, real or imagined, would only be shown once, it was never overlooked and it was never forgotten. The day you showed weakness, you were finished.

Contemplating retirement would be considered showing weakness. Geordie's relationship with his only son had the potential to be viewed as a sign of weakness. Ironic then that it was Will who had provided a possible solution to the retirement problem.

Geordie signalled left and turned off the main road, another two corners and he would be home. Moving to the south of the city went against the conventional wisdom that stated you must live in the very community that you exploit to look after your assets and as a show of strength. Geordie was from the north of the city. It was an act of bravado but also intent, setting up home in the territory of a rival. The house proved to be most suitable for his purposes. It was big and impressive to the chosen few who were invited inside but largely hidden from the street, sitting on a hill with its back to the road. The previous occupant was a Pakistani restaurant owner, rarely seen by the neighbours, who did not speak to him anyway. Geordie bought the restaurateur's Mercedes car along with the house and left it parked on the wide driveway. The neighbours did not even realise the house had changed hands.

When he arrived home, the doors of the attached garage opened automatically and he drove straight in. Geordie was still mulling over his exit strategy as he entered the house by the adjoining door. Perception was everything. He had to be seen to be moving on to something better, something more lucrative. That way it would not look like retirement, it would not look like weakness. The time was right for Geordie, bedroom cannabis factories and legal highs, amongst other things, had brought many new people into the business and they could not all be crushed. It was time to cash in his chips.

. . . . .

Despite waiting till ten past nine, Colette arrived first at the open mike. Unlike the Songwriters, there was no need to bring her own guitar. She made her way to the bar and ordered a pint of Guinness for Donny and a bottle of water for herself.

There was an empty table against the back wall and Colette took the drinks over, placing the pint of Guinness in front of an empty seat, where she draped her coat. Colette now felt comfortable enough to take notice of what was happening. The host of the open mike was walking round taking names and it looked like he had plenty of takers. She recognised a few faces. Two or three were like Donny, songwriters who would be trying out new material, others would do their party piece as they always did. Colette had her own ideas for tonight.

When the MC approached, she put Donny's name down as well as her own. The host had just moved on to the next table, when Donny pushed through the door carrying his guitar case. He spotted Colette and made his way over.

'You're late'

'Sorry I nipped in to Blackfriars to see if Jake was there.'

'The guy who played guitar for Cathy?'

'That's him, but he has not been in for over a week. Thought it was worth a try. If he is still working with Cathy, it would be our best bet for getting information..'

'Do you think he would help us if he is still working with Cathy?'

'Probably not, if he knew we were looking for something but if I could just engage him in conversation, you know, ask what he is doing, he might just tell me all about it. He loves to talk about himself. I'll keep trying. When he is not working, he is always in Blackfriars.'

'Sounds a good idea. What's with the guitar?'

'Me and John always do a duet. Don't we John?'

The MC, who was still taking names at the next table, turned round and smiled. 'Course we do. Highlight of the night.'

'Oh!' Colette was a little peeved but did her best to hide

it. 'What do you do?'

The MC winked. 'She'll just have to wait and see, won't she Donny?'

'Well worth the wait,' Donny added. 'Anyway I better tell you what I found out.'

Colette's irritation that Donny was likely to upstage her soon passed as Donny told her all about Stuart Williamson, The Willie Stewart Band and his trip to the drum shop. Colette in turn told Donny everything she had found out about Will and Geordie McSwiggen.

'I think we can safely say that there is something dodgy about all this, if that's the type of people Cathy has got herself involved with,' Donny concluded.

'I agree. Do you think we should just forget it?'

'We probably should.'

'Is that what you want to do?' Colette asked.

'No.'

'I'm so glad you said that.'

'If we do keep going Colette, we will need to be very careful, if what your friend said is true.'

'Oh Crawford knows what he is talking about.'

'OK we will keep everything to ourselves from now on. Who knows we are looking?'

'Well, Crawford of course, and Derek.'

'I don't think Derek will say anything. He knows what the McSwiggen's are like and it was him who put us on to them in the first place. No, Derek will keep quiet.'

'Same goes for Crawford. What about Billy Bongo? Him and Cathy are good friends.'

Donny thought for a minute. 'No, I never let on to him I had any suspicions about Cathy's songs, I always knew they were mates. Shit!'

'What is it?'

'There is someone Colette. Someone that we did blab to, and the worst possible person at that.'

'Who?'

'Pat.'

'I don't think we said much to him.'

'He's a journalist, or at least he thinks he is. We didn't need to say much, it's his job to pick up on these things.'

'He may know we are suspicious but we didn't say we were looking for evidence.'

'That's true. All the same we must be very careful what we say to people from now on.'

Neither of them had noticed that the pub had filled up during the time they had been talking. They had also barely noticed the half dozen or so singers who had already taken the stage.

'Can we have Colette up next.' A startled Colette turned to her friend.

'I didn't think I would be up till the second half. I don't think I am ready.'

'You'll be fine.'

Colette took a deep breath, rose from her seat and squeezed past the tightly packed tables to get to the stage. Her plan had been to do two of the songs she had done with the tribute band at the weekend. It would make a change she had thought from the dreary material that was all too common at open mike nights. It had however also been her intention to gauge the mood of the room first, before performing songs that were hits way before most of the audience were born. It was too late for that now.

Colette needn't have worried. She went down a storm, 'The Tide is High' followed 'Hanging on the Telephone'. Both covers, even when Blondie recorded them. She returned to her seat to loud applause. The host wisely announced there would be a short break.

'Good choice. That was brilliant.'

'Thanks Donny. I knew the audience in here were not really singer-songwriter types. I wanted to go on in the second half when they had a few more drinks inside them but it seemed to go down okay.'

'Certainly did.' Praise from Donny was always genuine and gladly given.

'What do you think we should do next then?' said Colette, returning to business.

'I have the phone number for Dennis, the bass player in the Willie Stewart Band remember, but it's his house phone and there was no answer any time I tried. He's a taxi driver so I expect he is working. I'll keep trying.'

'Will he know anything that the drummer guy didn't?'

'Don't know, but we better find out. I don't think he will be in contact with Stuart Williamson but he might know something.'

'That's Willie Stewart?'

'I explained all that Colette. Willie Stewart changed his name to Stuart Williamson.'

'I know, I was just checking. It's a bit odd and a bit of a coincidence don't you think, that he changed his name and so did Cathy?'

'I must admit I did think the same thing but it is pretty common in the music business, probably just a coincidence. Anyway I'll contact Dennis. I doubt that he is still in contact with Williamson but you never know. He might however know something about the tapes that Dan had. You know the ones that Cathy got hold off.'

'What about trying to contact Stuart Williamson direct?' Colette asked.

'Thought about that but remember we don't know if he is involved with McSwiggen in some way. Best to leave that for now.'


Donny was called to the stage for his duet when the audience was at its maximum, as Colette had suspected. She was however surprised when he opened his guitar case and removed his D hole gypsy guitar. Donny had spoken often about his beloved Django Reinhardt but Colette had never heard him play that style before. MC John was evidently also a devotee of the French swing jazz style. Both played with aplomb, competence and enthusiasm, grabbing the attention of a crowd who had been showing signs of singer-songwriter fatigue. 'I'll See You In My Dreams' followed by 'Swing Guitars' and 'The Sheik Of Araby'. Donny left the stage ten minutes later to the same show of appreciation afforded to Colette.

'That was fantastic.'

'Cheers Colette.'

# Chapter 15

Dan had remembered someone in the band saying that Paul McCartney had dreamt the song 'Yesterday' and when the Beatle woke up he had the whole melody and structure formed in his head. Lyrics were added later. Dan was having some similar experiences. Tunes would suddenly pop into his head. During the three hundred metres walk from his place of work to his home, he would regularly compose the melody to a song, entirely in his head. The hard part was getting it out of his head. What sounded fantastic, while locked in his imagination, somehow lost its magic, once he tried to play it on his guitar. Dan could never quite capture in the real world what he heard inside his head. Was McCartney simply a better musician, able to translate what was in his brain to notes played on an instrument? Was it an innate skill or would it come with practice?

The young musician pondered these questions often and was more than a little concerned that there may be a finite number of tunes that he was capable of summoning, apparently from nowhere, because many melodies had already been lost. The reality was that if the first effort at delivering the song into the physical world sounded wrong, the melody could never be fully recaptured, even in his head. Every subsequent effort, whether in the real or imaginary world, would drive the melody further and further away.

Lyrics thankfully were different. Once the line, phrase or single word that came with the tune was written down, the theme of the song was secured. It would simply take time to turn that thought into a lyric. It was, as Miss Wilson said in the O level English class, decide what you want to say, make a plan, expand on that plan, make your first draft then redraft until it is as good as you can make it. Dan had discovered that what had worked for school English assignments, worked for song lyrics. It was nailing those tunes that was the problem.

Today was Dan's ultimate McCartney moment. While waiting to cross the road, opposite his tenement home, his eye caught the street sign attached to the wall of his building, Main Street. There it was, the hook perfectly formed in his head, melody and lyrics. Walking down Main Street, Talking to the people that I meet, Walking down Main Street. He could sense the rhythm, hear the backing vocals and the instruments. He could feel the song in his soul, it was about who he was, it was about where he lived, it was about what he knew. It was there, it existed. He just had to hold on to it. He hurried across the road and into the common close hoping not to meet anyone for fear that if he had to stop and talk, the song would disappear from his mind as quickly as it had arrived. Luckily none of the neighbours were about and he reached the flat with the song still in tact.

'Is that you Daniel?'

'Aye it's me. See you in a minute, I need to go to the lav.' Dan locked the toilet door, pulled down the lid and sat down. The verses were coming now, the melody and some key words. He must not let this one slip away, he knew that for certain. Over and over again he repeated the chorus in his head then into the verse with just the odd word in place. He could feel the rhythm da di, di di, da di, di di.

'Are you OK Daniel?'

'I'm fine.'

'Dinner will be another half hour.'

Dan pulled the flush, opened the bathroom door and crossed the hall to his room. 'I need to record something. Don't come in.' That should stop her talking, he thought. The Echo acoustic rested against a chair. Dan stared at the instrument frightened to pick it up, for this was the point where it always went wrong. The notes on the guitar never matched the ones in his head and the more notes he tried on guitar, the faster the ones in his head faded. He lay on the bed letting the song play on a loop inside his brain but he would need to get it out of there soon. He could make an excuse to avoid talking to his mother but the band had a gig tonight and the van would be here to pick him up within the hour.

Talk of using the tape recorder was only a ploy to avoid his mother but now that he thought about it, it was worth a try. He got the machine from under the bed, plugged it in and waited for it to warm up. He felt a little foolish preparing to sing, unaccompanied and with few words, a song he had only heard in his imagination. Dan rested the small microphone on the pillow pressed simultaneously the play and record buttons, then sat on the bed with his eyes shut and his hands covering his ears. He let the song complete another loop in his head before singing out loud. Where he had no words, he just hummed the tune, over and over again. His fingers were now pressing hard against his ears and the voice he heard sounded like it came from inside his head. Instrumental breaks, harmonies, base-lines and drum parts were all mimicked by voice and captured on the tape. In the end, there was about twenty minutes of singing, humming, la la'ing, whining and screaming down on tape. Dan rewound back to the start and without hesitation pressed play.

What he heard sounded strange and would cause much hilarity should anyone hear it but it was most definitely what was in his head, caught for the first time. The strange noises made perfect sense to Dan and he had every confidence that he could, at his leisure, find the right notes and chords on guitar and complete the lyrics. What he would do with the completed song was another matter. His family and his girlfriend viewed songwriting as not for the likes of us. The band looked on Dan as the baby, and did not take him seriously. He had made the mistake of playing an original song in its raw state to some friends once and it was met with derision. It was not a pleasant experience and Dan resolved that he would only expose his songs to public scrutiny again once they were perfect, absolutely perfect.

. . . . .

It is quarter to one in the afternoon and Donny is standing at the bus stop opposite his flat, waiting for the number 34 bus. He is on his way to Cardonald, where Dennis Lindsey lives. The one time bass player in the Willie Stewart Band had agreed to meet as long as Donny could come to his house before he started work at half past three. Dennis had sounded quite excited that someone was interested in his old band when they had talked on the phone. Donny hoped he had not got the wrong idea. Musicians, in his experience, rarely think they are past it and still believe opportunity may yet come knocking.

The bus arrived more or less when the timetable said it would but the journey across the south side seemed to take for ever due to heavy lunchtime traffic. This did however give Donny some time to think. He did not want to give too much away but he would need to explain his interest. The simplest thing to do of course would be to let Dennis hear the songs Cathy had been singing and ask if he recognized them. The problem was, what would Dennis do if he did recognize them. In the end Donny decided he would only play the recording obtained from the stall in the Barras market and play it by ear from there.

Donny got off the bus on Paisley Road West and continued in the same direction till the junction with Lammermoor Avenue. The house he was looking for, he had been told, was about two hundred yards along on the right hand side. Three minutes later Donny had walked up the empty driveway where he had expected to find a taxi and had rung the doorbell.

'Dennis?'

'Aye that's me. Donny is it?'

'I thought you must be working when I didn't see the taxi.'

'My brother shares it with me. He's been out since five this morning. Come in.'

Dennis lead Donny to the upstairs flat. He was younger looking than Donny expected but he did not look like a musician nor a taxi driver, more like a librarian. When they reached the living room, which faced the back of the house, Dennis signalled for Donny to take a seat.

'What is it you want to know about?'

'I came across some old reel to reel tapes down the Barras and I think they may have been made by Daniel Quick, who I believe was in your old band.'

'Wee Dan eh! Do you know he died?'

'Yes I knew that.'

'He was a good guy Dan. Terrible shame what happened to him.'

'It was.' Donny agreed. 'I have a CD I would like you to listen to. Perhaps you can confirm or not that it is Dan.'

'I don't have a CD player.'

Some people would find it strange that a musician would not have have a CD player, but Donny did not, for he knew musicians from that generation who had no music collection of any description, no CDs, no vinyl, no mp3 or any other format. Odd, but true.

'What about a computer?'

'Aye sure, the laptop. Hang on a minute.'

Dennis left the room and did not return for fully five minutes.

'Sorry, I knew it would be nearly out of charge and I couldn't find the lead.' Dennis readied the laptop and Donny passed over the CD which was inserted into the machine.

After half a minute Dennis said. 'Aye that could be him.'

'But you're not sure?'

'Its been about forty years.'

'Of course. Listen to some more, there are a number of versions of the song.'

Dennis did as he was asked.

'I'm pretty sure it is him.'

'Jump to the last track, it's an instrumental.' Dennis clicked on the final track.

'Oh that's Dan all right.'

'You sure?'

'Definitely. We used to do that as a warm up at rehearsals.'

'Do you know if Dan ever did any songwriting?'

'Aye he did. After Willie left he could have joined another band straight away but he said he wanted to spend his time, working on his own songs.'

'Did you ever hear any of them?'

'Nah. I never really saw him much after the band split up, but any time I did bump into him he was full of it, wanted to form a band just to do original material. He asked me if I was interested.'

'Were you?'

'No. Fifteen quid between us in the Burns Howff and the like. Even in the seventies that was shite. Naw, I needed the money so I passed it up.'

'Fifteen quid to split between you. I know bands that pay to play gigs these days.'

'So I've heard. Well more fool them. Anyway Dan got knocked down before he got the chance.'

'Is there anyone you can think of who might know about

Dan's songs? Maybe some musicians he was intending to form a band with.'

'I don't know if he had started to rehearse a band or not but there is his girlfriend Brenda, she would know about his songs I suppose.'

'Do you know how to contact her?'

'Afraid not, I can't even remember her second name. She got a house in the Whitevale flats beside my old dear, you know the Gallowgate twin towers. I would sometimes see her and the wean when I was visiting but my mother died in ninety-two so I never saw Brenda after that.'

'Brenda had a child? Was it Dan's?'

'Aye. She was pregnant when Dan died.'

'I spoke to a neighbour of Dan's mother in Bridgeton. He never mentioned that Dan had a child.'

'No he wouldn't. Mrs Quick, the old battleaxe that she was, refused to accept that the wean was Dan's. She even stopped Brenda going to the funeral.'

'Surely she couldn't have stopped her going to the funeral.'

'Brenda was only a wee lassie. Mrs Quick said she hadn't to go and that was that.'

'What about when the baby was born, did she not come round then? It would have been part of her son, after all.'

'Not how the old devil saw things. The embarrassment of having an illegitimate grandchild would have been too much for her. Appearances, that was what mattered to her and nothing else. It's pathetic but as far as I know she never did acknowledge the wean's existence. It was a girl. Brenda called her Daniela. She even gave her Dan's surname, Daniela Quick.'

'That could be useful. Unusual name.'

'I see what you mean.'

'How did Brenda manage? What about her own family?'

'She did her best. As I said, she got a council house in the same block as my mother, but it must have been hard. She had a job, I remember that. Maybe her mother watched the wean. I suppose she must have.'

'Could they still be living there now?'

'Definitely not. The flats have been demolished.'

Donny remembered now. It had been on the news. The flats were an east end landmark that were once the tallest in the city. They had to be taken down floor by floor, instead of an explosion, the council's usual preference, because of the proximity of other buildings and the railway line.

'Don't suppose you have any idea where they might be living now?'

'Not a clue. The last time I saw them was more than twenty years ago.'

The journey home took even longer than the one coming. The bus was already full when it arrived at the bus stop and there seemed to be a few schools along the route. The upshot being that the bus was forever stopping, either to let people off or to pick up new passengers. Donny had to stand for the first mile. He eventually got a seat next to a elderly lady, whom he guessed had been visiting at the hospital at the end of the bus route, which made him think about Colette. He would call her later and tell her his news but she would not be finished work till early evening. A brief text was sent to whet her appetite

To pass the time Donny checked his emails. A wedding

gig had been confirmed for May and there was an enquiry about guitar lessons, but there was still no news about his submission to the film production company. He logged in to his Facebook account only to find endless posts from other musicians and songwriters self promoting, and friend requests from people he had never heard of. Donny found the whole Facebook experience a bit unpalatable, chancers on the make and people trying to force their views on everyone else (God save us from another referendum), but most of all, it just seemed too much like hard work. He searched for a Daniela Quick and found two, one in Australia and surprisingly one in Finland but if their profile was to be believed, they were too young. He was ready to log off when he decided to check out the Kate Rydelle page.

Donny had been mostly leaving it up to Colette to keep an eye on Cathy's web presence. He found nothing he didn't already know about, logged off and put the phone back in his pocket spending the rest of the journey wondering, had he really found his man. Everything did fit. Dan, it appeared, was a songwriter after all and his old tapes could easily have been sold down the Barras, probably with the rest of his belongings after his mother died. Cathy did buy a reel to reel tape recorder and a box of old tapes, almost certainly Dan's. If Brenda, Dan's partner, could be found, all he would have to do is play her a recording of the songs Cathy has been singing and that would be that. Kate Rydelle would be exposed as a fraud.

What then? Donny wondered.

What then indeed. With Dan dead there was no longer the opportunity to learn from a master, there would be no` informative debates over a pint about what made a great song, no chance to see a genius at work nor would there be someone to ask for advice and obtain that elusive, genuine constructive criticism. Donny also thought about the Cathy he knew before her rebirth as Kate. The Cathy he remembered, was a mate of sorts. Her songs were dreadful and his spirits sank every time he had to endure them but Cathy had always been a nice person. She had been good company and when she could be persuaded to sing covers, a good performer. Could Kate revert back to Cathy if her new material was snatched away from her? Was it even fair to do so? After all if she hadn't discovered the material on those tapes, and more importantly recognized their quality, the songs would have been lost forever. For all he knew Cathy may have tried to track down the writer, may even have found Brenda and Daniela and got their permission. Donny considered this last point but dismissed it. Even if Brenda did not understand the financial implications of letting someone else assume copyright, surely she would demand that Dan's work got full recognition.

Back in the flat he opened his laptop and resumed the search. There was no Daniela Quick in the phone directories nor one on the electoral register. A google search combining Daniela Quick with combinations of the words Brenda, Whitevale and Dennistoun came up with nothing, before he had to close the lid on the laptop and answer the door to the first of that day's pupils.

When Colette got the chance to check her phone at half past four that afternoon there was a text from Donny. All it said was, 'It's Dan.' Like Donny her first reaction was one of disappointment, if the writer was dead there could be no co-writing opportunities for example, but unlike her friend she quickly realized that with the writer deceased, copyright would be held with the next of kin. Donny had spoken about a sister. Perhaps a deal could be done with her. It was another four hours before Donny called.

'Hi Colette. Sorry I didn't get the chance to call earlier. I had lessons one after the other.'

'It's Daniel then. Are you sure?'

'Pretty much. Dennis recognised the instrumental track, said the band used to play it as a warm up at rehearsals. He also knew that Dan had been spending all his time writing after the band split up.'

'Did you tell him about Cathy?'

'No way. With McSwiggen involved we keep things to ourselves for now. I asked him if he had heard any of the songs but he said he hadn't. He only met Dan a few times after the band split.'

'But he knew Dan had started writing?'

'Yes. He was most definite about that.'

'OK Donny but we still don't have any proof. I was thinking, you said he had a sister.'

'That went to Blackpool and never came back.'

'Maybe we could track her down.'

'Possibly, but we may not have to.' Donny told Colette everything he had discovered.

'Well, Daniela Quick is an unusual name. Surely we should be able to find her.' Colette said.

'You would think, but I was on the internet for two hours.'

'I better have a look.'

'Be my guest.'

'Come on Donny. Social media is not really your thing, is it?'

'Fair point. Let me know how you get on.'


Donny headed to the kitchen, he hadn't eaten since lunchtime. The fridge was well-stocked but a proper meal would take at least half an hour to prepare. Best bet, he decided, was a takeaway. Donny put on his coat and woolly hat and made his way downstairs.

Mount Florida was well served as regards fast food; three Chinese, three chippies, two Indian restaurants that did takeaways, a kebab shop and a pizza place, all thanks to the proximity of Hampden Stadium. Tonight it would be pizza and Donny strolled up Cathcart Road.

Stefano's was quiet with just two people waiting. Donny ordered the twelve inch Riviera then, while it was being prepared, walked up to the Spar to buy the paper. On the way back to the pizza shop his phone rang.

'Hello.'

'Donny?!'

'Yes.'

'Its Dennis Lindsey, you were up to see me this afternoon.'

'Aye Dennis. How are you doing?'

'Fine thanks. Listen. You want to find Brenda don't you?'

'Yeah I would.'

'Well, her name's Murphy. I asked my brother when he brought the taxi back and he remembered. I forgot that he was still staying at home when Brenda moved into the block. Anyway he thinks she still lives in the area but doesn't know where exactly. Is that any help to you?'

'It is. Murphy you say?'

'That's right. I thought if there was any chance of something happening with Dan's music, she would be dead chuffed and if there was any money in it, you know.'

'She deserves a break?'

'Aye, that's what I was thinking.'

'Well thanks again Dennis, I'll try to find her. Cheers.'

Donny ended the call and re-entered Stefano's.

Unlike her daughter, Brenda was easy to find. She was in the phone book. Donny had her number and her address before his black olives and mushroom pizza was ready.

# Chapter 16

Three months previously

The lawyer picked up the small strip of paper lying on top of his antique mahogany desk. Turning it over revealed a telephone number. He picked up the phone, dialled the number on the piece of paper then sat back in his padded leather chair and waited for someone to answer.

'Can I speak to Mrs Marie Blackman please.'

'Who is it?'

'My name is Angus Johnston from the firm of McQuarry and Johnston. Am I speaking to Mrs Blackman?'

'What is it you want?'

'It concerns your late brother Daniel.'

'Dan!' Marie was bewildered. 'What about him?'

'He was a musician I understand?'

'He played in a band if that's what you mean?'

'Did he make any recordings?'

'Do you mean records?'

'Precisely.'

'No. He played in pubs. I think they were good but not what you might call big time, if you know what I mean. Look what's this about. That was all a long time ago.'

'No recordings then. That's a pity. Our client is a music

publishing company, specialising on lesser known artists but they would need recordings. You don't have any home recordings perhaps?'

'No, he's been dead for forty years. Are we talking about the same person, Dan Quick?'

'Any notebooks or any scraps of paper he may have jotted down ideas on. Anything at all in his handwriting?'

'I don't have anything. Wait a minute. Are you saying if I had any of this stuff someone would want to buy it? They would be worth something?'

'Oh not a great deal, perhaps a few hundred pounds. Our clients buy copyrights from hundreds of musicians, or their beneficiaries if they are dead. Musicians that have yet to earn any royalties. If in the future some of their work is used in a film, a television program or of course on a hit record then they can claim the royalties.'

'I see.' Marie was regretting being so candid but she had been taken by surprise.

'But if you don't have any recordings or written work, I'm afraid my clients won't be interested.'

'He did write songs before the accident. He got knocked down by a lorry.'

The lawyer smiled. This was the part of the conversation he had been leading up to. 'I am sorry to hear that.' The lawyer almost sounded sincere. 'Do you remember any of these songs?'

'Not really. I remember him playing the guitar in his room but I didn't pay much attention.'

'What about any of the titles to his compositions. Do you remember any?'

'No.'

'What about any of the subject matter or perhaps parts of the melody?'

'I don't remember anything.'

'In that case I'm afraid I have been wasting your time. That's unfortunate, I find that a few hundred pounds are always welcome at this time of year, with the cost of Christmas soon and those winter fuel bills coming up.'

'You're telling me.'

'Quite. Listen I'll tell you what. You say that his band were good though not, as you put it, in the big time.'

'They were very popular around the pubs in Glasgow.'

'Well there you are then. I will pass that on to our client. I will say that Daniel Quick was a popular musician in Glasgow in the seventies and that the copyright is available for, shall we say two hundred pounds?'

'Could we make it three?'

'I'm afraid my client won't go as high as three. Without any hard copy two would be the limit. It is what they term, taking a punt. It is a paltry sum I agree and if you don't wish to proceed I fully understand.'

'No.' Marie tried not to sound too desperate. 'Might as well go ahead.'

'A sensible decision Mrs Blackman. It is money for nothing, that's what I say.'

'When will I get the money?'

'Not long. I will pass on your details today. Can you first confirm that both Daniel's parents are dead.'

'Yes.'

'And you are his only sibling?'

'What?'

'He had no other brothers or sisters?'

'No.'

'Lastly. Was he married or had children at the time of his death?'

'No.'

'Thank you Mrs Blackman. You have been most patient. There will be some papers to sign, then a cheque will be issued. It should all be completed in no more than ten days. It has been a pleasure talking to you.'

'How did you get my number?'

Angus Johnston had already ended the call. He looked at his client sitting on the other side of the desk. 'I think that went well.'

'What if she demands more money?' The client said with a smirk.

'I'll be surprised if she doesn't. We may have to go as high as two hundred and fifty.'

Both men laughed.

. . . . .

It was true what Dennis had said. Brenda still lived in the area. Her home was opposite the site once occupied by the high rise flats. Donny pressed the button on the door entry system and waited for an answer.

'Hello.'

'It's Donny McNeil. I spoke to you earlier on the phone.'

There was a click as the lock on the heavy door gave way. 'Its the first door on the right.'

There had been no answer from Brenda's phone when Donny tried to contact her the night before. Nor was there any response on his first three attempts the morning after. On his fourth attempt Donny left a message explaining that he had come across an old recording of Dan's and that Dennis Lawson had given him her name. Donny's phone rang within a minute.

'Hello.'

'Hello. You just rang my number.'

'Are you Brenda Murphy?'

'Aye.'

'I've been trying to contact you but there was never any answer.'

'I don't generally answer the phone if it's a number I don't recognize or if it's withheld. It's usually a scam or somebody trying to sell something. If it's important they can leave a message. That's my thinking anyway.'

'I know what you mean.'

'You said it is about an old tape of Dan's. Daniel Quick I suppose your talking about.' Brenda sounded very surprised. 'How did you get hold of that?'

'They were sold along with a tape recorder down the Barras.'

'When was this?'

'About four or five months ago I think.'

'Are you sure it's Dan?'

'Yeah. Dennis Lawson recognized it.'

'Now there's a blast from the past. I've not heard that name in years. It's just that I was always told that Dan's tapes were recorded over.'

'I can let you hear the one that I've got. I can make you a CD copy if you like.'

'Oh would you? I'd like that. '

'I could bring it over to your house if that's OK. I would like to ask you about Dan if you wouldn't mind.'

'Any time you like son. I'm usually here.'

'No time like the present. If you're not doing anything this morning Brenda?'

'You can come straight over.'


Dan pushed open the heavy door and walked along the passageway to Brenda's front door. When she opened it he got quite a shock.

'Come in son.'

Donny had worked out that Brenda would be in her late fifties but the women holding the door open looked nearer seventy. She had a walking stick in her right hand and when she led the way down the hall she did so with difficulty and was obviously in some pain. Donny guessed multiple sclerosis.

'You find it OK?'

'Google maps, dead easy.'

'Have a seat.'

Donny sat in the middle of a three seater couch, Brenda took one of the single seats.

'That's Dan in the picture.' Brenda nodded towards a framed photograph sitting on top of the fireplace.

'Do you mind if I have a closer look?'

'On you go.'

Donny took three steps over to the fireplace and lifted up the five by seven frame. A young boy sat on a bed holding a guitar.

'That was New Year's morning nineteen seventy-two.'

'Would you mind if I get a picture of it on my phone?'

'Be my guest.' Donny took the picture and put the phone back in his pocket. He would have a closer look later.

'You didn't move far then, when the flats came down?'

'Oh I've been here for fifteen years, long before they emptied the flats. I needed the ground floor on account of my M.S.'

'Right. Sorry to hear that.'

'No need for you to be sorry. I can get up to Duke Street for the shops and my daughter takes me in the car if I need to go further than that.'

'That would be Daniela. Dennis told me you named her after Dan.'

Brenda's head moved backwards slightly and her eyes narrowed. 'Aye I did.'

Donny decided he better explain.

'Someone I know has bought an old tape recorder and a bunch of tapes from a stall down the Barras and I think they had belonged to Dan.'

'And they still have Dan singing on the tapes?'

'I think so.'

'The auld bastard.'

'Sorry?'

'Oh don't mind me son. Dan's mother, it's a long story and I'll not bore you with the details. She claimed that all Dan's tapes had been recorded over. I wanted them to keep for the wean.'

'For Daniela?'

'Aye, something real to help her know who her father was, when she was older like. But that was Mrs Quick for you. Would your friend let me have the tapes, they would be no use to her, would they? The truth is I didn't exactly encourage Dan with the music. I was jealous of the girls that followed the band. A bit daft I suppose, but there you are. Anyway I never got to hear the songs he had written before the accident. Do you know about the accident?'

'Yes I know.'

'I think he thought I wouldn't like them. Wanted to get them perfect I think, then I could hardly object to him continuing with the music. So it would be wonderful to hear them now. I could pay your friend for them.'

'The thing is she has been learning the songs and singing them at gigs and on the radio.'

'On the radio! That's brilliant, I'd love to hear her.'

'Well just local stations so far.'

'All the same. Wait tae ah tell Daniela.'

'Why don't I play you some of the songs see if you recognise anything in them first. I made a CD up for you. Do you have a CD player?'

'Aye just behind you.'

Donny lifted the lid on a nineties style radio/Cassette/CD player, placed the CD inside, closed the lid and pressed play. 'It's a session she did for a radio station. You can still listen to the whole thing online but I just put the songs on the CD and missed out all the talking.'

Brenda clasped her hands in front of her and leaned forward in her seat.

'This is called Main Street. It's about Main Street in Bridgeton.'

'That's where Dan lived.'

'I know.'

Brenda listened all the way through without saying another word. When it finished she said. 'That was great and you're sure it's one of Dan's songs?'

'I was hoping you would recognize it.'

'Sorry. As I said he kept them all to himself and I didn't ask.'

Brenda recognised small things in the next two songs that Cathy had performed on the radio session but she was not certain.

'This is the last song. It is called 'I've Found You Now'.'

Brenda leaned further forward in her seat and listened intently. As the song progressed Brenda's brows narrowed, she unclasped her hands and formed two fists, listened a bit longer then suddenly burst out laughing

'You recognize it then?'

'Not exactly. I thought it must be about me, then I thought it was about someone else. Then I twigged, it was about searching for his missing dog when he was ten. He told me that story. That's what that's about'

'Really?' Donny was aghast. Like Brenda had done at first, he too had assumed it was about finding love but could now understand better the lyrics he was listening too. Had he learned one of the secrets of song writing, he wondered.

'This is from the tape I own.' Donny said. 'It's the only one with Dan singing,' Donny played 'The Die is Cast.'

Brenda struggled to hold back tears as she heard his voice for the first time since nineteen seventy-eight. 'Oh I know what this is about. The Work In.'

'What Brenda?'

'You know the Upper Clyde Shipworkers, the men occupied the yards and staged a work in. Dan was into all that stuff. He went on the marches while he was still at school, even went to a benefit concert in the Greens Playhouse the night before his O levels. I remember him telling me his mother went berserk when he got home. The names he mentions there, do you hear them. Billy and Don' Donny nodded. 'Well that's Billy Connolly and Donovan.'

'No Way!'

'Aye, they were on the bill at the concert. Dan told me all about it. In fact that could be the first song he ever wrote. I remember he told me that the first song he ever wrote was about the work in.'

When the CD ended Brenda lifted her head from the intense pose she had maintained throughout and wiped a tear with the sleeve of her cardigan. 'It was marvellous to hear his voice again. The girl is very good. Dan would have been that chuffed to have his songs played on the radio. Daniela won't believe it. Your friend wouldn't mind giving me the tape, she could copy them first. That should be OK shouldn't it?'

'There's a wee problem there Brenda'

'How do you mean?'

'A very big problem to tell you the truth.' Brenda looked confused. 'What it is Brenda is...' Donny didn't know where to start. It was clear that Brenda had no concept of copyright law and had not grasped the financial implications. 'Brenda this is the situation. These songs of Dan's are good.'

'I can hear that.'

'No Brenda, I mean really good and not just for nostalgia. This kind of music is popular again and has been for some time. These songs could be worth a lot of money. In fact I would say they are definitely worth a lot of money.'

Brenda sat with a blank expression, the penny had yet to drop. 'By right, any money should go to you as Dan's partner when he died or failing that to Daniela as his next of kin. I don't know exactly how the law works but one of you anyway.'

Brenda still looked confused.

'Before I get your hopes up I better explain that problem.'

'Sorry son, I'm not following. Are you saying that the songs belong to me and that they may be worth something?'

'Well you or Daniela. As I said I'm not exactly sure about the law but yes that is exactly what I am saying. However as I said there is a problem.' Donny explained about Cathy passing the songs off as her own, her rapid rise over the past few months and that she was on the verge of a major record contract.

'The wee madam! And never any acknowledgement for Dan?'

'Not a word.'

'I'll soon put a stop to that.'

'There is another problem Brenda.'

'What now?'

'She has put a guy called W McSwiggen down as co-writer. His father is called Geordie McSwiggen.'

'Oh my god!' Brenda raised a hand to her mouth

'You've heard of him then?'

'Lets just say his name was known in the flats.'

'Well you know what we are dealing with here. He won't take kindly to someone turning up and spoiling the party.'

'What are you saying, just let them get away with it?'

'No, I'm not saying that. It's just that we must tread carefully that's all. To take things further, you will need proof that Dan wrote them.'

'But I recognized some the things Dan wrote about didn't I? Surely that's proof enough. How could I do that if Dan hadn't told me? Tell me that?'

'That's just it, lots of people have heard the songs now. Cathy, that's the girl's name by the way, she has been singing them all over the city at open mike nights, small pub gigs and doing sessions on community radio. I think she has been told to do that so if anyone tries to claim copyright, she can say the songs have been in the public domain for some time.'

'But I know what these songs are about.'

'A lawyer would argue that you could have heard them on the radio or at a gig and just made up that you recognized things in the lyrics.'

'Do I look like I go to gigs?'

'They could say someone recorded the gig and let you hear it, and you can listen to the radio, can't you?'

'Well I don't know.' Brenda looked deflated.

'Listen. We're not beat yet. I'll help you prove it. There must be someone that heard those songs. All we have to do is find them.'

'Why would you do that?'

'Look Brenda, I'm not looking for anything. At first I thought the writer would be alive, I never considered that he might be dead. I did think it could be to my advantage to find him but that doesn't matter now. I'm a songwriter myself I don't like the idea of someone taking the credit for somebody else's work. I really would like to help. Tell me the names of anyone you can remember that knew Dan at the time.'

'I can't think. It's so long ago, they would all have moved away, how would you even find them.'

'I found you, didn't I? Don't you worry about that. Think hard Brenda, old school friends, other musicians. Anything?'

# Chapter 17

Four months previously

Cathy sat cross legged on the floor with her back resting against her bed. Outside an autumn sun shone in a clear sky filling the room with light and warmth. Cathy had her guitar balanced on her lap ready to spend whatever time was necessary to meet her goal for the day. A set of headphones were positioned over her ears, before she stretched out to press the play button. Placed in front of her, on a single page of foolscap, were the hand written lyrics and chords to the song she was about to learn. The five second delay before the music started was sufficient for Cathy to prepare herself.

With the first beat of the song, Cathy was ready and she came in on time. The song had a single guitar accompaniment, a pattern of alternating strum strokes and bass notes, quite difficult to learn but Cathy had resolved to put in as much effort as was necessary to do just that. She played along as best she could, trying to mimic the technique of the player on the recording, ignoring the vocal part for now. It was the same strategy she had always used to learn songs, though never before had she strived to be note perfect. This song was special.

Four hours later, and with the finger tips of her left hand showing deep trenches created by holding down the strings, Cathy was satisfied that the guitar part had been mastered. She would now turn her attention to the vocal. The singer on the recording was male, making the key too low for her to sing along with comfort. She did try an octave above but that was too high. Her usual method in these cases was to transfer the track to the computer and use some technology. Her basic Audacity program could pitch shift, meaning the song could be transposed to a key that suited her voice. Cathy would then sing along to the altered recording, copying the singer's phrasing. This time Cathy did not want to do that. She wanted to impose her own stamp and the best way to do that was to stop listening to the recording, once the melody had been memorised. The male vocal was not quite there and Cathy saw some scope for improvement.

After a break for a cup of herbal tea and a slice of toast, Cathy once again picked up the guitar. This time she placed the capo at the fifth fret and played the same bass strum pattern as before. It was much easier to play in the new position but more importantly, the key had now been raised five semitones which suited Cathy's vocal range perfectly. The song was remarkably easy to sing despite having a complex structure. The words always had the exact number of syllables to fit the melody and rhythm with no exceptions. It was also easy to find places to take a breath. It was difficult however to maintain the guitar part and sing at the same time. In the past the solution would have been to simplify the arrangement, probably dropping the bass line but this time Cathy would persevere. She was on a mission as her old boyfriend might have said.

This dedication to her art was prompted by an email that had arrived that morning. Cathy had been awaiting its arrival for some weeks. She had hesitated before opening it, so much was resting on what it said. Was the dream over or was it only just beginning? The answer was only a click away. Cathy had taken a deep breath before she made that click. The reply was longer than expected. Everything that had been asked of the man had been granted and a detailed critique of the song she had sent was supplied, though he did point out it was not his usual genre. There was praise for the structure of the composition and the quality of the lyrics. The hook was singled out as particularly impressive. He liked the tempo, the rhythm and the use of a key change. It was suggested that the D chord in the chorus could be replaced by B minor and he felt a fade out on a double chorus would be better than a definite ending. Every aspect of the song came under scrutiny and was commented on, it really was extremely kind of him to put in so much effort. It had not been expected. He even said how much he liked her voice.

Cathy had read through everything once more to make sure. When she had finished, she was satisfied that Stuart Williamson had never heard the song before and had not recognized that the song was about him. It had been a chance she had to take. If the famous record producer did not notice the work of his former band mate, then no one else would. She still did not know the writer's name but was now confident that, as stated on the final page of his journal, he had not yet let anyone hear his songs.

.　.　.　.　.

'My forefathers fought with Wallace, they fought with Bruce, they fought with Montgomery. They just couldn't get on with anybody.'

Loud laughter, a few whistles and some banging of tables.

'As you know I joined the family business straight from school, forty three years ago next month, and I don't regret a single day of it. That day was twenty-second of August nineteen eighty-six.'

More laughter and some people are on their feet clapping and cheering.

It is the first booking of the year for the function band. A retirement do for one hundred and fifty guests at a hotel in Hamilton. After Donny had returned from the east end he had called Colette and brought her up to speed with events. It took the rest of the afternoon to prepare for the gig. Over an hour just to put new strings on the Strat and find enough working leads to connect the effects pedals. Then he had to relearn songs that had been second nature to him only three weeks previously. By the time that was done it was nearly six o'clock, and he had to start moving the equipment downstairs for the six fifteen pick up, then a half hour drive along the motorway to the venue. That only left forty five minutes to get the gear in, set it up and have a sound check before guests started to arrive for the eight o'clock start. It was a hectic but well practised routine which was completed on time. Next came the most boring part of these evenings as the band had to pass the time, waiting to play, without getting too drunk in the process.

At a quarter to ten, the musicians were given the nod to get ready.

'As soon as Bob finishes his speech, straight in with Simply The Best. You got that boys? Straight in mind, before he leaves the floor.' That was the instruction from Bob's brother and organizer of the event.

'When dad decided to retire nineteen years ago and hand the reins of the business on to myself he gave me three envelopes and said if the company was ever in trouble I should open the first envelope. Well in my second year in charge profits did take a dip and the family were starting to ask questions. I opened the first envelope. It said BLAME YOUR PREDECESSOR, which I did and we got over that difficulty. Then five years ago when the bank was getting nervous about the size of the overdraft I opened the second envelope. It said, REORGANISE. This I duly did and the bank backed off. Last month I realized I would need to open that last envelope.'

Bob pauses, the room becomes quiet.

'It said.'

Another pause. Bob looks very serious. The room is completely silent.

'PREPARE THREE ENVELOPES.'

Loud cheering and everyone is on their feet.

'One Two. Simply The Best.' Gary launches into a passable impersonation of Tina Turner while playing bass guitar at the same time.

The dance floor is soon full and a circle has been formed with Bob in the middle. More cheering, more applause, a little whooping and a few tears. Donny scanned the crowd, well fed, well lubricated and well up for a good time. He smiled at the others. It was going to be an easy night.

Donny returned to Kingspark Road a little after one o'clock on Sunday morning and the equipment was soon packed away in a cupboard. The next gig would be a golf club dance in two weeks time, unless the band picked up something from an agent before then. It will be March before things pick up again. He settled in a chair and sipped a glass of Glenfiddich, twelve year old single malt, freshly poured from the triangular shaped bottle, a present from a grateful pupil. Donny took the phone from his pocket and selected the last picture taken. It was the snap of the photograph Brenda had. The framed one that sat on top of her fireplace, Dan in the early hours of New Years day nineteen seventy-two. The fifteen year old is sitting on his bed, the new guitar he got for Christmas, resting on his lap. His right arm is raised and his hand is holding a can of Tennent's lager, the ones that had a picture of a model printed on the side. The drabness of the room with its fifties furnishings had been transformed by covering the walls with album covers. Donny was envious of the long haired teenager in a tie-dyed, long sleeved granddad shirt.

Donny zoomed in thinking to himself, this was the time to get into music and pick up a guitar for the first time. Not amid the Mersey Beat boom or in the summer of love. Not when punk exploded in seventy-six nor during the Factory years and certainly not during the Britpop era he himself emerged into clutching a Chinese Telecaster. No, seventy-one was the best time and the teenager's wall was testament to that fact. Donny could make out 'Sticky Fingers' by the Rolling Stones. The Who's 'Who's Next', John Lennon's 'Imagine' and Rod Stewart's 'Every Picture Tells a Story,' all released within the previous twelve months. Donny was well aware of the year nineteen seventy-one having read the David Hepworth book on that magical twelve months. Perhaps hanging on the unseen walls, he speculated were Carole King's 'Tapestry', Bowie's 'Hunky Dory', Joni Mitchell's 'Blue' or Don McLean's 'American Pie,' which were also released in that unique year. Albums that sold in their millions at the time and just kept on selling, seeing off Disco, Punk, New Wave, Rave, Grunge, Hip Hop, Indie and the rest and are still selling to this day with no sign of their popularity waning.

Donny sipped his whiskey and imagined how Daniel Quick may have progressed. Despite all the albums decorating his wall to use as inspiration, it would not have been easy. Things had changed so much since the seventies. There would be no internet to turn to for tutorial videos for a start, no local teacher who would be au fait with the new music that was engaging. He would certainly struggle to find much in the way of books on the subject. No, Dan would only have himself to rely on. He would have to pick it up by ear and by trial and error. Yet somehow he went from absolute beginner to master songwriter in no more than six years. Astonishing really. Was it a diet of only the very best in sonic nourishment that developed such a talent? Perhaps it was. As a child he would have subconsciously absorbed so much amazing music, the Beatles, Stones, Motown, Beach Boys, Dylan.

Donny emptied his glass and poured another. He glanced at his own music collection, mainly CDs, a technology unimaginable to the young Dan but somewhere on those shelves were most of the albums that could be identified in the picture. New technology, same great music.

Donny was remembering more about that year. Was that the year of the first Glastonbury festival? He reached for his laptop.

# Chapter 18

Leonard Cohen and Colette sat on top of two high stools. They were both playing nylon strung guitars and they stared into each others eyes while singing 'That's No Way To Say Goodbye'. Colette had dyed her hair black and it looked longer somehow. She wore a ridiculously short light blue dress and was barely recognisable. Leonard wore a jacket over a woollen polo neck sweater looking, Donny thought, incredible for a man who must be in his eighties. There was not a grey hair on his head.

Donny was sitting beside Billy Bongo in an unfamiliar pub, unsure how he had got there. It seemed a strange choice of venue but it was Colette's night so what could he say. He looked round the dingy room which clearly hadn't been decorated since the seventies. About twenty friends of Colette's, mostly unknown to him, were paying scant attention to the legend performing on the makeshift stage. Seven or eight pub regulars were paying no attention at all. 'What's the matter with these people, that's Leonard Cohen for fuck sake?' Donny exclaimed. Billy placed his hands on his knees, bowed and shook his head, exhaling slowly.

Donny could hear a second source of music coming from the back of the room. 'Do you hear that?' Billy nodded. Donny went to investigate. Someone had started up a reel to reel tape recorder connected to a small guitar amplifier. The song being played was 'That's No Way To Say Goodbye'. 'You have got to be kidding me.' Donny pulled the lead from the guitar amp. Twenty heads turned and glared at him. 'What?' The owner appeared from somewhere, stared disapprovingly then turned and walked away down a long corridor. On stage, Colette and Leonard were oblivious.

Donny was making his way back to his seat when his phone went off in his pocket, the reggae mouth organ ringtone competing with the singers on stage. He tried to switch it off but the buttons wouldn't work and it was not switching itself off automatically after ten seconds as it usually did. People were staring and some were shouting at him. 'It won't switch off,' Donny explained. In panic, he started pressing all the buttons at once which for reasons unknown triggered a drum and base track which was now blaring out over the PA, drowning out the pair on stage, who did not seem to be bothered.

Donny now realized why he hadn't recognised the pub. It wasn't a pub at all. It was Southern Music. With all the amps pushed to one side it looked different. The door of the shop opened and what looked like roadies for a heavy metal band carried in two huge speaker cabinets and were taking great exception to the drum and bass track. They growled at Donny who in desperation tried to disconnect the battery from the phone which is still playing the reggae mouth organ tune. Unfortunately he dropped the phone and it skidded under a wardrobe. Everyone unites to express their annoyance with Donny

On stage, Colette has disappeared and Leonard is

appealing for calm. 'I just want to entertain you' he says into the mike before launching into a version of Classical Gas. Donny ignores the mayhem going on around him and moves closer to the stage. Despite years of trying, he had yet to master this guitar classic. Mr Cohen was not known for such proficiency on the guitar and Donny had to concede that he had slipped another place on the guitar playing order of merit.

'Afternoon temperatures could reach as high as ten degrees Celsius in places but there is a chance of showers particularly in the west.' What is Colette on about Donny thought, and where is she?

The radio sitting on the chair next to Donny's bed had burst into life and he slowly entered the first stages of waking up.

Donny had forgot to reset the alarm. It was only nine o'clock, way earlier than he intended getting up. He lay in bed and half listened to the radio thinking he would make the most of the day now that he was awake but could not stop himself dozing off a few times. He promised himself he would get up after the ten o'clock news.

Donny had spent much longer on the internet the night before than he had planned and only made it to bed at a little after three. That gave him more than six hours rest, his less than fully functioning brain worked out. Prime Ministers run the country on less than that. He only caught snippets from the ten o'clock news bulletin as he continued to slip in and out of sleep.

As if from a place far away Donny heard the words, 'the line up for this year's Newcomers Award at Celtic

Connections has been announced.' Donny was fully alert in an instant. It was not until the last name was read out that he heard what he had been waiting for, Kate Rydelle.

Donny leapt out of bed, picked up his phone and called Colette. After only two rings she answered.

'Hi Donny. A bit early for you on a Sunday. What's happened?'

'Just heard the final line-up for the Newcomers Award.'

'Is she on it?'

'As expected. The first finalist to come from the open stage in seven years.'

'I thought she might withdraw if she was picked. I mean what if she doesn't win? It would take the shine of things a bit after everything that has happened.'

'Maybe.'

'Its this evening isn't it? Perhaps she won't turn up.'

'She'll be there. They contact you first to see if you want to take part. If you say no, they move on to the next person on the list. They probably only contacted everyone last night. It might be the last chance we get to talk to her.'

'What will you say Donny?'

'Don't know. Maybe just say we are there to lend our support and wish her all the best. Say we think her songs are great and does she have any tips for her old friends at the Songwriters Club. See what she says. Don't worry, I won't blurt out anything we have found out.'

'Don't you think she will be kept well away from anybody who might ask difficult questions?'

'You're probably right on that one. I'll have a think about it. Anyway are you able to go?'

'Wouldn't miss it for anything. I need to prepare for a

meeting with some students tomorrow, apart from that, it's a day off. When does it start?'

'Five o'clock, but it is bound to be even busier than usual, so we better get up there early. Do you want to meet me in Blackfriars this afternoon? Say about three. There is a chance that Jake might be there, might even have the band with him. It's worth a try anyway.'

'I might be a bit late but I'll get there as soon as I can.'

'No problem. See you then Colette.'

Donny shared Colette's surprise that Cathy, or more likely, whoever was pulling the strings, was prepared to take a chance on appearing in the final. The winner certainly gains a lot of prestige plus a barrel load of publicity, and not just in Scotland but world-wide. However what if she didn't win? Cathy was certainly taking a giant risk, with all the momentum that Kate Rydelle had built up in the past two weeks. The roots of the festival were in traditional music and although it had diversified over the years the judges were just as likely to pick some virtuoso fiddle or accordion player as an up and coming singer-songwriter, no matter how big the buzz was surrounding her. Cathy would soon find out if her decision was wise or not.

There were two lessons for Donny to rearrange and both were happy to come along early. Each of the learners were at the beginners stage so there was no need for preparation. Thankfully, Kenny was safely back on the rigs so the following week would seem like a holiday. One of the snippets Donny did catch from the news bulletin was that the slowdown in the North Sea oil industry was continuing. The thought of Kenny being paid off and available for lessons every week, did not bear thinking about.

. . .

Colette's friend Crawford, the criminology student, had got in touch saying he had some information for her and they had agreed to meet for coffee on Sunday afternoon in a place the other side of the park from her flat. She set off in good time for the two o'clock appointment realising she had a busy day ahead of her.

This time it was Colette who arrived first. She ordered an Americano and took a seat on one of the high chairs, facing the window. Crawford arrived on the stroke of two.

'Sorry. Am I late?'

'No, you're fine. I have to meet someone later, I wanted to make sure I wasn't late that's all. I have only been here five minutes.'

Crawford ordered himself a Latte then climbed on to the adjacent high chair. Taking the hint that Colette did not have much time, he came straight to the point.

'I was talking to a contact in the Specialist Crime Division about something I am researching at the moment. I took the opportunity to ask her if there was anything new that Geordie McSwiggen was up to. She said that the only new piece of information she had on Geordie McSwiggin was that a pub he owned was up for sale. She only knew that because she drank in it.'

'You think he might need the money.'

'Unlikely. Criminals like Geordie are always looking for places to hide cash, not raise it. It is a bit unusual and it made me think. Last year the Fiscal's office were trying to put together a case against Geordie, under the proceeds of crime act.'

'That's the subject of your PhD?'

'Exactly. The case didn't get off the ground but I got to know some of the details. One of the details I remembered was that Geordie owned a large number of pubs, nine to be precise. I had managed to get a list of them and I still had it. When I got home I went online to the commercial property sites and the auction sites and found another one of his pubs was up for sale.'

'It's the smoking ban, there are pubs closing down all over the place.'

'That's true, you can see what the clientèle are like by the line of smokers standing outside. It has put me off going into some pubs, I can tell you that.'

Colette laughed. 'That's not what I meant but I know what you mean.'

'Anyway I did a bit more digging and found out that he only owns three of that original nine. He may be getting rid of other things too but I don't have any information on the extent of his assets. I only managed to get hold of the list of pubs.'

'Why do you think that's important?'

'Nothing on its own but if he has also been very quiet recently, and that's what my contact was implying, then add to that what you told me last week, I think I recognise the pattern. I think he might be getting out.'

'You mean giving up crime?'

'Career criminals like him never stop. Not completely anyway, but they do move on. These pubs were places to do business in relative safety, if they didn't make any money over the counter, other money, dirty money, could be channelled through it. They were also a reminder to people of who held the power in some communities. If Geordie is getting rid of them it is because he doesn't need them any more and perhaps it means he is not going to be around to keep an eye on things. He has kept the best ones, the ones in the city centre though, they make too much money.'

'What do you think he is planning?'

'Well that's where I think you can help me. You told me your friend was involved in the music business and has got herself mixed up with the McSwiggens. There is a lot of money to be made out of music.'

'For some. I'm still waiting.'

'Gigs at the Hydro every week. Fifteen thousand people at sixty pounds a ticket. It is just the kind of thing that would interest him. Merchandising that the tax man doesn't get to know about, ticket touting at inflated prices, it is right up his street and easier than all the things he has to deal with at the moment. Don't forget, he is getting on a bit. Getting out on his own terms, that's the point. It would be like a freedom fighter moving into mainstream politics, it would seen like progressing not quitting.'

'Why can't he just quit. He must have plenty of money to last the rest of his life.'

'Not how it works Colette. There will be a lot of people out there ready to pounce if it was ever thought that Geordie couldn't hack it any longer. They would swoop in like vultures. If he is moving on, and I suspect that he is, it would be the worst possible time to get in his way. He can't afford, for whatever it is he is up to, to fail because once he makes his move he can't turn back.'

# Chapter 19

Six days previously

Stuart buttoned up his overcoat and put on his furry hat before the lift reached ground level. He may be Scottish but thirty years in California had softened him as far as resistance to the cold was concerned. When the doors opened onto the ticket hall at Belsize Park underground station, the January chill hit him hard.

Outside on Haverstock Hill Stuart noticed that no one else seemed to be as troubled by the weather, the numerous coffee shops on the street still had seats outside and some even had customers sitting on them. He tried but could not remember what they all had been before they were coffee shops. Perhaps he would visit one, sitting inside of course, he was way too early for his appointment. The irony of not going straight to the house he had owned for thirty-five years did not strike him, for he had long ago stopped thinking of it as a house. It was now only an asset, or more accurately *the* asset.

Stuart crossed over to the NatWest and withdrew sixty pounds from the cash machine. The sustaining qualities of the hotel breakfast were beginning to wear off and he remembered a restaurant from last year where he had taken the kids for pizza. Stuart made his way up Haverstock Hill, crossed the road and entered the unusual restaurant, it had been converted from a semi-detached house. The last visit had been during a family holiday. It was the only time they had stayed in the London house, vacant for a month between the old renter moving out and the new one moving in.

A seat was chosen as far away from the door as possible. Stuart ordered a coffee and said he would choose something to eat later. When the coffee arrived, he sipped it slowly while considering his lot. Despite all the years of success, the pot was now empty and here he was back in London to kill the goose that laid the golden eggs, meaning sell it.

Starting a family at the age of forty-nine when his best earning years were behind him, was not the smartest move Stuart realised but he had made his bed and now he had to lie on it, as his mother used to say. He was sixty-four years old, with a wife twenty years his junior and four children, all of school age, all of private school age.

Before Stuart left California, he asked his accountant to tally his career earning. It totalled just shy of twenty-nine million dollars. Current bank balance, less than zero. The rent from the London house had once made up the shortfall from dwindling royalties but the gap between earnings and expenditure kept getting wider, until the rent was no longer sufficient. Two remortgages gave some temporary respite but they had to be paid back adding to his expenditure. An attempt at a third remortgage had failed which was why he was passing time before a twelve thirty appointment with an estate agent.

The house had been bought in the early eighties when the first royalty cheques came in. Thirty thousand pounds cash plus a twenty-three thousand mortgage from the Halifax, to be paid over twenty-five years. Two stops on the tube from Camden but like a different world.

Stuart's seven years in London centred on three stops on the Northern Line, a squat in Camden, a bedsit in Camden followed by a rented flat in Chalk Farm, then the house in Belsize Park. Friends in California would have described it as a doer upper but it was the norm for the time. The house was almost completely untouched since it was built sixty years previously, apart from some painting and decorating,. He and Kay had spent less than a year in its eleven rooms before what was meant to be a temporary move to America.

Someone at the record company recommended a firm of property managers and Mr Hatton of Hatton and Sons was entrusted with finding tenants, and taking care of repairs. The vague instruction of collect the rent, pay the bills and spend anything left on the upkeep was taken most seriously by Mr Hatton. The best renters he could get at first were three nurses from the Royal Free Hospital which soon became four then five. The first year surplus was spent on the roof where Mr Hatton engaged a tradesman of the old school who, section by section, removed each slate, turned them upside-down and refitted with all the damaged and chipped corners now covered by the overlapping slate. The result was a watertight roof that functioned like new while retaining the original character. Mr Hatton knew all manner of craftsmen, and the next year the sash windows were systematically restored. Over a ten year period, the house was improved in steady increments. The quality of renter mirrored these improvements and the nurses made way for some junior doctors and they in turn were replaced by an American banker and his large family. There was now money left over at the end of each year and that revenue formed a substantial part of Stuart's income.

That income had kept the wolf from the door and the house's final act of benevolence would be to fund his next and perhaps last big project in music. Once the bank was paid off from the eighteen million asking price, there should be just about enough to cover what he needed.

. . . . .

Blackfriars was unusually quiet, no more than a dozen customers and no Jake. His drinking buddy was there however, a lone figure standing at the bar and the only one with a pint glass, everyone else looked like they were in for lunch or to read the Sunday papers over a coffee. Even though he knew it would be a waste of time Donny decided to try anyway and wandered over to stand beside the man of few words.

'You all right?'

'Aye fine.'

'Quiet in here today?'

'Aye.'

'I've not seen Jake in for a while?'

'Naw, he's still away.'

'With the Kate Rydelle band?'

'Don't know.'

'Have you heard from him?'

'Naw.'

'They are playing today up at the concert hall. Are you going?'

'Naw.'

Donny ordered a pint of Amstel. 'Can I get you something?'

'Naw, I'm OK.'

'Well if you see Jake tell him I was asking for him.'

'Sure.'

Donny lifted his pint and took a seat at one of the many empty tables. It was a lonely half hour before Colette arrived.

'Sorry. I met Crawford for coffee.'

'Oh aye!'

'Nothing like that but I didn't like to rush off.'

'That will only encourage him.'

'Stop it. I've told you he's a friend, that's all.'

Donny went to the bar and came back with another Amstel and a glass of tap water. Jake's friend had disappeared.

'Crawford sent me a text yesterday, said he had some information so I said I would meet him.'

'About the McSwiggens?'

'Well about the father. Crawford has been doing some research and he is convinced that he is winding down his old businesses and moving into something new'

'Kate Rydelle?'

'I never mentioned her name. All Crawford knows is that Will has put himself down as co-writer on some songs by a new artist.'

'Dan's songs.'

'Yes I know, but Crawford knows nothing about that. He

is only speculating that there are lots of scams in the music business and, as he put it, it's right up Geordie's street.'

'If he is prepared to give up his other stuff and put his energy and money behind the myth that is Kate Rydelle, he must be very confident that he will make one hell of a lot out of it. It makes you wonder just how many songs Cathy is sitting on.'

'What about Dan's girlfriend? What does she think?'

'As I said on the phone Brenda didn't get to hear any of them. He kept it all to himself. She said he was completely immersed in his music. Apparently, he was really clever at school but left at the end of fourth year, after picking up the guitar. From then on, his life revolved around music.'

'If he kept it all to himself, how are we going to find any proof?'

'I can't believe he never let anyone else hear them, can you? The band he was in, well they were that bit older and I don't think they took him too seriously, so I can understand why he just kept working away on his own. Brenda even said he wanted the songs to be perfect before he would let her hear them, that way she couldn't object to him pursuing a career in music. That however only explains how the band and his girlfriend didn't get to hear anything, there is still his other friends and remember he was trying to form a band to do only original material just before he died. He must have let them hear his songs.'

'We don't know how far he's got. Maybe he hadn't got to the rehearsing stage yet?'

'Let's hope he did Colette, it might be the only chance we've got. Well, maybe his sister.'

'I tried to find her on the internet. If she is still around she does not do social media, not under the name Marie Quick anyway. What about the producer guy, are you sure he is not mixed up in this somehow?'

'Stuart Williamson? I don't see how. I am pretty certain that Cathy simply got lucky when she bought that old reel to reel and all those tapes.'

Colette was not so sure. 'What are the chances that what might turn out to be Scotland's most successful songwriter, even though he is dead and what you tell me is Scotland's most successful producer... You know what I'm trying to say.'

'I know. I have thought about that too, it seems too much of a coincidence but I just can't see how. If he had access to that material he would have done something with it before now, don't you think? Lets say he did have access and was waiting for the right moment to release it, why would he pick Cathy and why would he have anything to do with the McSwiggens?'

'Could it be he is connected to them in some way?' asked Colette

'I don't think there is any connection. I think it is just a coincidence.'

'In that case he may be the person to help us.'

'I know. I did think of that.'

'But you are not completely sure he is not involved?'

'Well not one hundred percent, and if we were to show our hand?

'Geordie would come calling.'

'Exactly.'

They both sat in silence for a few moments, each considering what they were getting into. Colette still clung to the hope that she might yet get the chance to record those songs herself. If anything her chances had improved. More chance of persuading Brenda and Daniela to give permission than it would have been persuading some reclusive songwriter. It was dangerous, foolhardy even, to take on someone as ruthless as Geordie McSwiggen but the rewards could be substantial. Such an opportunity would never pass her way again.

Donny thought about his safe, comfortable life in his top floor flat on Kingspark Road. He was not rich but made slightly more money than he spent. He was content with that life and would be happy to return to it but he also thought about Brenda. He had to help her. Fate had dealt her a very cruel blow that afternoon in nineteen seventy-eight. Pregnant at eighteen, the father dead, his family refusing to acknowledge the baby. Her own family barely surviving as it was she left pretty much on her own to bring up a child. It had been a struggle, he had seen it written on her face though Brenda herself would never have said so. On top of all that, she ends up with MS. How could he not help.

It was Donny that broke the silence.

'Listen Colette, I think you have done enough. It is too dangerous and for what?'

'No more than it is for you.'

'But you live on your own.'

'So do you.'

'I know, but.'

'Look I want to keep going, we will both need to be careful. If we find some proof all we can do is pass it on to Brenda and Daniela anyway. It will be up to them to get a lawyer and get it all sorted. If they want to go to the media, that will be their call too. Won't it?'

Donny hadn't given the details much thought. He was prepared to blow the whistle and take his chances but Colette was right, in the end it would need to be Brenda and Daniela that pulled the trigger even if it was him that placed the gun in their hands.

'OK, but if there is anybody that has to stick their heads above the parapet then it's me. You keep your head down.'

'Yes sir.' Colette saluted.

'It's not funny.'

'I know.' Colette draped her arms around her friend and gave him a hug.

'What's that for?'

'For being such a good friend, that's all. I'll be careful don't you worry about that. Now have we anything at all to go on?'

'Not much. Brenda gave me some names of old pals from Bridgeton but she has no idea where to find them. There's been no time to look for them online yet. We could try after the gig.'

'OK. We can go back to my place and I'll make us something to eat.'

'Sounds good. We can also keep trying to find musicians who were around at that time.'

'Was Dan in any other band before the Willie Stewart Band?'

'No. According to Brenda that was his first band. He had been learning guitar for three or four years she thinks, but Dan thought he wasn't good enough to join a band. I think he was a bit of a perfectionist. I formed a band at school as soon as I could play three chords. Different times.'

'Is it really? Haven't people always done what you did, form a band as soon as they could string a few notes together. Skiffle, Rock and Roll, Punk?'

'Yes, but not in nineteen seventy-one they didn't. You have got to think how high the bar was then.'

'How do you mean?'

'The Beatles had just split up and every band thinks this is now our chance to be top dog and then what happens?'

'What?'

'The individual members of the Beatles all bring out solo albums, even Ringo, and they are dominating the charts all over again. George Harrison brought out a triple album at the end of nineteen seventy, can you believe that? How long had he been sitting on those songs? Anyway that was the bar raised another notch. You know some of the albums that were released that year and either side of it.'

'Yes you told me on the phone.' Colette could have said that he often went on about the early seventies but she decided to bite her tongue.

'I didn't tell you half of it. I was up till three last night finding out stuff. Did you know that was the year of the first Glastonbury festival, there was also the concert for Bangladesh. The Rolling Stones and the Who played Glasgow that year and they were at the very top of their game. Imagine seeing that then picking up a guitar. I think I would have given up. You would say to yourself, how can I match that?'

'My dad was at both those concerts, he still talks about them,' Colette remembered.

'Wow! That's amazing. Your dad saw the Stones and the

Who in their hey day. Did he form a band?'

'No, he became a maths teacher.'

'That would have been the easier option at that time. Did you know that Queen were formed that year?'

'They must have missed those gigs.'

'Yeah, lucky for them. Come on we better head up to the concert hall.'

# Chapter 20

The area around the concert hall was busy with Sunday shoppers, well wrapped up against the cold. A lone busker was braving the weather and making a good job of Paolo Nutini's 'Let Me Down Easy,' to the total indifference of passers-by. Unexpectedly, there was no sign of a queue. The busker recognized a soft touch when he saw one and Donny's display of interest was rewarded with a smile and an extra dose of soul injected into the chorus. The special effort was rewarded with a pound coin and a thumb's up.

'That's odd. I thought there would be more people about.' Donny observed.

'They will all be inside if they have any sense, it's freezing out here. Come on'

Donny and Colette climbed the stairs and pulled open the door leading to the foyer. The place was deserted apart from two people asking questions at the ticket desk.

'Are you sure you have got the right time?' Colette enquired.

'Definitely. I'll check at the box office.' Donny walked over and waited behind a French couple, struggling to understand the assistant's Glasgow accent. Behind Donny a door opened and he turned round hoping to find someone to ask.

'Pat!'

'Donny.'

'Are you here to see the gig?'

'Yeah. I'm covering it for the paper. I've just been talking to the organizers. Actually I'm glad I bumped into you. '

'Have I got the time right? It does start at five?'

'Yeah it starts at five.'

'I thought there would be a queue by now. That's why we came up early, to make sure we would get in.'

'It's tickets only. Did you not know?' Colette had moved across to join them.

'Did you hear that?'

'I heard.' The French couple had moved away from the box office, apparently satisfied. Colette turned to the assistant. 'Excuse me. Do you have any tickets for the Best Newcomers show?'

'Sorry, it's sold out.'

'Don't worry I've got some comps, you can have one each.'

'Thanks Pat. I didn't want to miss it. You said you were glad to have bumped into me. What is it?'

'There's some seats round there.' Pat led the way to a quiet spot where they could talk.

'Your tip about Kate Rydelle. You know, about her co-writer. I've got some news for you. You will never guess who W. McSwiggen is.'

'Son of Geordie McSwiggen, notorious Glasgow gangster.' Pat looked deflated as Donny stole his thunder.

'How did you find that out?'

'Somebody that knew Cathy told us. How did you find out?'

'I mentioned his name at the paper. Everybody knew who he was. That's what I wanted to talk to you about. I remembered what you had said at the Songwriters.'

'About Cathy not writing those songs?'

'That's right. You were not the only one by the way, others had also cast doubts. Anyway, I had a listen to some old tracks she had submitted to the blog for review.'

'And.'

'Well they were shite. To be fair, the singing and the playing were all right but the songs themselves were terrible. The last one was sent in last June and it was as bad as the rest. I agree with you she is getting help, but not from W McSwiggen.'

'I think we are all agreed on that.' Donny was not giving anything away.

'Do you have any ideas as to who that person might be? You're the expert in that field.'

'It is no songwriter that I've ever met, that's for sure,' Donny said in all honesty. 'You're the journalist, have you come up with anything?'

'Well, not yet. I went to the news editor and told her that I might have an interesting story, linking the son of a local gangster and Glasgow's next big thing in music. I tell her what I know, which isn't much but she is interested. She tells me to contact Mi.P for comment and see what they say.'

Donny raised a hand indicating that Pat should stop talking. 'Mi. Publishing? In America? One of the biggest music publishers in the world?'

'Oh you don't know?'

'Know what?' Colette interjected.

'Kate Rydelle has signed a publishing deal with them. It is to be announced at the end of the show today. That's why I'm here.'

Donny had the breath taken from him. He kept his hand in the air to prevent Pat continuing, before he had recovered. 'Mi.P. That's like a footballer signing for Real Madrid.'

'I know, that's why I think I have a great story with the songwriting credit McSwiggen has claimed. So I call the office in New York and ask to speak to whoever is handling the Kate Rydelle deal. I can't get past the switchboard. I'm given an email address and told to submit any enquires that way. So I do that. I ask if William McSwiggen is indeed the co-writer as stated on promotional material.'

'What did they say?'

'I got a reply the next day. It only had one line. It said currently copyright on all Kate Rydelle songs reside with K Rydelle and W McSwiggen. Nothing else. I looked out the promotional CD and true enough it does not use the words songwriter. It only said copyright K. Rydelle and W. McSwiggen.'

'Did you ask for confirmation of who the writer was?'

'I did. I emailed back asking that very question. I also asked if there was a co-writer or co-writers involved. I specifically asked what part W. McSwiggen played in the creative process. I also asked for comment on the fact that W. McSwiggen is the son of a crime boss. The news editor is getting excited now, she knows when someone is being evasive and thinks there could be a good story here.'

'Did you get a reply?'

'Not from New York. Friday morning I get a call telling

me to get in a.s.a.p. to see the editor of the paper. Well, I've barely met the man before and we have never had a conversation. I'm freelance, I only do the odd piece and review gigs as required, I hardly ever go into the office, so I think I must be on to something.'

'Well what did he say?' Colette was getting impatient.

'When I get in to see the editor, one of our lawyers is with him. They tell me that the legal department from the parent company in London have been in contact saying that if we go ahead with any story, there must be no suggestion of anything illegal or anything untoward concerning the copyright arrangements for Kate Rydelle. It was linking Mi.P with a known gangster that set the cat among the pigeons. The publishers had engaged one of the most expensive legal firms in London.'

'Are you saying the paper has been got at?' Donny challenged.

'Not exactly. Mi.P's London lawyers had all the details of the deal signed by McSwiggen and Rydelle and they were prepared to show it to the parent company's lawyers under a confidentiality agreement. The legal department say they are satisfied that there is nothing illegal or in any way suspicious in the deal.'

'And your paper went along with this?' Donny was aghast.

'Well, the parent company did, who are American owned by the way.'

'Brilliant.'

'So you have to drop the story.' Colette asked.

'Not exactly. I can still use it if I find out who is helping Cathy but if I can't link it to a Geordie McSwiggen racket, then it won't make the news pages. 'Young artist gets help.' Not exactly a scoop is it?'

Colette glanced at Donny who remained stony faced. Pat continued. 'So that's why I am here early. I wanted to catch the sound check, see who was with Cathy and try for an interview.'

'Any luck?'

'No. I was told Kate Rydelle would not be doing a sound check.'

'What?' Donny said. 'That's crazy, the band won't like that.'

'No band. She is performing solo?'

Colette was aghast. 'I've seen Cathy perform. Great songs or not, on her own she won't win.'

'You have not seen Kate.' Donny reminded her. 'If she is to perform solo there will be a reason for it. I don't know who has been advising her but they haven't put a foot wrong so far. Perhaps the big production thing with the band has done its job. She has the publishing deal. A record contract will be assured if it isn't already in the bag. Just a question of picking the right one. With Mi.P already on board they will be clambering over each other to get at her.'

'You're right Donny. It's mission accomplished. It's a bugger that there will be no band. I had already written a first draft of my piece based on the radio podcast for the last show. I figured they would play the same set.'

'Thanks for the insight into the world of music journalism.' Colette sighed sarcastically.

'Anyway the sound checks are about to start. I need to get back in and get some quotes from the other finalists.' Pat took two tickets from his inside pocket and handed them to Donny. 'Remember if you have any ideas about who is helping Cathy, let me know first.'

Once Pat was out of earshot, Donny turned to Colette. 'Mi.P, can you believe that? That's a big deal.'

'Do you think they know about Daniel? They must have done some research into Cathy's past.'

'You would think so. I don't see a company like that taking any chances. If they say that the copyright issue is all above board, they probably believe it. They must also be sure they have the proof too, if they can convince a newspaper not to go ahead with a story.'

'What do you think?'

'I don't know.'

# Chapter 21

There was an hour to kill before the doors were due to open so Donny and Colette decided to wait in the café-bar upstairs, it was too cold to go back outside. Donny sent a text to Pat letting him know where they would be. A bowl of soup and some bread filled an empty space and helped to pass some time but the next half hour dragged in. Conversation between the two friends had always come easy but the only thing on each of their minds was Cathy and at the moment, there seemed nothing new to discuss. When Pat appeared, he was welcomed with some enthusiasm.

'Get what you were looking for?' Colette inquired.

'Well I got the full S.P. on the rest of the field but nothing on the favourite.'

'So she is going on without a sound check? That's a bit of a risk.' Donny was a bit puzzled.

'It's only acoustic guitar and vocals. The sound guy insists he has all the settings saved from the first gig, so there should be no problem.'

'But Cathy is the only one to take a chance. There's confidence for you.'

'According to the organizer she is coming back from out of town and won't get here till after the start.'

'So she will need to go on last, the best spot. Very convenient,' Donny observed.

'Actually it's a band that's going on last. Kate Rydelle will be second last. There is a fiddle player from Orkney accompanied on piano, another singer songwriter who is actually pretty good, a Canadian group made up of guitar, banjo and fiddle who all sing and a group playing Galician pipes and drums. There is someone else but I can't remember what they do.'

'Sounds very traditional. What about the band?'

'Trad.'

'It might go against Cathy if that's the way the judges are thinking,' Colette suggested.

'It would certainly put a damper on any publishing company announcement,' Pat agreed. 'They would probably postpone it if she doesn't win. Anyway I better get back in, just wanted to let you know the state of play. Hopefully I'll get my interview at the end.'

'Will you ask about her co-writer?' Donny inquired.

'You bet.'

'You will let us know how you get on?'

'It will all be in the paper tomorrow.' As Pat left, Colette noted there was still fifteen minutes till the doors open and another half hour after that, before the first artist took to the stage and suggested another coffee. Donny agreed. Twenty minutes later they made their way back downstairs.

Only a handful of people were already inside the performance space. Donny noticed there were more seats and fewer tables laid out than on his previous visit. Two seats over to the side with only a partial view of the stage were selected. The advantage was that they could also see into the back stage area which was actually at the side of the stage and only separated from the audience by a few screens.

'Do you want something from the bar? I'm going to have a pint.'

'No, I'm fine Donny.'

As Donny waited to be served he watched a man, who was on his own, leave the bar with two bottles of mineral water but only one glass. The man had drawn his attention because he was so wrapped up against the cold. He had an Ushanka hat on his head with the ear flaps down, a heavy black overcoat still buttoned up and a red knitted scarf round his neck. He had only removed his leather gloves to pay for his purchases and to carry them away.

It was winter in Glasgow, it was hardly Siberia. Donny's watched the man as he selected a seat in the middle of the room, equidistant from the PA speakers and with a good view on to the centre of the stage. When the man removed his hat, Donny recognised him at once. It was Stuart Williamson.

When proceedings got under way, the first four acts received polite applause but little else. It was clear who the majority of the audience were here to see. The crowd was mostly under twenty-five which Donny knew was unusual for such an event and few looked like they had any interest in traditional music. Every time someone was introduced that was not Kate Rydelle, there was a rush towards the bar. Donny and Colette had spent the first hour and a quarter watching Stuart Williamson who seemed to be enjoying the music while scanning the room, perhaps looking for any sign of Kate Rydelle or the McSwiggens, of which there were none. They could see Pat sitting at a long table, that had several empty places, set up just behind the judges. As the fourth act, the Canadian trio left the stage, those empty places were suddenly occupied. At the bar it was now easy to get served.

Already Donny realised that Kate had made the right call in deciding to perform without the band. The electric guitar and keyboard set-up would have been all wrong in this company. What was required was a more subtle approach and besides the judges had already experienced the full on band sound and been bewitched along with everyone else. A toned down set coupled with a bit of humility was all that was needed to seal the deal.

Colette gave Donny a nudge. Cathy had appeared at the side of the stage looking more like her old self than the power-dressed diva of ten days previously. She could be seen between the gap in the screens standing with two men who had their back towards the audience. 'What do you think, the McSwiggens?'

'I don't know.' Donny pushed back his chair. 'I'm going to go over.'

'What will you say?'

'I'll wish her luck. Say we are here to give our support. I'll ask her if she is coming back to the Songwriters Club.'

'Fat chance of that.'

'I know but it will be a chance to get her talking.' Donny stood up and began to squeeze between the tightly packed seats, which took some time. He was beaten to the side of the stage by someone who had the same idea. It was Billy Bongo and he was shouting 'Cathy' into the gap between the screens. His path was blocked by one of the two men.

'I'm a friend. I just want to say hello and wish her luck.' Ten feet away, an embarrassed looking Cathy mouthed the word sorry. The young man said 'Miss Rydelle is not able to meet anyone at the moment.'

Donny had stopped short and observed as Billy's protestations fell on deaf ears. When Billy gave up and moved away Donny approached him.

'Hello Billy'.

'Bastards! Did you see that? I only wanted to say hello.'

'That's what I was coming over to do but I don't think I'll bother now.'

'No, you would be wasting your time.'

'Who was that anyway?'

'That's her manager. His name is Will McSwiggen. The older guy is his father. It was the father that put up the money.'

'Right.' Donny could see that Billy knew a thing or two and he wanted to find out what. 'I'm over there with Colette. There is a spare seat if you want to join us.'

'Thanks, I'll do that. I've got a pint back there, I'll go and get it.'

Donny made his way back to Colette. 'Did you see that?' Colette nodded. 'Billy confirmed it's the McSwiggens alright. He's coming over. Hopefully he can tell us something.'

Billy Bongo approached, repeating apologies to people as the dangling sleeves of the bikers jacket he was carrying brushed over their heads and his pint glass dripped lager on their laps. 'What do you make of that? Ten years I've known her, backed her at gigs, never taking a penny. You know that Donny?'

'True Billy.'

'Ten years. Now she can't even say hello.' Billy was more than a little pissed off and Donny and Colette knew better than to interrupt his rant. 'She has not answered any of my calls or texts. I think she has even stopped using that number. I've sent emails. Nothing. I'm not looking for anything. I think it's brilliant what's happened to her. I was doing gigs with her only three months ago. I don't believe it. I just don't believe it.' Billy took a long slug of his pint and shook his head.

Donny waited till he was sure Billy was finished. 'Maybe it's that manager guy.'

'Damn right it is, but it's no excuse.'

'Will McSwiggen. Is that not Cathy's landlord? I think Derek, you know, Cathy's old boyfriend, mentioned him once.'

'Aye, that's him. Son of Geordie McSwiggen, a Glasgow 'businessman' as they say in the papers.'

'Right, it's coming back to me now. Isn't he the idiot son that hides behind his father's reputation?'

'I don't know who told you that. He's as sharp as a tack.'

'I thought he just did odd jobs for his father, that he was a bit of a plonker.'

'I can assure you he is the mastermind. He went to one of those private schools up the West End and has a lot of contacts, especially in the media. He also knows exactly how the music business works.'

Donny and Colette exchanged glances. It seemed neither Derek nor Crawford had the measure of the gangster's son. Billy Bongo would be pumped for more information later as the interlude was over and the compère was at the microphone.

'Next we have a young lady who blew us all away when she first appeared on this stage. She has flown up specially from London where she is recording her first album. We're very grateful for that. So one more time, a big Glasgow welcome for Miss Kate Rydelle.'

There was wild whooping and cheering from the younger element in the audience. Pat and his fellow reporters were quite taken aback. To a man they all turned round, as did the judges, missing Kate Rydelle's entrance. Donny leaned over and spoke into Colette's ear. 'Now that's weird.' Colette agreed.

Cathy had certainly toned down her appearance but still managed to look stunning. She wore a cream Arran knit jumper over a green tweed skirt with a subtle check and brown knee length boots. Her red hair had a slight curl and rested on her shoulders. She looked like a grown up sophisticated Katie Morag. She had placed her guitar on a stand and was now standing at the mike, her hands clasped behind her, accepting the acclaim.

'Thank you so, so much. That's the warmest welcome I've ever had.'

Billy Bongo's face was a picture as he turned to Donny and Colette. 'Course it is, she was playing in pubs to twenty people at a time, up until a month ago.'

Colette gave a nervous laugh. She hoped that Billy would not make a scene.

When the noise died down, Kate Rydelle thanked everyone for coming out on such a cold evening and apologized for the band not being with her, stating that they were so disappointed but had to stay in the studio. She then said how amazing the first four acts had been.

'How do you know? You only arrived ten minutes ago.' Billy was getting more and more agitated with every word. Donny was more impressed than anything else. Once again she had the audience eating out of her hands. Kate Rydelle's praise for her fellow artists had drawn another round of applause. Even the judges and the press were drawn in. When the noise died down, she announced that her first song would be the traditional Celtic ballad 'She Moved Though The Fair' and it would be done unaccompanied.

'Now that's genius.' Donny looked at the other two for affirmation. The whole room was behind her now, she could do no wrong. 'Now That I Found You' was followed by 'Main Street'. Both attracted rapturous applause and not just from her young fans. Kate then announced that she would do a song that she had never sung live before. It turned out to be of equal quality to the previous two. She ended her short set with Rabbie Burns 'Green grow The Rashes, O' encouraging the audience to sing along. Her set was gauged perfectly, ticking all the boxes. The traditionalists were pandered to, the fans had their show stoppers to get them all excited and the press were lured into the trap with the exclusive of a song, never before performed in public.

A minute into a standing ovation that looked like it could go on all night, Kate Rydelle clasped her hands in front of her, moved forward to the edge of the stage and bowed, before gracefully exiting stage left.

Donny had not forgotten about Stuart Williamson. He had kept an eye on him during the set. Williamson had sat impassive throughout not even bothering to clap, as he paid more attention to the reaction of the crowd than he did to what was happening on the stage. When everyone eventually sat down, Donny expected to find him still in his seat, sipping his glass of water but Stuart Williamson was nowhere to be seen.

Donny leapt out of his seat without saying anything to the other two. He still had no idea how Stuart Williamson fitted into things but he had to find out. It was hard to believe that someone with such a massive reputation would get involved in something so underhand especially involving an old band mate. It could hardly be for the money. Donny squeezed past the same people as before, finding them less accommodating this time, and hurried over to the side of the stage shooting a glance at the bar just to check there wasn't a simpler explanation for the producer's absence. The gap between the screens was now unguarded. Donny tentatively popped his head round. There was neither Williamson, the McSwiggens nor Cathy. Instead the five members of the final act stared back at him.

'Sorry I was hoping to find Kate?'

'Through there.' One of the musicians pointed to a door.

'Oh. Er, thanks.' Donny walked over to a set of double doors faking confidence, took a deep breath and pushed them open.

He found himself in the concourse which was busy with people gathering for a concert in the main auditorium. Donny could not see Williamson nor any of the others. There were stairs going up, stairs going down and the foyer continued round corners both left and right. Donny searched all the possibilities but came up with nothing. He returned to the hall via the main entrance.

'Did you see her?' Billy Bongo asked.

'No, there must be a room somewhere that they can wait in.'

'The other finalists are all in here.' Colette pointed out.

'They don't have Will McSwiggen for a manager.' Billy chipped in.

'Very true. Actually it was someone else I was after. Did Cathy ever mention someone called Stuart Williamson?' Billy shook his head.

'Don't think so. Who is he?'

'He was a top producer back in the day and I spotted him here tonight, sitting in the middle about ten rows back from the stage. He was here right up to the last song. He must have left when everyone was on their feet.'

'Did he go to see Cathy?' Billy asked.

'I don't know.'

# Chapter 22

Three months previously.

'What are you doing in my room? Get out'

'Cathy. Is that any way to talk to your manager?'

'I told you I don't need a manager. I'm doing fine on my own.'

'Not quite on your own though, is it? You're forgetting Daniel Quick.'

'What are you talking about?'

'His name is Daniel Quick. Had you not found that out?'

Cathy froze. 'Found what out?'

'Cathy I can help. I want to help, so you might as well drop the act. I read the diaries.' Cathy's eyes darted involuntarily to the empty box at the foot of the bed. 'I read them two weeks ago Cathy. You should have locked them away before.'

'You've no right being in here and no right touching my things.'

'You're right, I don't, but I've done it and if you listen to me you will be glad that I did.' Cathy said nothing. She was thinking about her landlord's first offer of help. He had arrived one evening to collect the rent in the middle of a rehearsal with Billy Bongo. He said he liked her sound and asked if she had a demo, claiming he could get it played on the radio. Five days later a rough version of 'Now that I've Found You' was played on an afternoon arts program very much to Cathy's delight and surprise. Since then Will McSwiggen had been turning up at open mike nights and offering his services as a manager. Now here he was standing in her room in possession of her big secret.'

'OK, I'm listening.'

'That's more like it. I really can help you know. I got your demo played didn't I?'

'Did your dad make them an offer they couldn't refuse?'

'As a matter of fact I was at school with the presenter. All I did was ask her to listen to the demo. She played it on air because it was good not because she knew me and it had nothing to do with my father.' Cathy was succumbing to the flattery. 'I was able to get your music listened to, that's all. The rest was down to you. Oh, and Daniel Quick.' Cathy's face was burning, part anger but mostly embarrassment. 'How did you think you could get away with it?'

'I thought you had read the diaries.'

'I did.'

'Well you know how.'

'Just because he said he had never played his songs to anyone you can't be sure no one has heard them can you? If we are to work together, we would need to be sure that no one can come along later and claim the copyright.'

'And how do we do that? Not that I'm saying I want to work with you.'

'I think you are Cathy. I think you are.' Cathy was

realising she had few options, it looked like Will McSwiggen understood that only too well. There was no way she could continue passing off the songs from the old tapes as her own if he knew the truth. The choice was, work with him or quit, and she did not want to quit. Life had been too good the past few weeks, she had tasted success for the first time and she liked it. 'Let me explain the situation Cathy. Daniel Quick died in a road accident on the twenty fourth of May nineteen seventy-eight.'

'That's just after the last entry in his diary.'

'Exactly.'

'Then that means he never did get to play his songs to anyone.'

'Perhaps. There were two pages torn out. Do you know anything about that?'

'No. It was like that when I got it?' Cathy managed to keep her voice even.

'Not that it matters.'

'How did you find out his name?' Cathy asked.

'That was easy. I checked the death notices in old newspapers up at the Mitchell Library for the days after the last entry in the notebooks. There was only one for a young man from Bridgeton. It said he died in a road accident. When I checked the papers for the day after the accident I found a report, Bridgeton musician killed by lorry on London Road.' Cathy felt sad at hearing the news.

'I'll just cut to the chase Cathy. My father bought the copyright to all compositions by the late Daniel Quick from his sister. She is his next of kin.'

'He what?'

'He owns the copyright on 'Main Street' and everything

else Daniel wrote. It's all above board and legal. It doesn't matter if someone recognises the songs anymore, they are legally his.'

'How did he manage that?' Cathy did not know what to make of this new turn of events.

'It wasn't easy. She is living down south.'

'Well how did he do it then?'

'My father has some influence in the Bridgeton area. He sent someone down to ask questions and they came back with a name. Geordie has friends who are good at finding people, even when they don't want to be found.'

'And she was willing to sign the songs over, just like that?'

'More than willing, I can assure you.'

'How much did he pay her?'

'Confidential.'

'Sure.'

'The point is Cathy that the songs are his to do with as he pleases. Now you know as well as I do, they are special. I played those recordings you gave me to someone in the business yesterday, and he is desperate to get his hands on them.'

'Another school friend?'

'It was a very exclusive school.'

'It's not what you know but who you know. Is that it?'

'Good job you know me then.'

'Yeah. Lucky me.'

'Cathy I'm offering you the chance to have first go at those songs. Geordie will put up the money for a band and recording sessions. We'll give you a complete makeover, website, the lot. You can still put your name to the songs.'

'But he'll get all the royalties.'

'There is still the performing royalties, which could be substantial.'

'I'll need to think about it.'

'Look Cathy. You have done a great job with the songs that's why I am offering you a chance, but there are a lot of singers out there, if you are not interested.'

'What if I record some proper demos in the studio, you could take them to one of the big publishing companies and they could offer them to someone with a big name.'

'We might end up doing just that, but what have you got to lose. If the demos sound good, there could be a recording contract in it for you.'

Cathy had already made up her mind to accept the offer. As the man said what did she have to lose. She did not however, want to give in too easily. 'Like I said, I'll think about it.'

'I'll take that as a yes. Be ready at ten tomorrow, you have a rehearsal with your musical director.'

.　.　.　.　.

'What are you for?'

'Something to get rid of the bad taste. Make it an Addlestones. Cheers Donny.'

Donny and Billy Bongo were back in Blackfriars. Colette had returned home to prepare some food for herself and Donny, who had promised to be no more than an hour.

To no one's surprise, Kate Rydelle took the award for best newcomer at the festival. The compère announced Kate had signed to the London record label AnStar and had a publishing deal with Mi.P before the singer took to the stage one more time, thanking her manager Will McSwiggen who she described as also her collaborator. There was praise for those that had helped her back in Oban, for her family and for the musicians in her band. It was as if her life in Glasgow as Cathy Riddle never happened. There was no mention of the Songwriters Club or any of the musicians who had supported and encouraged her over the past ten or so years. The evening was brought to a close with a triumphant version of 'Main Street' after which Kate Rydelle was whisked away by two mean looking thugs, dressed in suits for the occasion, ignoring questions from the assembled press. Stuart Williamson did not reappear, nor did Geordie McSwiggen. Will McSwiggen approached the press table at the end of the evening, saying unfortunately Kate had to catch a plane back to London but he would stay and would be happy to answer any questions. The stewards prevented any earwigging by emptying the hall. When Donny suggested a drink, Colette realised it was a ploy to get Billy Bongo talking and was astute enough to know he would be more forthcoming if that conversation was man to man.

'She could at least have mentioned the club. I can't forgive her for that. Can you?' Donny shrugged his shoulders. 'Well, I remember when it was the only gig she could get. We supported and encouraged her when her songs were, well, lets say not great, and now she can't even say hello.' What Billy was saying was certainly true for himself. He had gone out of his way to help Cathy. It was little wonder he was so disgruntled.

'That's something I wanted to ask you about. How come

her new songs are so good when her old ones were,' Donny hesitated, 'well, bad?'

'What do you mean?'

'Well, don't you think it's a bit odd. To be blunt, do you think she really wrote them?' It was evident Billy had never considered this possibility.

'She said she did. They didn't always sound that good. When she first asked me to go to some open mike nights with her, they didn't seem that much better than her old stuff, apart from better lyrics. She only had two songs then but she got better and more confident as the weeks went on. By about the third week, they sounded really good.'

'How often were you playing?'

'About three times a week. It was just the same two songs at first then she started to introduce a new one every week. The new ones were always well-rehearsed before I got to hear them then we would practice together before going out to do an open mike.'

'When did the manager appear?'

'Not too sure. Probably about three months ago. She gave up her job soon after. He decided she should perform on her own so that was that for me.'

'How come?'

'I don't know. I thought we were sounding good together.'

Donny knew perfectly well what was going on. McSwiggen did not want anyone from Cathy's past around who might start to ask awkward questions. That would also explain why she had not been seen for months at the Songwriters Club before her Celtic Connections warm-up appearance. The pieces of the jigsaw were beginning to fit into place. The one piece that would not fit was Stuart Williamson.

# Chapter 23

The Range Rover slowed down quickly, cut across the path of oncoming traffic, crossed the pavement and came to an abrupt halt in the driveway. In the twenty minute drive from the concert hall, not a word had passed between Cathy and her driver.

'Boss said you have to stay in, he wants to talk to you.' There was no particular malice in Gaz's voice, just enough to convey that he expected the instruction to be followed.

Gaz remained in the driving seat while Cathy removed her guitar case and holdall bag from the back seat. When she slammed the door shut, the driver reversed into the road and drove off at speed in the direction of the city centre.

Cathy opened the door of the house that had been home for the past ten days. It was beginning to feel more like a prison. The house belonged to Will's mother and was where he had grown up, a four bedroom, three reception rooms, red sandstone villa in the affluent suburb of Bearsden, five miles, north west of the city centre. His mother spending the winter in Tenerife, Cathy had the place to herself.

Cathy left the guitar case in the hall and took the holdall upstairs. She was still wearing the clothes she had worn on stage, an outfit put together by one of Will's school friends who, 'knows about these things.' Cathy did not bother to remember her name. She was just another in a procession of people in the know that had been called upon to create Will's vision of what a pop star should look like.

On the upstairs landing Cathy paused to look at herself in the full length mirror. She had to admit the look was good, but did she recognize the person looking back at her? Cathy continued to the room overlooking the back garden that had been allocated to her. It was roughly the same size as her old room in the tenement flat back in Partick, but that was where any similarity ended. All the furnishings were of the highest quality and as far as Cathy could tell they had never been used. The biggest difference however was that the room was always warm.

Back in her casual clothes, Cathy came downstairs to the well-appointed kitchen, the only room in the house she used apart from the bedroom. She had some thinking to do and liked to do that with the aid of a cup of her herbal tea. Gaz had said the boss wanted to speak to her, but which one was he talking about, he had the annoying habit of referring to both Will and Geordie as boss. Hopefully he meant the son this time.

The elation of winning the award lasted all of thirty seconds, once she had departed the stage. It ended when she came face to face with Stuart Williamson. Will had initially kept it to himself that the producer had tried to make contact. He had not answered Stuart's emails, playing hard to get. There had been many enquiries from all sorts of people trying to get in on the act these past two weeks. It was only in passing that Will mentioned Stuart Williamson to Cathy, who nearly choked on hearing it.

Cathy had to tell her manager that the Willie Stewart in Dan's diaries and Stuart Williamson, the legendary producer were one and the same. To say Will was spooked by this revelation was putting it mildly.

Cathy had to bluff it was common knowledge in the Songwriters Club that Stuart Williamson had changed his name from Willie Stewart. 'And you never thought to tell me about this' Will had bawled at her. 'If he has recognized any of these songs we are fucked. I can't believe you never told me. This could ruin everything.'

That had been the perfect opportunity to come clean and put Will's mind at rest. All she had to do was explain that she had already tested that theory and tell him that Stuart Williamson had already been sent the one song. A song he would be certain to recognize if he had heard it before, as it was written about him. Cathy could state that Williamson had heard the song, had even critiqued it and that he suspects nothing, proving that what was written in the diary was true, Dan had not let another soul hear his songs. She could have done that, but she had not.

Sitting at the kitchen table with her hands clutching her warm cup, she wished she had told Will. That way he could have talked confidently to the man and respectfully declined his offer, instead of just ignoring him. The reason she kept quiet was because it would mean explaining how she knew that 'Cut And Run' had been written about Williamson. It had been on the final two pages of the journal. the pages Cathy had torn out. The pages that also revealed Dan's girlfriend was pregnant at the time of his death and that Dan most likely has an heir. An heir that could claim the rights to their father's compositions.

That information was Cathy's insurance policy. She could have wiped the smirk off Will McSwiggen's face there and then that day when he triumphantly declared that he alone held the copyright to the songs she had been parading as her own.

Deciding when and how to cash in that policy would be a tricky decision. Geordie in particular had become increasingly jittery these last few days. He had invested quite a sum already and was committed to further substantial injections of cash before he would see any return. Perhaps he is not as wealthy as everyone had presumed.

While sipping her second cup, Cathy decided on what she would say when whoever it was, Will or Geordie, turned up to talk. How she hoped it would be Will. She would say that she worked out that 'Cut And Run' must have been about the guy who quit the band and headed to London.

Cathy was still rehearsing her story as the Range Rover sped into the driveway once more. When the front door to the house opened, Cathy could sense that two people were entering the hallway.

'You have some explaining to do, young lady.' It was Will's voice. His words sounded ridiculous to Cathy. Will was four years younger than her for a start and it was hardly the language you would expect from a gangster's son in the middle of a scam. As the two men entered the kitchen it was clear Gaz thought the same.

'What do you mean?'

'Don't play the innocent. That American arsehole has just told me you sent him a demo.'

'You know he is not American.' Will ignored the correction. 'It was way before you got involved and I did it for a very good reason.'

'Oh do tell.' Gaz had to swallow his laugh.

'I explained to you who he is.'

'You never said you had contacted him.'

Cathy glanced at Gaz then back to Will.

'It's OK, you can talk.'

'Right. I was only doing what you should have done. I was testing if what was in the diaries was true and Stuart Williamson was the one person that might have realized that Dan Quick was the writer.'

'You should have told me that you had contacted him.'

'I know I should. I'm sorry, but it was before you got involved. I didn't think it mattered. I got a reply. He didn't suspect anything.'

'Let's see the emails.'

Cathy switched on her phone and passed it to Will. 'I got it ready for you.'

Will carefully scrutinized the email Cathy had sent, then the long critique she got in reply. As he did so, Cathy was weighing up whether this was the time to say Williamson had made further contact suggesting that she sing on one of his projects and that she had closed that account preventing, she assumed, any further contact. She watched Gaz who was reading the email over Will's shoulder. As things stood, the minder might report back to Geordie that she had been smart in testing the information.

'How come you only sent the one song and why that one?'

'I worked out that the song was written about him. If you

235

read the lyrics it's obvious, someone leaves his mates behind and heads for the big city to seek fame and fortune. That's exactly what Willie Stewart did.'

'And you didn't think that was an important piece of information that I should know about.'

'What was it you said? You do the music, I'll do everything else.' Gaz was enjoying this.

'You should have told me.' Will's voice had mellowed, perhaps realizing that Geordie would blame him for not finding out about people who knew Daniel Quick and not rely solely on what he had written in his journals. Cathy began to relax.

'And that's the only time he contacted you?'

Shit! It was Gaz that asked the question and that was what caused the millisecond of hesitation.

'You better say hen. The Boss'll no' like it if you hold anything back.'

'There was one other time.'

'Christ, Cathy you should have told me everything. You're a fucking idiot.' Will was now sounding like a gangster's son. 'What have you done? He is the last person on earth we want taking an interest.' Will had risen from his seat, knocking it over in the process and was clutching clumps of his hair with each hand.

Gaz, who had remained standing throughout, was unmoved. 'You better let us see the other email.'

Cathy felt sick. 'Give me a minute' She reached out her hand and Will slapped the phone into it. He wanted me to try out for some song he was recording. He wasn't interested in me as a songwriter. I didn't want to get close to him, I'm not daft, so I saved any important stuff and closed the email account. He didn't even know my name, I never signed the email and you couldn't work it out from the address. I only said I was from Glasgow to attract his attention.'

'You did that alright.'

'There were three emails. I only answered one and said I was not involved in music any more. That's when I closed the account. I don't know how he found me.'

When Cathy had located the email, it was Gaz that took the phone from her. This time it was Will who read over Gaz's shoulder. When they had finished reading, Gaz put the phone in his pocket. 'The Boss will want to see this. You better write down any passwords.'

Cathy did not protest. 'Don't think you will need any but it is always oban101, lower case.'

'What?'

'Small letters for Oban'

'Right.' Gaz turned to Will. 'We better get back.'

'In a minute.' Will turned to Cathy. 'You heard of a reporter called Pat Cullen?'

'Yeah, he writes a blog on local bands and singers.'

'Has he ever written anything about you?'

'Don't think so. I've sent in some demos and he has covered some Songwriters nights.'

'But he knew you from before. Before you got Quick's tapes?'

'I suppose so. Why?'

Because he was at the Concert Hall tonight and he has a meeting with Stuart Williamson lined up. That's why.'

'I don't understand.'

'No you don't, do you?'

'But you own the copyright and the deals have already been signed. Haven't they?'

'The record company and the publisher know about the copyright. They have seen the contract signed by his sister and the lawyers have been all over it. That is not the issue.'

'I still don't see the problem.'

'The problem Cathy is the public, the fans. They won't be so interested if they find out you are not the writer. It is all about perception. A singer/songwriter is perceived to be worth more than just a singer.'

'I do write, remember.'

'Shut up Cathy. We can spin them along for about five years with the songs we have but if they were to find out you were not the writer, they won't be so keen to buy your recordings or come to your concerts. We have invested too much already creating Kate Rydelle for this to fail.'

'Boss, we need to go now.' Gaz was walking towards the door.

'You better hope you haven't blown this Cathy. Geordie has gone out on a limb for us. We better not let him down.'

When the front door slammed shut, Cathy burst into tears. What she wanted to do was head straight for Oban and into her mother's arms but she was aware that Geordie was not a man you could run away from. She would have to stay and face the music, as it were.

Pat Cullen, sticking his nose in, was not good news. What she did not tell her manager was that Pat had written some pretty damning reviews of her performances at the Songwriters Club. Then there was Donny McNeil another person she did not want to see and to make matters worse he was with Billy Bongo. Donny was certain to be suspicious.

Cathy pulled herself together and walked over to the sink to wash her face. The two hundred pound make-up job was no longer so impressive. When she finished Cathy went into the hall and brought her guitar case back into the kitchen, sat it on top of the table and opened the lid. Cathy squeezed her fingers between the thinnest string and the edge of the sound hole. The folded up final two pages from Daniel Quick's journal were still safely secured to the inside by a piece of gaffa tape.

# Chapter 24

Donny picked up a taxi on Albion Street just outside the bar, a lucky break as he had stayed longer than intended with Billy Bongo. It was not that the Songwriters Club compère and long-term friend and collaborator of Cathy Riddle had any vital information. It was because the man was down in the dumps and Donny felt the least he could do was commiserate over a pint in the time honoured fashion of the city of Glasgow. By the time Billy downed his third pint of Addlestones (7% volume) and Donny had switched to half pints of lager, the percussionist was in a more optimistic frame of mind. It was all the fault of Will McSwiggen, Cathy would not turn her back on her old friends. Donny felt it kinder to agree to this assessment, declining to point out that Billy himself, while still on his first Addlestones, confirmed that Cathy was well on her way to changing her image, and had developed a single minded determination to succeed before Will McSwiggen appeared on the scene. As his cab made its way across town Donny considered the powerful unholy trinity of Cathy, Will and Geordie McSwiggen he had witnessed this evening. The ambition of a singer thrown a lifeline for a career long dead in the water, a manager with the guile and the contacts, and a backer with the money and the muscle to make it happen. It was a sobering thought to think that this was what he had pitted himself against.

When Donny pressed the button on the entry system to Colette's flat, his head was almost clear.

'Only an hour late. I had planned for double that.'

'Is that smell what I think it is?'

'Its kedgeree, if that's what you are thinking?'

'You know it's my favourite.'

'I can cook other meals you know.'

'I'll tell you if I ever get tired of it. You're the only person I know that can cook it. You're probably the only person I know that's even heard of it.'

'You are the most appreciative dinner guest I've ever had but tell me did you find out anything from Billy Bongo?'

'Only that Cathy had set the ball rolling long before McSwiggen appeared, her reinvention that is. But it was only when McSwiggen was on board that she cut all ties to her old life. It was probably his idea to change the name.'

'Do you think it was Cathy that asked him to get involved or do you still think it is the McSwiggens that are forcing her?'

'Don't know, could be either way. My guess is that Cathy knew that Will McSwiggen had the contacts and she tried to use them. Will spots the potential and takes over.'

'Did Billy Bongo know of Stuart Williamson's involvement? That's got to be the most important question.'

'I tried to press Billy on that one but as he said at the gig, he had never heard of Stuart Williamson. There something that just doesn't fit there. I can't see him and the McSwiggens together. Why would he need them? Why would he need Cathy for that matter?'

'What if Cathy discovers the tapes, makes the connection between Stuart Williamson and Dan Quick then contacts Williamson, perhaps only to find out who owns the copyright and it is Williamson who suggests Cathy passes off the songs as her own but him taking a share of the royalties?'

'There's a few problems with that theory. First he would be stabbing an old mate, or at least the family, in the back.'

'What if he needs the money?'

'Hardly. The last time I read about him 'Over The Castle Wall' was still bringing in a hundred thousand a year.'

'When did you read that?'

'OK, it was a while back. Three or four years, maybe more.'

'Have you heard it on the radio lately?'

Donny had to admit that the song that was all over the television and radio when he was growing up, and for years afterwards, had disappeared off the radar in recent years.

'What about his production royalties, do they bring in much these days?'

'I take your point but he has made millions over the years.'

'Maybe he has spent millions.'

'That may be true but my second point was why not go to Brenda and Daniela and get their permission to record the songs? They would certainly have agreed.'

'So he can keep all the royalties, I suppose.'

'You know the old saying, where there's a hit, there's a writ. He has got to suspect that Brenda or Dan's sister or someone else would recognise the songs once they became well-known.'

'Cathy and Will McSwiggen seem willing to take that chance. Could it be that Stuart Williamson is playing it clever, letting them front the scam and he keeps in the background.'

'Possibly. It's just that I can't see why he would pick the McSwiggens as partners. They're not the kind of people to mess with. Geordie, remember, is used to staying in the background himself and letting others take the risks. Williamson's millions would not save him if he were ever to cross Geordie McSwiggen, if we go by what your friend Crawford has been saying.'

'There is something we have got to find out. Why is Will McSwiggen happy to put his name to the songs and why is Stuart Williamson happy to appear in public in Glasgow as part of the audience when Kate Rydelle is performing? They must be very confident that they will not be found out. The reason for that, is what we need to know.'

'Is that kedgeree ready? My brain's like mush trying to figure all this out.'

'Just a couple of final touches. I opened a bottle of Chardonnay, it should be ready to drink now. Pour yourself a glass and a half glass for me. Oh and get the plates organised.'

# Chapter 25

As many a deposed leader might attest, when a coup takes place, it is when you least expect it and it happens fast. One minute you are in power and feeling secure, the next you are out. It was most certainly true in the world that Geordie McSwiggen inhabited. He had mounted several coups himself in his time, all of them successful. Geordie like many before him did not see it coming.

At seven thirty a.m. on the morning after Kate's victory at the Newcomers Awards, an anonymous 999 call was received at Police Scotland. The caller said there was a body in a car on the forecourt of the garage on Canal Street. The call was then ended before any further information could be requested. The senior officer on duty recognised the address as the garage belonging to Geordie McSwiggen.

The first police car on the scene arrived at 7:33 with instructions to wait for the armed response unit. An ambulance had also been dispatched with the same instructions. When a second police car arrived it blocked off the street at the corner, one hundred metres from the garage. The first car then closed the road at the other side, about 50 metres away from the entrance. The ambulance arrived next and drew up on the main road about 20 metres from the blocked off corner. When the armed response unit arrived, it did not wait for the uniformed officers to move the car blocking the street, but mounted the pavement before returning to the road and coming to a halt across the entrance to the garage. There were about forty cars of varying ages, all looking pristine, available for sale on the forecourt. It did not require the team to leave the armoured vehicle to spot what they were looking for. In the second row back from the street, three cars in from the end was what look like a man sleeping in the passenger seat of a two year old Skoda Octavia. The only thing that suggested otherwise was the dark spot in the middle of his forehead.

Within half an hour, screens had been erected and scene of crime officers had begun their work. Uniformed officers were diverting traffic and taking details from people arriving for work in the various industrial units nearby. Only three people acknowledged that they worked at the garage.

At 7:45 Jim Burnie, the garage manager could see the police car blocking the street as he approached. He did not indicate but drove straight past. As he did so, he glanced to the left beyond the car blocking the street and could see what was obviously an armed response unit van in front of the garage. He could also see a lot of activity around the cars on the forecourt. He took the first turning on the right and found a parking space.

Jim Burnie was essentially an honest man, a car mechanic by trade who had worked for Geordie for more than thirty years, starting soon after the garage opened. He knew of course that Geordie had many other interests and that the garage was kept mainly to facilitate them. He also knew when to ask questions and when not to ask.

The garage manager quickly took his phone from his

pocket cursing himself, for he was certain that he had missed a call or a text. He was both surprised and alarmed to learn that he had not. After a moment's hesitation, he tapped a memorized number into his phone.

'It's Jim, Boss. I've just got here. How do you want me to play it?'

'What are you talking about?'

'The garage. The police are all over it.'

'What?'

'It's the armed response unit.'

'Fuck!'

'There was nothing from Rab, not a thing Boss. Do you think they are here for him?'

Geordie knew the answer was no. Rab looked after the premises at night and supervised the comings and goings of cars outside normal business hours. He dealt with the side of the business that needed to be conducted away from prying eyes and evidently did so efficiently, because he was now doing this work elsewhere, and for a new employer.

'Look just turn up like normal and see what they say. Get back to me when you know something.' Geordie hung up. From his pocket he took out a pay as you go phone and pressed the only number in the memory. There was no answer. From another phone he tried another number. Again no answer. The same from a third phone.

'Boss. The cops are at the door.' It was one of Geordie's minders. 'What do you want to do?'

'Let them in. Bring them to the kitchen.' Geordie crossed the hall and down the side of the stairs to the largest and most impressive room in the house. It was the work of Jackie, his current partner and only his second after the break-up with his wife. It occupied the space of two former rooms plus a conservatory extension. Geordie poured himself a coffee and sat down at the breakfast bar. Two plain clothes policeman were shown in.

'Mr George McSwiggen?'

'You know who I am. What do you want?'

'DS Martin Collins and this is DC Caroline Woods. Can you confirm that you are the owner of Sighthill Motors?'

'Just get to the point.'

'I believe that Andrew Ward is an associate of yours.'

'I know Andy. Sometimes we go to the game together, been to his clubs a few times, but we're not in business together.'

'Drop it Geordie, it's us you're talking to.'

'I prefer it when we play the game Inspector.'

'It's Sergeant.'

'I'll say it to you DC Woods, your pal doesn't listen. I have no links to any criminal activity in this city or anywhere else. I am a legitimate businessman.' Geordie had been waiting these past three weeks for the opportunity to recite that line to an officer of Police Scotland. He had said the same thing or similar many times in the past, but this was the first time that it was true.

'Let's cut the crap. At seven fifty-two this morning a dead body was discovered inside a Skoda Octavia on the forecourt of your Garage. We have reason to believe that the body is that of Andrew Ward.'

'I can't believe it.'

'Well you better believe it.'

'That is shocking.'

'Yes it is shocking.'

'Andy always drove a BMW.'

'Aye very good.' DS Collins was well aware he would get nowhere but went through the motions anyway. Geordie kept up the front, as he always had done, when interviewed by the police. It was a well-practised routine performed on autopilot but this time he was shaken. Andrew Ward had been his chosen successor. The youngest of his lieutenants, but the smartest and the strongest. Geordie had found a way out into something better, something more prestigious and potentially more lucrative. Andy understood Geordie's thinking, it was, in the younger man's eyes, a master stroke. Make your money then become a gentleman, that's what Andrew's grandfather had told him. That was what Geordie had done and that was what he intended to do himself one day.

Geordie had struck a deal with Andy in the week before Christmas and initiated the process of replacing key personnel and making introductions to contacts, while eyes and ears were distracted over the holiday period. When the New Year's festivities subsided, there was a new order in the city's underworld. Geordie's two other lieutenants received the news straight from the horse's mouth. 'I've sold out to Andy. No one will lose out but Andy will be in charge.' The news was received without emotion. Neither assent or dissent was expressed.

After the two detectives were shown to the door the minder returned to the kitchen.

'They've left a couple of uniforms in a car outside.'

'Thought they might. Andy's dead.'

'I know Boss, been on the phone. It's Ricky.' Geordie did not react.

'What about Johnboy?'

'Just Ricky, Boss. Johnboy's in Majorca. He'll no' be coming back.'

'And the rest of the team?

'All gone with Ricky as far as I can tell.'

'Just you, me and Tam then.'

'Just you and me Boss.'

'What!'

'Tam left while the cops were in. He said he's sorry but, you know.'

'What stopped you?'

'Ricky never asked me.'

'Don't spare my feelings son.'

'Sorry Boss.'

'What's up with you then? You're a better fighter than Tam.'

'Shagged his daughter at that New Years party.'

'So did Tam. He told me.'

'Aye but Ricky caught me.'

'Nae luck.' Geordie was assessing the new reality in his head. 'I think we better get out of town for a bit.'

'I think that's a good idea Boss.'

'Take Jackie's Mini, drive around for a bit to make sure you are not followed, then leave it in the roof car park down at the arcade. Go through the arcade and cross over to King Street, you'll see a black Corsa,' Geordie tossed Gaz the key. 'Bring it back this way and I'll meet you at the other side of the pedestrian bridge. Get there at exactly nine o'clock. Exactly nine mind.'

# Chapter 26

Colette rose at seven thirty, fifteen minutes before the alarm was set to go off and only four hours since Donny left by taxi. A second bottle of Chardonnay had been opened as Pat's latest blog was posted on the internet. All the details were there, first album to be released in April, first single to be 'Main Street', released next month. The record deal was for four albums, one every two years and the publishing deal would last for ten years. When asked how they had come to be together as a songwriting team, Will said they had been friends for a number of years and that it was natural for them to become collaborators. Asked about his father's involvement, Will replied that Geordie knew more about negotiating contracts than anyone, so it was great that he had come on board with the project.

The wine had been consumed in the ratio of three to one in Donny's favour but Colette still felt that was more than sufficient to push her over the limit, having had so little sleep. She had resolved to travel to work by train, there would be no time for a run. Twelve minutes brisk walk to Charing Cross, two quick stops to High Street, then another ten minutes up the hill to the Royal Infirmary.

Colette entered the complex and began to make her way through the warren of corridors heading to the Coronary Unit with its unfortunate view of the Necropolis on the other side of Wishart Street. Her route took her near Casualty.

Walking towards her, decidedly unsteady on his feet and sporting an array of bandages, was Pat Cullen.

'Are you all right?' Pat took a few seconds to recognise who was talking to him.

'Oh, it's you.'

'What happened?'

'Last night this guy, I never seen him before in my life.' Pat hesitated and seemed to forget what he was going to say.

'What did he do?' Pat opened his eyes wide and spread his hands out as if to say, 'this!.'

'For no reason?'

'He said something about me and his mate, I can't remember exactly.' I said, 'I think you've got me mixed up with someone else.' He said. 'It was you alright and then he hit me smack in the face.'

'He must have done more than that.'

'He did but I was out cold. Next thing I know a taxi driver is standing over me and saying there is an ambulance on its way.'

'What about the police?'

'Yeah they were there too. I tried to give a description but it happened so fast.'

'Where did it happen?'

'It was outside the office at about half twelve. I had to get the article written up for this evening's edition.'

'Did you do something to this mate of his?'

'Course not. He either got me mixed up with someone else or he just used that as an excuse to hit someone.'

'Have they said you can go home?'

'No not yet. I have to wait for the result of some tests.'

'You should be on a ward for observation.'

'They said that, but I refused. I just want to get up the road.'

'You really should be in a bed.'

'I'll be fine. I'm feeling better already. Really.'

'Well you better rest when you do get home and don't drive. Don't even think about going into work.'

'I'm freelance remember, no work, no pay, but I will take it easy. There is a gig at the Hydro to review on Wednesday, should be fine by then. Unfortunately I missed a breakfast interview with a famous record producer this morning, that's a bugger, but there you go.'

'It wasn't Stuart Williamson by per chance?'

'Yeah. How did you know that?'

'I saw him last night. I think he was there watching Cathy.'

'Well done, you. None of the other guys noticed him.'

'Gold star for you, me and Donny then.'

'Only for you and Donny. I'm not sure I would recognise him. It was Stuart Williamson that contacted me. He wanted to get the gen on Kate Rydelle. He said he has been unable to contact her or her manager.'

'Can't you reschedule the interview?'

'Too late. He's catching a flight back to America this morning, that's the reason for the seven thirty meeting. I've got an email address. I can try and contact him and perhaps set up a phone interview.'

'Listen Pat, take care. I better get a move on.'

'No problem Colette. Thanks for the advice.'

When Colette rounded the first corner she took out her phone and called Donny. It rang out, going to voice mail. She tried another twice before a very hungover Donny answered.

'It's me. Listen carefully. Stuart Williamson is flying back to America from Glasgow Airport today. It could be our best chance of talking to him. Remember what you said last night. Donny did you hear that?'

'Yeah I heard. What flight?'

'I don't know. There is probably only one flight to America today. He might even be catching a connecting flight via London or somewhere. You will need to get there fast and hope you can spot him.'

'OK I'll get ready. How do you know this?'

'I met Pat coming out of casualty. He got beat up last night.'

'Shit. Is he all right?'

'He will be in a day or two. It was him that told me. I don't have time to explain. Stuart Williamson could already be on his way to the airport and he is not involved with the McSwiggens.'

'Did Pat tell you that?'

'Yes he did. Donny I need to go and so do you.'

'Right, OK.' Colette ended the call.

Donny was still waking up. He looked at the time on his phone. It was only eight thirty. He had less than five hours sleep and he was feeling rough. He checked the pockets of the trousers he was wearing the night before and found a twenty pound note and some change. Hopefully that would be enough for a taxi. He phoned a local firm and was told the taxi would be there in five minutes. Donny was not in the habit of working that fast. He ran to the bathroom, had a pee, no time for a wash, returned to the bedroom to get clean pants and socks from the drawer, next to his bed. He pulled on the clothes discarded earlier, as they were conveniently placed on the floor beside his bed. On his way out, he grabbed a bottle of water from the fridge and snatched his coat from a hook on the wall. As he pulled the front door closed behind him, only four minutes had passed since he had made the call. He waited another six on the street outside. 'Why do they always say five minutes?' Once the driver confirmed a fixed price of £17.50 to the airport, Donny relaxed. The roads around Mount Florida were busy but it was only a mile to the motorway on-ramp and most of the traffic would be heading into town.

Donny took out his phone and found Pat's number. Pat answered immediately.

'Hi Donny. Did Colette tell you what happened?'

'She did Pat but I don't know the details, she had to meet some students.'

'Well it's three cracked ribs, a broken finger, a head the size of a basketball and stitches across my cheek. I'm black and blue all over and everything hurts.'

'But apart from that?'

'Apart from that, I feel great.'

'No I'm really sorry to hear what happened.'

'Thanks.'

'Can I ask you something. It's about Stuart Williamson. Have you been in contact with him?'

'He read my blog on the Glasgow music scene and thought I would know something about Kate Rydelle. He asked if we could meet. He was finding it impossible to get in contact with her. I could only make it this morning, I had to write up my piece for the paper last night. It was outside the office I got jumped.'

'This might sound daft but did the McSwiggens know you were going to meet Stuart Williamson?'

'I did mention it last night. I suggested Williamson as a producer for the album and said I had a breakfast interview with him before his flight back to America. I just wanted to rub it in to the other journos. They can be a bit snooty because I'm freelance. You know how it is. What is it you're getting at Donny?'

'I think the McSwiggens might have good reason for keeping Stuart Williamson in the dark about the sudden blossoming of Cathy Riddle as a songwriter.'

'You think I was beat up to stop me making that meeting?'

'That's exactly what I'm thinking.'

'If you know something Donny, you've got to tell me.'

'I will Pat. When are you getting out?'

'They're keeping an eye on the swelling in my head but I expect this afternoon.'

'I'll call you later today Pat. I'll tell you everything.'

Donny ended the call before Pat had a chance to ask any questions. He was regretting using the name McSwiggen in earshot of the driver. Taxi firms, he had been told, were notorious for links to criminals. The driver had not reacted in any way to what had been said, but Donny took the first opportunity to casually mention he was catching a flight to Dublin.

'Have you not got any luggage?'

'No.' Donny hadn't thought of that. 'It's my girlfriend

I'm going to see. She works there. I keep clothes in her flat, it's better than carting a case back and forward.'

'Right. How long are you going for?'

'Two weeks.'

'That's a lot of holidays to take so soon after Christmas and New Year. Is your employer happy about that?'

'I have days left over from last year. You need to take them before the end of January or you lose them.'

'What is it you do?' It was now obvious to Donny that the cabbie was not any kind of underworld spy, he was just a nosey bastard.

'Quantity surveyor.' It was his father's occupation and the only proper job Donny had any knowledge of. It was also so boring that any mention of it would usually kill any conversation stone dead. Not this time.

The driver showed a keen interest in his passenger's pretend occupation and that of his fictional girlfriend, the nurse who worked in the Dublin Infirmary. Donny was more than relieved when the taxi drew up at the drop-off point. The cabbie's scepticism had stopped just short of calling Donny a deluded fantasist.

Inside the terminal building, the destination board showed no flights to America. There were however upcoming flights to Heathrow, Paris, Amsterdam and much to Donny's delight, Dublin. At least that part of the story was plausible. All these airports could accommodate connecting flights to America. Donny went first to the queue for the security check, but there was no sign of Stuart Williamson. Donny returned to the main check-in area and there he was, second last in line at the KLM check in for Amsterdam.

Donny approached. 'Mr Williamson?' Stuart Williamson gave Donny a look that suggested the cabbie had issued a warning that there was a lunatic on the loose.

'I'm a friend of Pat's. You had an appointment with him this morning?' Stuart Williamson was acclimatizing to the Scottish weather, the flaps on his hat were up but otherwise he looked the same as when he entered the concert hall the previous afternoon. The cold averse producer looked even more startled and seemed to be in something of a dilemma in deciding whether to say yes or no.

'I'll come straight to the point. Were you aware that all the original songs sung by Kate Rydelle last night were penned by Daniel Quick forty years ago?' Stuart Williamson looked dumbfounded and did not know how to respond. It was clear he had no knowledge of this.

'Written by Dan. You have got to be kidding.'

'If you can spare ten minutes I can tell you the whole story.'

Stuart Williamson did not have to think twice and immediately left the queue.

# Chapter 27

Cathy rose early on Monday morning. Early for her at any rate, it was only nine thirty. She had been awake half the night, managing no more than four hours sleep. Her first action of the day was to reach for her phone sitting on the bedside table.

Checking on twitter, she discovered that she had in fact risen at seven and was already at a London recording studio, currently in the middle of a recording session. In between takes, she had taken the time to tweet, keeping the fans both informed and involved in her day. This despite having celebrated her award at an unnamed London club till three in the morning. Cathy was impressed with herself. She went over to facebook to check out the pictures and thought she looked pretty good for someone who had flown up to Glasgow, played a gig, won an award and flown straight back to London. Also there did seem to be a lot of celebrities in the club last night. 'Had they all turned up just for me?' she mused. Reading the carefully crafted text, she could almost believe that they had.

Cathy pulled on a dressing gown and put the phone in the pocket before going downstairs for breakfast. Sipping a herbal tea, she caught up with all that had been happening in the wonderful world of Kate Rydelle.

Cathy had no access to any of the social media accounts. That was the sole preserve of a professional publicist, hired by Will and whom Cathy had never met. She was the one charged with building the right image and creating a false history for Scotland's new rising star, achieved with the aid of photoshop and a web of fictitious friends and followers. The very name, Kate Rydelle, was now a registered trademark owned by Geordie McSwiggen. When Will had said 'you do the music and I'll deal with everything else,' that was exactly what he had meant. Cathy did not even own her own name.

A car could be heard in the driveway outside and a minute later, the front door of the house opened.

'Cathy? Cathy, get up'

'I'm in here.' Will walked down the side of the stairs and into the kitchen. He seemed to have lost his usual swagger and the bravado of the night before had gone.

Cathy waited for him to say something but he just sat down on the opposite side of the table and said nothing. 'What's up?'

'A body has been found at Geordie's garage. It's his partner, Andrew Ward.'

'That's awful! Is your dad alright?'

'He's OK, but everything is falling apart. I don't know what's going to happen. Anyway that's not why I'm here. It's that reporter.'

'What, Pat?'

'I started to deal with the backlog of emails last night. There was one from Mi.P. He's been on to them asking questions about me and Geordie.'

'Right.'

'They obviously don't see it as a problem or they would have called but if this guy keeps digging then they might get nervous.'

'What was Pat asking?'

'What part I played in the writing.'

'What did they say?'

'They put the lawyers on to it. They were more concerned about the connection to Geordie becoming public. Just answer these questions Cathy, don't hide anything.'

'Of course Will. What is it?'

'When was the last time you spoke to Cullen?'

'Never. I've never spoken to him'

'Have you ever sent him any demos?'

'Yes, I think I already told you that.'

'And he never got back to you?'

'No, never. Look he is probably just trying to get a story.'

'No, he knows something. If it was just a story he was after he would have come to me, all the other music journalists have done that. No, he doesn't want to show his hand, that's why.'

Cathy could see the guitar case sitting in the hall. Maybe this was the time. If Pat had found out about Dan Quick and he puts it in the papers, then the girlfriend might come forward. Was this the time to cash in that policy?

'What are you thinking about?'

'Nothing.'

'If there is something I don't know about Cathy, you better tell me.'

'Donny McNeil.'

'Who?'

'Donny McNeil, I saw him last night. He thinks he is an expert on songwriting. He will never believe it was me that wrote the songs.'

'Has he contacted you?'

'No, that's what's odd. Everyone else at the Songwriters Club had lots of questions but he didn't ask a thing. It was when you said Pat did not want to show his hand. Maybe it's the same with Donny McNeil.'

'Where can I find him?'

'Well every Tuesday night at the Songwriters Club in Blackfriars.'

'And his house?'

'I might have his address somewhere.'

It had been on the tip of Cathy's tongue to come clean about the two missing pages in Dan's journal, but for some reason it was 'Donny McNeil' that came out of her mouth.

# Chapter 28

Geordie poured himself another coffee and sat alone in the giant kitchen, he had much to think about. He had maintained a façade for the benefit of the police and also for Gaz but in truth he had suffered one body blow after another in the last half-hour. If anyone were to make a move he would have expected it to be Johnboy, a man not so different from himself. The fact that he had moved to Majorca could only mean, he had spotted an opportunity and had thrown his lot in with the South American cocaine gangs. Had he struck a deal with Ricky? Possibly. At least that would make sense. The second and third calls Geordie had made earlier had been to these men. When no one answered, Geordie knew everything had changed. The first call had been to Andy.

What a mess, and so unnecessary. Andy was the smartest, the other two would surely concede that point. Even if Andy took the top cut as Geordie had done, the rest would now be divided two ways and not three. Logic unfortunately, rarely comes into it, but why did it have to be Ricky?

Richard Mullen was tough, no doubt about that, fearless even, but not so smart. He was the only member of the quartet, not to have some legitimate businesses. He liked to flaunt his ill-gotten gains, especially in front of the police. When others feared the Proceeds of Crime Act, Ricky adopted a strategy of spending it as fast as it came in before they could get their hands on it. The younger boys in the team all liked Ricky, he talked like them, dressed like them and acted like them. It was just that he was 20 years older than them.

Losing Tam was a hard one to take. He and Gaz were like sons to Geordie. It had been intended that they were to look after the remaining businesses, with Andy as back-up. They would make an example of anyone who had their fingers anywhere near the till. They would also encourage slow payers to cough up on demand, just as they had done when Geordie was around. Ricky had fucked things up somewhat, in the short term at least. As usual the prick had not thought things through. He may think he has all the contacts, but they went no higher than what might be described as middle-management. The men at the top among the Ukranians, the Colombians and the Manchester boys were known only to Geordie. Even Andy was to be drip fed this information over time. That was Geordie's guarantee.

Geordie glanced at his watch, 8:40, time to go. Ricky had certainly thrown a spanner in the works. The problem was the city was full of people, who bore a grudge. Now they all knew Geordie was on his own. He walked through to one of the rooms facing the street to see if the patrol car was still there. It was.

Had Geordie received the two detectives in any room other than the kitchen, they would have noticed how bare the place looked. All personal items had been removed and were now in Florida with Jackie. By the end of the week that's where Geordie intended to be.

Geordie left the house without wearing a coat. He also left the heavy storm doors open. Both actions were to give the impression he was popping out but would return home soon.

When the Volvo pulled out of the drive and turned left then left again at the first corner, the police car followed. Geordie headed to the nearest shops, about half a mile from the house, and parked up outside a convenience store. The police car parked behind. When Geordie entered the shop, one of the officers got out to check there was no back entrance. Geordie emerged from the shop a minute later carrying two newspapers and two litres of milk, then got back into his car. He watched the traffic approaching and pulled out in front of the line of cars at the last minute, forcing the police car to wait till they passed. It would take a left then a right turn before Geordie was back in his own street. When he made the first turn, the police car was one hundred metres behind. The Volvo's right indicator went on early signalling that Geordie was heading home. The police car did not try to reduce the gap. When the turn was completed, Geordie put the foot down. There was a bend in the road so the police would not be surprised that the Volvo was out of sight when they made the turn. When the police car came round the bend, the Volvo was almost out of sight. The blue lights and siren were switched on and the police car sped up, but Geordie had already reached his destination. Fifty metres past the house, a path lead to a pedestrian bridge that crossed a dual carriageway. There was no direct access from Geordie's street on to this road.

The Volvo had been abandoned and Geordie was running towards the bridge. The young officers made chase but the twenty second start Geordie had created was just enough. Gaz was in place as instructed and the Corsa sped away with Geordie inside. Behind, an out-of-breath police officer could be seen relaying details into his radio, for all the good it would do. Geordie and Gaz switched cars a minute later, in a residential street devoid of any CCTV cameras.

# Chapter 29

Donny suggested a coffee upstairs. Stuart looked at his watch and said, 'Sure.'

In the café Stuart insisted on paying and ordered a decaf with soya milk for himself and a plain white coffee for Donny. 'I've had some surprises in this business but that one takes the prize. Are you sure about this?'

'Yeah I'm certain. They may have been reworked a bit, I don't know, I haven't heard the original recordings.'

'Is Kate related to Dan?'

'No, she is not related.'

'What's the deal then?'

'I'll tell you everything I know. I'll be as quick as I can.'

'You just take it nice and slow. I think I'm going to stick around a while longer.'

Donny told him the whole story. The night of Cathy Riddle's triumph at the Songwriters Club, the chance discovery that Main Street was actually about the Bridgeton of forty years ago, Derek's revelation that Cathy purchased some old tapes and appeared to be learning songs from them, getting hold of a misplaced tape from that collection, Big George identifying the guitar sound, finding that guitar, discovering that it once belonged to Daniel Quick who died in nineteen seventy-eight, the Willie

Stewart Band and Dan's connection to Stuart himself. Donny detailed Cathy's transformation into Kate and revealed everything he had found out about Will and Geordie McSwiggen, finishing with the news that Dan's girlfriend Brenda was pregnant when he died and that Dan had a daughter, Daniela.

'That is quite a tale. Have you ever thought of going into the detective business. Sounds like you're a natural.'

Donny laughed. 'Maybe you're right I've had more success at detective work than as a musician.'

'Everybody needs a break in this business, that's all. You hang in there.'

'Will do. Can I ask you something? If you didn't know any of this, what are you doing here? It can't just be a coincidence, can it?'

'No it is not a coincidence.' Stuart took a deep breath. 'I've got an interesting tale to tell you.

Four months ago my office in L.A. received an email with an mp3 attached. We get dozens everyday but someone always reads the email and has a listen to the attachment just in case. Anyway the email mentions Glasgow. Now they all know in the office that I read everything that comes in from Glasgow, which is actually very little these days. So Carly, that's my P.A., has a listen to the song. It's nothing like my style, so no chance of a plagiarism suit somewhere down the line. It is forwarded to my personal email account and I pick it up at home. There is no name on the email and the address doesn't help but the writer says that they know I was originally from Glasgow, the same as them, and asked would I listen to this track. She said that any feedback I could give would be very much appreciated.'

'Did she say she wrote it?'

'No. That kind of request comes into the office all the time and I wouldn't normally go near them with a barge pole. You admit you have heard something or worse commented on it and then any similarity, no matter how tenuous, to anything you do in the future and you'll be getting that letter. You know the one. That was so clever of you to incorporate such and such of mine in your recording of bla bla bla. Anyway Carly has cleared it and I think, what the hell, if I can help some young kid from back home that would be nice. So I open the file. It's a good song, the voice sounds really good though it's just a live recording of guitar and vocal. There was no mention of a title in the email but I figure, it's a cover of a country track. I don't really know that genre. It's such a good song it could be really well known for all I know. I concentrated mostly on the performance but gave her my opinion on the song anyway and some tips on how she could make a decent recording of it. And that was that. As I said, it wasn't my style of music.'

'Did you hear from her again?'

'No.'

'But what brought you here then.'

'I started a new project soon after. I've been gathering a whole heap of material that somehow got overlooked in the past. Some fantastic songs Donny, real good. I start thinking about potential vocalists and I'm speaking to record companies. It was Carly that suggested the girl from Glasgow, if she had the right image of course. I say OK, get in touch. Just a tentative inquiry. Carly tries but there is no reply. It would generate some great publicity, you know, the Glasgow connection. Radio and TV love that kind of thing.'

It would also work wonders for invigorating Stuart's back catalogue, Donny thought to himself.

'We wait a day or two. Still nothing, so we try again. This time we give more away, we say we have a particular song in mind. We get a short reply saying sorry but she was no longer pursuing a career in music. I can't understand this, so I sent a personal email. It bounces back. Account closed.'

'When was this?'

'Ten days ago, or thereabouts.'

'So how come you're here?'

'I was curious, wasn't I. Who turns down a chance like that. I passed the demo she sent to the intern in the office and I say the girl is from Glasgow or at least Scotland, see if you can track her down. Two hours later, he has the name Kate Rydelle and the name of the song, 'Cut And Run' credited to Rydelle and McSwiggen. He shows me this slick website and her social media presence. Well I know I'm onto a winner if I can persuade her to record for me. I even think I could do a job for her on 'Main Street' if not her other songs. For the past week I have been trying to set up a meeting but they won't talk. Stonewalled at every turn.'

'So you flew to Glasgow to try and sign up Kate Rydelle.'

'That's about the size of it. I was already booked on a flight to London, I had some business to attend to, but I have been here for three days. I got in touch with my old mucker, Ronnie Gibson, he has a drum shop on the Trongate. Ronnie has been trying to help but her manager won't talk. He did not respond to emails and wouldn't talk on the phone. I even got Ronnie to call for me but as soon as my name was mentioned, the manager made an excuse.'

'Well you now know the reasons why.'

'But I never got to hear any of Dan's songs back then and besides it was them that sent the demo to me. What was all that about?'

'Have you not worked it out yet?'

'No. None of it makes any sense to me. What is it?'

'It was when you said the song that she sent was 'Cut And Run' it all made sense.'

'Maybe to you.'

'Boy drops everything for a new start in the big city. Does it not remind you of someone?' Stewart looked blank for a few seconds, before the penny dropped.

'Well, fuck me.'

'Four months ago Kate Rydelle was plain old Cathy Riddle and learning a bunch of songs she found on tapes bought in the Barras market. I don't know how she found out that you were in the same band as Dan but if anyone was going to recognise the songs after all this time, it would be you and the one song you would be sure to remember was the one written about you. How she knew it was about you, I have no idea, but Colette and I found out things so she could have done the same. When you responded with advice but did not mention you recognized the song, she would think she was in the clear. I've spoken to your friend Ronnie and also Dennis.'

'Ronnie said someone had been in asking about the old band. He couldn't have made the connection.'

'I never mentioned Kate Rydelle, only that I had a tape that might be of Dan. The point is neither he nor Dennis had ever heard any of Dan's songs and as far as I know nobody else has.'

'You're wrong there. I know of about a hundred.' The look of disbelief on Donny's face eclipsed the expression Stewart had displayed when he heard that Kate's songs had actually been written by his old band mate forty years ago.

'That's exactly what I've been looking for. That's brilliant.'

'Well, perhaps not. I haven't a clue who any of them are and I would say there's one chance in a million any of them remember.'

'Who are these people?'

'It was in a pub on Sauchiehall Street, The Ship it was called. It was only two days before the accident. I was up from London, mainly to see my folks, but by that time I'd started scouting for one of the big labels. They were giving me ten pounds a day for expenses and the promise of a thousand pounds if they signed anybody that I brought to them. I had told them that I had some bands in mind back in Glasgow, which was partly true, but mainly it was so they would keep giving me the tenners. They must have thought there would be plenty of foul mouth yobs that could spit up in Glasgow, because they gave me fifty quid for five days and another fifty for the train fare. I used the overnight bus and pocketed the rest.

I got in touch with Dan while I was here. I remember telling him it was still all punk in London and that the labels were not interested in anything else. He said it wouldn't last, it was all shite. I agreed with him but I knew it would not go back to the dreamy hippie stuff, he was into.'

'But it did.'

'It took a long time but you're right. There's no genre

that dominates any more. All sorts of things sell these days but back then in nineteen seventy-eight the labels wanted Punk. Where was I?'

'You were meeting up with Dan.'

'Right. It was in the Ship, a music pub that we used to play in. I wanted to talk to the boys in The Alert. They were the band that took over our regular spot in the pub. I thought I could get them a deal if they were prepared to change to playing punk and take on the image. Anyway I arrange to meet Dan straight from his work. I was catching the night bus back to London and would have to leave early. When he turns up, he has his guitar with him so he could have a jam in the dressing room with the boys, before they went on. Anyway the band haven't turned up and me and Dan have sunk about five pints each, when one of the waitresses comes over and asks if we would do a half hour spot, just until the band turned up. I had already hung on too long as it was and said I had to go but to my surprise Dan says I'll do it.'

'Did he do his own songs?'

'That was the second surprise. He said to the waitress, 'Can I do my own songs?' Well I remember she looked very doubtful and said she would need to ask. To tell the truth I was glad I had to leave, I can remember that. If Dan was going to embarrass himself, I did not want to see it. He had never mentioned that he had written anything. I think I did try to talk him into doing some easy covers instead, but he said he didn't know the words of any covers. By the time I'd downed my pint, he was already on stage giving it one two, one two, into the mike. I'm afraid I couldn't get out quick enough.'

'If any one of those people remember those songs, Brenda and Daniela can claim the copyright.'

'I don't want to burst your bubble Donny but you will need a heck of a lot more than that.'

'But it's something. It's more than I had this morning.'

Stuart poured more cold water on Donny's optimism, but stopping the McSwiggens was becoming something of a crusade for Donny. No one deserved a break more than Brenda and Daniela. It was also an affront to his artistic principles seeing someone waltz in and claim the spoils for the doubt, toil and pain every songwriter endures in pursuit of that hit song. More than this though, was the opportunity to outwit a privately educated smart arse.

Stuart said he would return to the Radisson for a couple more nights and see what happens. He also offered to meet up with Brenda and give her some advice, however he was still stressing that they would need better than some vague reminiscences of a one-off rendition, forty years ago.

Donny and Stuart agreed to share a taxi back into the city but first Stuart had to go to the KLM desk and change his arrangements. Donny had to locate a cash machine, after which he would contact Pat. It was time to put him in the picture.

When Donny came back to the KLM desk, Stuart was waiting for him. 'Did you get it all sorted?'

'I decided to leave it open. I'm going to hang around a while, see how this pans out. I'd like to help you guys, if you'll have me.'

'Yes, of course. You have helped already but you know the reputation of Geordie McSwiggen, don't you?'

'Yeah I know. Ronnie told me he has some shady

dealings.'

'It's a lot worse than that. I had never heard of him before last week but Colette, that's the girl that I've been working with, she has a contact that knows all about him. He is dangerous, very dangerous. I am pretty sure that Pat got beat up on his orders so he couldn't keep the appointment with you this morning.'

'You sure about that?' Stuart was not looking quite so composed any more.

# Chapter 30

Glasgow Royal Infirmary is a collection of buildings modern and old, connected to each other by a confusing array of corridors. It was also built on a hill meaning what was the second floor in one building could be the fourth in the next. Donny was having difficulty locating Pat who was sitting in a cafe waiting for the all clear to go home. Donny had to ask for help twice, then twice got lost again. Twenty minutes after entering the labyrinth, he came upon the cafe by chance.

'I must have walked a mile since I came through the door. I hope you know how to get out of here'

'Hi Donny.' Donny got a shock when Pat looked up.

'I didn't think you were as bad as that.'

'Thanks. I needed cheering up.'

'Should you not be in a bed?'

'Been through all this with Colette. They suggested that, but I refused. I just want to get back to my flat. I said I would wait for the results of the tests and see another doctor at eleven.'

'It's nearly twelve now.'

'I know it's only down there,' Pat nodded towards a corridor. 'The nurse said she'll come and get me when they were ready.'

On the wall to the side, a TV was tuned to the news channel with the sound turned down but with the subtitles on. Neither were giving it much attention as Pat explained to Donny what had happened. On the screen a police incident of some sort was unfolding. There were a lot of striped police cars with blue lights flashing but whatever was going on was hidden behind large screens. It was only when Pat recognised the reporter that he began to take notice. It was the girl that always did the reports from outside the Glasgow courts.

'I think that's Glasgow on the news there!' Donny turned round and they both tried to follow the subtitles, the words moving position as new text was added. They managed to catch, 'Unconfirmed reports say the body is of a man concerned with organised crime in the city.'

'That's the Springburn flats you can see in the background,' Pat observed.

'That's where Geordie McSwiggen has a garage.'

The two men stared at the screen but it was evidently the end of the report and the programme had returned to the studio.

'Do you think it's Geordie?' Donny speculated.

'I don't know.'

'Excuse me Donny I need to phone the paper. We can link this to my piece about the Newcomers Award. I might make the front page after all.' Pat hurried deep inside the cafe to get away from the noisy hospital corridor frantically scrolling his contacts list. Donny used his phone to check the Internet. It confirmed that the premises did belong to Glasgow businessman George McSwiggen and that the body was not his. There was some speculation of a gangland war and comparisons to another incident, some years earlier. Donny remembered what Colette's friend, Crawford had said about Geordie preparing to get out. It appeared that process was not going well. Was this how Geordie dealt with problems?

Pat returned after only a few minutes.

'That was quick.'

'It's a news story, just wanted to let them know about the connection to Kate Rydelle, I know my place. They have Graham Dunsmuir on the story he's the top news man, there is no dedicated crime reporter these days. If he can link it to my article that will be good for me. It is going to be too late for the last of this evening's editions, bad timing unfortunately. The Dailies will be all over it tomorrow so by time we come out we will need an angle. The link to the winner of the Newcomers Award at Celtic Connections will give us something different. I don't think the other papers will know about that.'

'I checked on the Internet while you were away, it is Geordie's garage but the body is not thought to be his.'

'That's a pity, it would have been a better story if the body was one of the McSwiggens. I'm going to skip the doctor. I want to get into the office, there could possibly be something for me in tomorrow's paper. I can't pass up a chance like this.'

'Pat you're in no fit state for that.'

'Are you joking. This is the first time I have been anywhere near a news story. This is a break for me.'

'If you promise to take it easy and wait for the doctor I've got something for you. Remember I said on the phone.'

'I forgot about that. What is it?'

'I'll tell you but we wait here till you get the all clear to go home. It will be worth your while. Agreed?'

'It better be good Donny.'

'I can assure you it is.'


By the time a nurse eventually came to collect Pat at ten minutes past one Donny had divulged the whole story. Everything from Cathy's appearance at the Songwriters club to his meeting with Stuart Williamson. It would be no understatement to say Pat was excited. 'That is incredible,' he said more than once. The account of the events of the past three weeks had worked wonders for Pat's condition. He was looking like his old self as he was led down the corridor.

Donny sent a text to Colette, bringing her up to date as best he could. It was strange to think she was in the same building. As expected, there was no reply.

Pat returned a quarter of an hour later with a detectable spring in his step.

'What did they say?'

'No brain damage that wasn't there already. I promised to take things easy for a few days, so they said I can go.'

'And will you take it easy?' Pat ignored the question.

'I've got an idea. We get Stuart Williamson on the radio to appeal for anyone who was in the pub that night.'

'And how do we do that?'

'We just ask them.'

'And they are going to say yes, just like that?

'Are you kidding. It will make a great show. I know the perfect programme, Tom Martin, nine till eleven, he plays a lot of seventies stuff. He'll go nuts if we offer him Stuart Williamson or more importantly his producer will.'

'Slow down, we will need to ask Stuart first.'

'You said he was willing to help.'

'I didn't say he was prepared to stick his neck on a chopping block.'

'What do you mean?'

'The McSwiggens. Have you forgotten the news report?'

That brought Pat back down to earth but he was not for giving up on his scoop.

'OK, we don't mention anything about songwriting, we simply say that was the last time Stuart was together with his old band and that Dan got up to do a few songs and does anyone remember it. If anyone calls in, we get their number and talk to them ourselves.'

'I don't know. We could ask him I suppose.'

'Right I'll get on to it then. Give me five minutes.'

Pat took his phone to the same corner that he utilised before, while Donny sipped the dregs of his third cup of tea. While Pat was away, he checked the internet for any updates on the incident at the garage, but there was nothing new.

Pat was back ten minutes later. 'Sorted. Spoke to the show's producer, if Stuart is willing to do it, he can go on tomorrow night.'

'What reason did you give for him going on the show?'

'What do you mean?'

'How did you explain that Scotland's most successful record producer was suddenly willing to give an interview?'

'She never even asked. It's a commercial station and I was offering something for nothing. She probably thinks he is coming to publicise a tour or a book, happens all the time. Don't worry about that. Think about how you are going to persuade Mr Williamson to appear.'

# Chapter 31

Brenda and Daniela were sitting at the kitchen table. Monday morning was their special time in the week and both mother and daughter always looked forward to it. Daniela's husband was at work and the children were in school. A certain bond existed between them, it was them against the world or at least that is how it seemed when Daniela was growing up. Single mothers were far from unique in the high rise council flats where they had lived, nor at the school Daniela attended but in the pecking order, weekend dads, fathers with new girlfriends and those that had simply disappeared, ranked above a parent no one had ever seen.

Brenda had spent almost every Sunday with Daniela and Steven since they married, fifteen years earlier. At first it was in a rented flat in Dennistoun, only ten minutes walk from her own home, but for the last eight years it was an end terraced house in East Kilbride bought to accommodate the three children, Amy thirteen, Karen eleven, and Paul ten. Brenda was proud of how her daughter had turned out, principally because Daniela had not made the same catastrophic mistake she had made by falling pregnant at the age of eighteen. She did however feel guilty that Daniela had always been old before her time, missing out on so much that other girls her age took for granted.

After the move away from the East End, Brenda would stay over on Sunday nights and be driven back home on Monday afternoon by Steven, when he returned from his job as a postman. There was plenty for mother and daughter to talk about at the best of times but today there was something new. Donny was barely out the door on Saturday morning before Brenda had lifted the phone.

Daniela quickly appreciated the financial implications of what her mother was saying. Her father's love of music had not been passed down but she did have a good head where money was concerned. Her part-time job in a call centre, operated by a bank, had taught her that there were more people than she had ever imagined with tidy sums in their accounts. Daniela did not know anything about the origin of these sums, but she suspected inheritance or some other form of windfall. Inheriting copyright from her father could be her windfall.

'How do we know we can trust this Donny?'

'He was a nice boy Daniela, well, man. He said he wanted to help and I believe him.'

'But what's in it for him?'

'I don't know but had he not called on Saturday morning we would be none the wiser, would we? Everything he has told us has turned out to be true, hasn't it?' Daniela had to concede that point.

Daniela possessed the computer skills that her mother lacked and it did not take her long to find Kate Rydelle on the Internet. All it had taken was the title, 'Main Street' and the name McSwiggen. When her mother arrived for dinner on Sunday afternoon, Daniela was able to play clips of the songs available on the Kate Rydelle website. They matched what was on the CD Donny had provided. The fact that Donny had referred to the girl as Cathy and not Kate had sewn the seeds of doubt in Daniela's mind. That and the fact he never mentioned anything about her being in the running for an award.

There it was in the newspaper, spread out in front of them, complete with photograph. The headline screamed 'Best Newcomer at Festival,' and led into an article predicting a glittering career and detailing a seven figure recording deal.

'He never let on about that, did he?' Daniela tapped the picture of Kate Rydelle.

'Maybe he didn't know about it.'

'He knew everything else.' Both women relapsed into silence, the only sound in the room coming from the radio.

'Did you never hear any of my dad's songs, mum?'

'I've told you before, I wanted him to give all that up. He had a good job in the plumbers merchants. All I wanted was a wee house maybe in Dennistoun, like the one you and Steven had. To tell you the truth, I was embarrassed when he talked about writing songs. I didn't think that anyone from Bridgeton could do that. I thought you had to be American or from London or somewhere like that but not people like us.'

'That's daft mum.'

'I know. but that's how people thought. That's how I thought, how my family thought.'

'Were people not allowed to have ambitions?'

'If you were a boy you were allowed to dream about

being a football player.'

'And what about the girls, did they not have any dreams?'

'They could dream about being a footballer's wife.' Daniela laughed.

'Ambition was something you kept to yourself.'

'And is that what my dad did?'

'That's it. Getting above yourself was the worst crime you could commit. It seemed disloyal or disrespectful somehow, to want to escape your surroundings.'

'That's crazy. Lots of people from Bridgeton did well for themselves.'

'I know they did, but it was best not to talk about it. Just do it. If your dad had told people he was going to be a professional songwriter he would have left himself open to ridicule. Remarks like, haven't seen you on Top of the Pops yet. You know that type of thing. I don't know what your dad's plans were exactly but he wanted to get them right before revealing himself. Having ambition and succeeding was one thing, having ambition and failing was something else.'

'What a life.'

'It wasn't all bad.'

'Another cup of tea?' Brenda nodded and Daniela rose from the table filling the kettle from the tap in front of the window. It was twelve o'clock and the radio presenter announced that they would be going over to the newsroom.

'The body of a man has been found at a north Glasgow garage in what has all the hallmarks of a gangland killing. The garage is owned by Glasgow businessman, George McSwiggen.' Daniela spun around and stared at her mother who had raised her hand to her mouth. 'The name of the dead man has not been released but sources say he is known to the police and that he has connections to organised crime in the city. Our reporter Heather Campbell is at the scene.'

# Chapter 32

Donny had phoned a taxi and was waiting on the pavement for it to arrive. He had called the same company that he had used that morning and was now regretting his choice. What if it was the same driver? What if all the drivers had been warned about the Kingspark Road, Billy Liar. What cover story could he use? Missed the flight to Dublin, fell out with girlfriend and caught the first flight home, forgot my passport. Do you need a passport for Ireland?

It was not the same driver thankfully but that did not mean he didn't know. Should he engage the cabbie in conversation,'I would be in Dublin tonight if it were not for...." Donny opted for staying quiet. The driver was either unaware of the Irish connection or he did not want to upset the lunatic.

A taxi was an extravagance for Donny but tonight he was happy to pay. He was on his way to pick up Brenda and then on to meet up with Stuart Williamson. The choice of venue was Brenda's and Donny liked her reasoning. It was West Brewery, a German styled beer hall and restaurant housed in part of a former carpet factory in Bridgeton. Brenda had said Dan's teetotal mother had worked there and would be turning in her grave now that it had been turned into a pub.

Donny phoned to say he was on his way and that he would be with her in ten minutes. Brenda was waiting at the entrance when the taxi drew up outside her building. Donny got out to lend a hand.

'I'm fine, I'm fine. Getting in and out of taxis is something I'm an expert in. How's yourself?"

'A lot has happened since I saw you on Saturday.'

'Aye, Willie Stewart back in Glasgow, now there's a turn up for the books.'

'That's not the half of it. I hope the West Brewery has a late licence there is lot to tell you and a lot to explain.'

'That's fine by me, I don't need to get up early in the morning.'

'You told me on the phone that you worked out that the girl I told you about was the one that was in the paper today?'

'Daniela had found her on the internet ten minutes after you left. You called her Cathy?'

'Her real name is Cathy Riddle, she changed it two weeks ago.'

'A stage name like? Kate Rydelle does sound more classy.'

'It does, but that was not her only reason. We can talk about that later. How did Daniela take the news?'

'Hasn't slept a wink since. Same as me.'

'We'll talk when we get to the pub.' Donny's paranoia about taxi drivers was coming back. The two passengers sat in silence for the remainder of the short journey. When they arrived Stuart Williamson was already there taking pictures of the elaborate brickwork of the Victorian building.

'I had forgotten that this building was so beautiful.

Brenda! Great to see you. You haven't changed a bit.'

'Hello Willie. And you haven't lost any of that charm. Does it work as well on the California girls as it did with the ones in the Ship?'

'Been a one woman man for the last twenty years Brenda. If you knew how boring I'd become, you wouldn't have agreed to come out with me.'

'Like I said, you've still got the patter.'

'Did Donny tell you not to eat?'

'Away ye go. I'm no' used to eating at this time of night. I had my tea at six, same as always. You boys go ahead, I'll be fine.'

'Perhaps we can tempt you with a dessert.'

'Aye, maybe you will.'

Donny suggested they move inside. As he was travelling there and back by taxi, he only put on a jacket. Brenda and Stuart were having a who can wear the most clothes competition.

'Good idea Donny. Brenda will you take my arm?' Brenda offered her left arm, she still had her stick in her right hand though she now appeared not to need it.

'This feels familiar Brenda, we must have done this before.'

'No, we bloody well did not, William Stewart.' Brenda had shed twenty years in two minutes.

'When we get to the door I want you to close your eyes, there's a surprise inside.'

'A surprise?'

'I phoned two of your old admirers and they jumped at the chance of meeting up with you again.'

'Old admirers, what are you on about?' Donny was

wondering the same as Brenda.

'You've got to shut your eyes.' Brenda reluctantly did as she was told and Stuart led her through the doors. When she opened her eyes, Ronnie Gibson and Dennis Lindsey were standing in front of her.

Donny took a back seat while the four old friends got reacquainted. Stuart's mid-Atlantic accent was disappearing as quickly as Brenda was shedding years. In their own little bubble, it was once again the mid seventies. Ronnie and Dennis had taken Brenda's cue and were addressing their old mate as Willie and the famous record producer did not object.

Stuart told Brenda and the boys about Dan's impromptu performance in the Ship and that he was going on the radio to appeal for anyone, who was there that night.

When food arrived, half an hour later in the form of haddock fried in beer batter and thick cut chips, Donny was brought back in to the conversation. For the third time that day he told his story, for the benefit of the newcomers. Both pledged their help but like Stuart and Brenda they could come up with very few names. Dan's sister Marie was suggested but Donny explained the move to Blackpool and the absence of any presence on social media. A private detective was proposed which seemed like a good idea but Brenda pointed out that Marie might not be cooperative, while Ronny warned she might even lodge a claim of her own.

# Chapter 33

'That was Simple Minds. I never get tired of hearing that song. 'They Promised You a Miracle', I promised you a very special guest and here he is.' The track was still fading in the background as the presenter spoke. 'I only have Stuart Williamson sitting beside me. That's right *the* Stuart Williamson, Scotland's legendary record producer. Welcome to the show, Stuart.'

'Thanks very much Tom. It's a pleasure to be here.'

'Now if there is any one out there that does not know the name Stuart Williamson then believe me you will be more than familiar with his work. In the studio tonight is only the man who wrote and produced 'Over the Castle Wall'. And he didn't stop there, he was also the producer on 'Turn to Me', 'Brooklyn Heights', 'The Chase', I could go on and on. Eight number one records, another thirty-two in the top twenty and three nominations for Grammy Awards. That's enough from me, lets hear from the man himself. Tell me Stuart just how many tracks have you produced?'

'Over a thousand Tom.'

'That is unbelievable.'

'It could have been more. There were a lot of great songs that I wanted to record but for various reasons it never got done.'

'How's that Stuart?'

'Mostly because I had other projects on the go. After 'Turn to You' and 'The Chase' I became known for power-pop so that's the kind of work I kept getting offered. So I didn't always get the chance to record the music I wanted to.'

'But you're doing that now?'

'That's right. I've collected all these great songs over the years and now I want to match them up to the right artist.'

'So will it be something that comes out under your own name this time?'

'Yes. It will be called 'Stuart Williamson and Friends.'

'Any friends you can tell us about?'

'Afraid not. Not at this stage. I am still finalizing the selections for the first album.'

'So there will be more than one album?'

'Definitely. The first one should be out by the end of summer.'

'And is that what has brought you back to Glasgow?'

'Well partly. There has always been great talent here. I have some people in mind. It all depends what songs I decide to record first, then it's a case of matching them to a suitable band or solo artist.'

'Any names you can tell us?'

'Too early for that Tom, but it would be great to work with some Glasgow musicians again.' Stuart winced at the clumsy link. Tom took it in his stride

'Because you started in Glasgow, didn't you?'

'I did, yes, back in the seventies. I had my own band, before leaving for London.'

'Now, not a lot of people know that,' Tom attempted a Michael Caine impression. 'That's because back in the day you were not known as Stuart Williamson, were you?'

'No, my real name is actually William Stewart. It's a long story.'

'And your band was called?'

'The Willie Stewart Band.'

'What else. If anyone out there remembers the Willie Stewart Band we want to hear from you. The phone lines are now open.' Tom reeled off the number, 'Meanwhile here's the Baggies with their number one hit, Over the Castle Wall.'

The track was already cued up to play. Tom pressed the button as he finished talking and the famous drum intro burst into life. The presenter indicated it was safe to remove headphones and talk.

'That went well. When the calls start coming in we will work the conversation round to....' Tom consulted the notes he had taken earlier when he had met Stuart to make preparations for the show.

'It's Dan.'

'We'll work the conversation round to Dan.'

Stuart had readily agreed to go on the radio when Pat and Donny put their plan to him. It was a natural thing to do after all, if you were in the music business and seeking publicity for a new project. As long as songwriting was not mentioned in relation to Dan, the radio appearance should not prompt the suspicions of the McSwiggens or so it was hoped.

Pat had fed the presenter and his producer the line that Stuart was back in Glasgow on a trip down memory lane, as well as scouting talent for his new project. They were told that the last time Stuart saw his old friend and band mate

Dan Quick was just before Dan went on stage as a solo performer for the first time, but unfortunately Stuart had to leave to catch a bus back to London, so never got to hear his friend perform. When the presenter heard that Dan had died in an accident a few days later he could barely conceal his delight at being gifted such good material for his show and wanted all the tragic details surrounding Dan's death.

While his most famous track was broadcast over West Central Scotland, Stuart supplied the presenter with some facts about the song. When the monitor screen indicated that only twelve seconds of the track remained. Tom put his headphones back on and prompted Stuart to do the same.

'What a great record that is. Am I right in thinking Stuart, that the drummer was none other than Ronnie Gibson, who operates the Big Beat music shop in the Trongate?'

'Yes that was Ronnie. It was actually just me and Ronnie that played on the record apart from the singer Gordon Cottle.'

'Yes, the Baggies had more or less split up at that point.'

'That's right. Everyone apart from the singer had gone back to Birmingham.'

'But they all came back to appear on Top of the Pops though they didn't actually play on the record?'

'Not the first time that has happened.'

'No it is not.'

'At least the singer in the Baggies actually performed on the record. More than can be said for some bands.'

'True, true. We'll say no more.' Tom decided to abandon this negative thread.

'I think we'll go to the first caller.' Tom consulted the

screen. 'We have Brendan from Pollok. You're through to the Tom Martin show. Tell me Brendan, what's your memories of the Willie Stewart Band?'

'I remember seeing the band round about nineteen seventy-six, seventy-seven. It was in the Doune Castle in Shawlands.'

'Do you remember that gig Stewart?' the presenter cut in.

'Hello Brendan, thanks for calling in. That was actually a regular date for us, we played there many times.'

'You were some band by the way. Especially the guitar playing.'

Tom butted in again. 'Was it you Stuart who played lead guitar?' The presenter had spotted the opportunity of steering the conversation in the desired direction.

'I did a bit Tom but I think Brendan would mostly be thinking of Dan Quick. He was a great player and the youngest member of the band. If you remember us for the guitar playing Brendan, it would be Dan's playing you remember.'

'I remember you were both good.'

'Very kind of you to say so Brendan, but Dan was the man with the guitar skills.'

'What did Dan do after the band split?' the presenter interjected. At the same time he nodded towards Stuart's microphone and widened his eyes, indicating this was his opportunity.

'Sadly Dan did not get the chance to fulfil his potential. He died in a road accident not long after the band split.'

'Oh I didn't know that,' the caller revealed. Brendan sounded sad and at a loss for what to say next.'

Tom was not going to let the sombre tone continue any

longer and seized control of the situation. 'Thanks Brendan for reminding us about the talent of the late Dan Quick. Let's listen to Jessica by the Almond Brothers Band, a staple in the Willie Stewart Band set, I think I'm right in saying Stuart?'

'That's right Tom, it really showed Dan's guitar skills.'

'Remember the phone lines are open. Perhaps you remember Dan playing this great guitar piece, better known as the theme tune to Top Gear.' Tom displayed both thumbs up and once more removed his headphones.

'Thanks.'

'No problem, we're all pros here,' replied Tom with a wink. On the other side of the glass, the producer was priming callers to talk only about Dan.

Over the next hour, Stuart supplied the tittle tattle expected of him. He had come armed with his best anecdotes from a forty year career, and allowed himself to be a little less discreet than was his usual style. Revelations were restricted to those about Americans who Stuart felt were unlikely to listen to local radio from Glasgow. If they were already dead, so much the better.

Donny listened to the show with Colette, sitting in her Land Rover parked on Albion Street. It was Songwriters Club open-mike night again.

The club was still enjoying a revival in numbers post Kate Rydelle though the press maintained the same lack of interest it had always shown. Billy Bongo had at least exerted his authority over the microphone hoggers by stating at the start of the night, that everyone had five minutes, no matter how long the song or how vital they felt the need to supply an introduction. Donny and Colette had both secured spots early on, while the club was very busy. Both promised to return later to support those at the end of Billy's list.

Outside they listened as Tom Martin milked the tragic tale of a young life cut short for all it was worth, and the calls kept coming in. The presenter had at the same time skilfully prevented Stuart from appealing for witnesses to Dan's performance at the Ship, experience telling him that once a guest got the plug they wanted they lost interest in the interview. There was only ten minutes of the program left when he eventually got to the point.

'Am I right in saying Stuart, that Dan was starting a solo career and you missed his first and only gig because you had to catch a train?'

'It was a bus actually, the overnight bus back to London. What happened was we were in the Ship waiting to see some old friends of ours play but they were late and the manager asked if me and Dan would step in and do a few songs. As I said I couldn't stay but Dan said he would do it.'

'And you never heard anything?'

'No. I was climbing the stairs as Dan was getting ready to start.'

'Well listeners, can anyone help out Stuart by telling him how Dan got on. Meanwhile let's listen to Stuart's first American number one, Brooklyn Heights'

Donny looked at his watch and shook his head 'There will only be five minutes left after that track. They have left it too late.'

'You never know,' Colette answered more in hope than anything else.

# Chapter 34

Tom Martin thanked his guest for coming on the program. 'It was a good show, you did really well. Those anecdotes were very funny. You certainly know some people, Stuart. It was like a who's who of pop history.'

'Thanks. If you have been in the business as long as I have you get to meet a lot of people. By the law of averages, some turn out to be famous one day.'

'Well the listeners certainly liked it. That's some of the best numbers we've ever had for a phone-in. Thanks again.'

'No problem.' Stuart was hiding his disappointment with how things had gone. It may have been interesting for the listeners and he did get some plugs in for his new project, but that had not been the point of going on the radio. By the time the presenter got round to specifically asking for calls about Dan's performance in the Ship Inn, the show was nearly over. When a caller was eventually put on air, she talked and talked and talked. 'Dan was amazing, the night was amazing, the band had always been amazing.' Could she remember any amazing details? No.

When the producer of the show led Stuart down the corridor on his way out he was tempted to say 'you made a right mess of that' but decided, what's the point. When she tapped in the code to the security door that led Stuart back to the reception area, all he said was, 'thanks for having me.' Pat was waiting for him.

'Sorry Pat, I screwed up. I should have saw what they were up to and made the appeal myself when I had the microphone.'

'What are you talking about? It went great.'

'What, one caller who knew nothing?'

Pat held up a sheet of paper. 'I've got four names and their phone numbers. That was always the plan. The comic turn at the end was selected half an hour ago. I doubt she was even there that night. This is what we came for.' Pat again held up the list. Every caller was asked if they were present that night. I've got a waitress that worked at the Ship with her sister. Two punters and a roadie for the band that never turned up. He told the producer you would remember him if they said tattoo. Do you?'

'Yeah I think I do actually. Jimmy something, he was called. I'm astonished he is still alive. They should have put him on instead of that idiot.'

'Well, no. The band never did turn up, a breakdown on the motorway, but he claimed to be a good friend of Dan's and said he was at his funeral.'

'Have you spoken to him?'

'No, it's in the notes here. I only got them two minutes ago. I thought the best thing would be to call all four of them and say I am doing a piece for the paper, which is true, this will make a fantastic story. I'm hoping I can even sell it on to the nationals when this is all sorted out. It is one incredible tale.'

'Please wait till I am safely back in the States before you do that.'

'It could generate some cracking publicity for you.'

'As long as I live to make use of it. No, you wait till I am on that plane.'

Both men laughed, though none really thought it funny. Geordie McSwiggen was a dangerous man to tackle and they both knew it.

'Listen the car is outside waiting for us. Are you going back to the hotel?'

'I better Pat. I've got some calls to make. It's only three in the afternoon in L.A.'

'I'll call these numbers on the way and see what we come up with.'

Pat sat in the back seat talking on the phone while Stuart sat in the front chatting to the driver.

The waitress remembered the night well. She said Dan played for nearly an hour, before a mobile disco was brought in to cover the rest of the evening. She remembered that Dan did play his own compositions but only because the manager had not been happy about it. She could not however, remember anything about the songs he sang but said she would ask her sister if she remembered anything. Pat asked for the sister's number but that was refused. He was told to phone back the next day. The two punters could not remember much beyond that Dan was on the stage playing an acoustic guitar, which was unique for the rock pub. They had recognized Dan from his days in the Willie Stewart Band. There was no answer from the tattooed roadie.

'You're not having much luck Pat?'

'I'll keep trying the roadie's number and talk to the waitress again tomorrow.'

The car supplied by the radio station delivered Stuart back to the Radisson. Pat asked to be dropped off at Blackfriars.

. . .

Will and Geordie listened to the broadcast together. Father and son had been in each others company since five that evening. It had been the longest time they had spent together that Will could remember and for the first time he believed what his mother had always said, he was not missing much. It was slowly dawning on the son just how uncultured, uninformed and down right uninteresting his father really was.

Geordie was staying in a small, top floor flat off Nicolson Street in Edinburgh, kept for when he needed to disappear. The neighbouring apartments had a high turnover of tenants, either let to students, workers on short term contracts or listed on Airbnb. Nobody noticed that one flat was always empty.

Glasgow had become a dangerous place in the past thirty-six hours and not just for Geordie. Ricky, his one time associate, was having to confront the flaw in his strategy. Previously he had been part of a gang of four. Geordie, Andy, Johnboy and himself. Now it was just him, and his stint at the garage had broadcast that fact. Rivals subdued for many years had suddenly become emboldened. For Geordie the problems started almost immediately after news of the body in the car broke. Several other cars in the forecourt had been vandalised before the police had even departed the crime scene. The whole lot, sixty-three cars in total, were hastily transported away, to be sold at auction. The three pubs Geordie had held onto in the city centre, were shut at short notice for 'refurbishment', as a precaution. The rental properties were more a problem for the tenants and the insurance companies, which just left those wanting to settle old scores in a more personal fashion, hence the move to Edinburgh.

Geordie would have joined Jackie in Florida a week earlier than had been planned, if it were not for the problem with Kate Rydelle. Many of his other interests had either been wound-up, sold or passed to Andy as part of the deal Geordie had struck. Anything not yet dealt with was left in the hands of Geordie's lawyer Angus Johnston.

Will had driven through from Glasgow in a silver VW Golf. Geordie had told him where to find it, parked in the Merchant City, complete with residents parking permit. Will thought the precaution unnecessary, Geordie insisted it was not.

When Will arrived, he found his father watching Pointless on a huge, flat screen TV. Any time Geordie proffered an answer, which was not often, it was the most obvious one scoring the highest number of points. The gangster was particularly weak on politics failing to name a single members of Tony Blair's first Cabinet. When Will said he would go out and get some food in, he discovered his father did not like Indian, Chinese or even Italian. Will was dispatched to a Sainsbury's Local with a shopping list comprising, principally of Heinz tomato soup and plain white bread. Will added some items of his own to the list. His father was not impressed by his choices.

Kate Rydelle's managers had listened to the Tom Martin

show with little comment between them. When the program ended, Will spoke first.'It could be what Cathy said.'

'Maybe.' Geordie retrieved Cathy's phone from his pocket and looked again at the three emails sent from California. It was true that Stuart Williamson and his P.A. did not seem to be interested in Cathy as a songwriter but only as a performer. That was good news, his son reassured him. Once they had used up all of Daniel Quick's songs, there was every chance that Kate Rydelle could continue making records. 'Why did they keep mentioning that night? They're fishing for something.'

'Fishing for what?'

'I don't know, but something. Why did he not go back to America yesterday?'

'We have only got that reporter's word that he was going back yesterday.' Will was becoming exasperated with his father, he was always suspicious, always seeing problems.

'I should have told you to bring those books'

'The diaries?'

'Aye.'

'You read them, you know what they say.'

'There were two pages torn out.'

'There were lots of pages torn out, they were his old school notebooks. The boy tore out all the used pages.'

'But the two pages after the last bit of writing? The lassie could have done that.'

'I told you I asked her. She said it was like that when she got it.'

'But I didnae ask her. Get her. Bring her here.'

'Its past eleven.'

'I want to speak to her.'

'What about Gaz? He's in Glasgow.'

'I want to leave Gaz where he is. You'll need to go.'

At that moment Gaz was sitting in a black Mini Cooper, two cars behind Colette's Land Rover on Albion Street.

# Chapter 35

When Donny and Colette pushed open the heavy doors to the Blackfriars basement they were shocked to find the place half empty. It was like pre Kate Rydelle times. Billy Bongo came over to meet them.

'What happened? The place was jumping when we left.'

'Newcomers! Once they realized that the press weren't coming and there were no talent scouts, they decided it wasn't worth the wait for a five minute spot. You can go back up if you want? I've got plenty spaces now.'

Donny accepted the offer. He had been neglecting his own songwriting lately.

'What about you Colette?'

'No thanks Billy, I'll leave it this time.' Colette never got up to perform off the cuff, she always prepared in advance.

'OK Donny you should be up in about twenty minutes.'

'I'll be ready.' It was Colette's turn to get the drinks in and she made her way to the deserted bar. Donny returned to the seat he had vacated an hour earlier, sat back and surveyed the scene. It was only the die-hards like himself who were left, the old dependables.

By the time Donny was called to the stage, the crowd had dwindled to little more than twenty. It was exactly like old times. Undeterred, he chose two of his most upbeat songs and decided to give it laldy.

Mid-way through the second song, Pat walked in displaying a thumbs up, indicating good news, then joined Colette at the back of the room.

'Hi Colette. Did you hear the program?'

'We heard.' There was disappointment in her voice.

'No, it worked. Well I got some members anyway.'

'We thought there was just that one caller.'

'No, she was picked to go on air for entertainment value only.'

Donny's efforts were rewarded with a warm display of appreciation, from Pat and Colette, that is. The rest of the audience barely made a sound. When Donny reached the faraway table he addressed Pat. 'Have you found something?'

'There are two good leads. A waitress in the bar that night and a roadie that claims to be a friend of Dan's.'

'Have you spoken to them yet?'

'Yeah, spoken to them both. The waitress can't remember too much but her sister also worked there. I'll call her back tomorrow once she has contacted the sister.'

'And the roadie?'

'Only got through to him five minutes ago. He's in town just now drinking and he has agreed to meet us in Maggie Mays at twelve. Are you coming?'

'Sure.'

'Count me out boys.'

Good nights said, Colette climbed into her Land Rover and drove off up Albion Street. Pat and Donny walked in the opposite direction paying no attention to the black Mini

Cooper or its occupants.

Maggie Mays is a late licensed bar sitting on the corner of Albion Street and Trongate. At ten minutes to twelve it was almost empty, half an hour later it would be packed to capacity.

'How will you recognize him?'

'You won't believe this but he said he looks like Ronnie Wood.'

'And he's proud of that?'

'I don't know but he should stand out.'

The look-alike was indeed easy to spot. At twelve midnight on the button, Jimmy, the tattooed roadie was granted entry by two bouncers whose decision was touch and go. Had the Stones septuagenarian guitarist not so famously taken such great care of his health and shunned the excesses of the rock and roll lifestyle, then Jimmy could very well have been his doppelganger. The man was painfully thin and looked ill. He was wearing a denim jacket with the sleeves cut off over a multicoloured shirt, black 501s and pointed toed boots with Cuban heels.

'Jimmy?'

'Aye. How you doing? Are you Pat?'

'Yeah, and this is Donny'

'Are you here to be interviewed as well?' Jimmy had spotted Donny's guitar case.

'He has already done his, I'm all ready for yours.'

'Eh, we never discussed a fee on the phone.'

'All depends if it gets printed or not. I'll go fifty-fifty on any fee if the interview makes it to print. It will depend on what you can tell me.'

'Well..." Jimmy was scratching the top of head, drawing attention to his grey roots.

'It is the same deal for Donny here.' Jimmy looked at Donny who nodded in confirmation.

Jimmy was thinking about it.

'What do you say I get you a drink in and we can get started?'

That did the trick. 'OK. I'll hae a Southern Comfort, a double. I'll go for a pee first.'

'An interview? What did you tell him?'

'Don't ask. I had to get him here, didn't I.'

When Jimmy returned Pat took him to a sofa and went though the pretence of conducting an interview. Donny remained at the bar, not noticing the casually dressed young man watching him and Pat, from a discrete distance. Had the man worn a suit, Donny would have recognized him as one of Kate Rydelle's minders at the Newcomers awards.

Donny watched Pat frantically scribble strange hieroglyphics in his note pad. He knew his friend did not do shorthand but Jimmy seemed impressed by it and was responding enthusiastically, his arms waving in the air, helping him tell his story. Donny sipped his pint alone for quarter of an hour before Pat returned. 'Anything?'

'Could be. Let's go or we'll be lumbered with Jimmy. I'll tell you outside.'

Pat gave a wave to the interviewee who was confidently pushing his way though the throng to reach the bar. Someone else with equal self-assurance was clearing a path for Jimmy. 'It's a double Southern Comfort isn't it?'

The few seconds it took to reach the door and pass through was about all the suspense Donny could bear.

Taxis were arriving, spilling more late-night drinkers onto the already crowded pavement, as bouncers decided what level of drunkenness was acceptable. Pat led Donny a little further along the street away from the mayhem.

'Well, what did you find out?'

'A lot more about drugs and groupies than I did before.'

'Stop taking the piss. What about Dan? What did he tell you?'

'Well he didn't know anything about Dan's songs but he did have one good suggestion.'

'What?'

'He said there was a blind boy that came into the Ship and would record the bands on a cassette recorder.'

'Did Jimmy think he would still have the recordings?' Donny thought it sounded a long shot at best.

'That's the thing. He collected the recordings, knocked out the wee plastic bit, so it could never be recorded over.'

'What about a name?'

'No, Jimmy couldn't remember but I think I might know of this guy. There is someone who puts live recordings of old bands at the Apollo on Youtube. It sounds like the same person. Jimmy said he would go to any big concerts in town and record them too.'

'I'll check out his Youtube channel, there may be some contact details.'

'Don't forget the waitress, they all knew this boy in the Ship apparently. I'll call her first thing and let you know what she says.'

'Great. Listen better call it a night. I'm going to grab one of these taxis.'

'I'll do the same. Speak to you tomorrow.'

While Donny's taxi performed a U turn, Jimmy could be seen through the bar's windows in animated conversation with someone. Probably bragging to someone about the 'interview', Donny wrongly assumed.

# Chapter 36

Geordie stood looking out of the window on to Nicolson Square. Edinburgh was an exotic place to him, different from Glasgow, like a foreign country. He had made a half-hearted attempt at checking the parked cars for any signs of occupancy, but in truth he was just killing time. The TV had been switched off because Geordie did not really watch television, there was no Hi-Fi system in the flat because he did not listen to music, and there were no books because he didn't read them. There was a laptop but that was only used for business.

Geordie had spent the past hour, since Will departed, mulling over events. Of all the things that irked him, Ricky was top of the list and he had already decided the arse hole would pay for his stupid stunt, when the time was right. With the garage and three city centre pubs, temporarily closed for business, Geordie was losing money, a state of affairs he was totally unfamiliar with.

His thoughts on the small crisis within his new venture were mixed. The three weeks, since relinquishing control of his empire, had been the dullest he could remember. His son had the Kate Rydelle bandwagon running like clockwork and requiring no input from him, apart from forking out the cash. Sunday night's difficulties had served as something of a stimulant. Now, there were again people to size up, figure out what they wanted, discover what made them tick and decide how they will be kept in check.

Music was an alien world to Geordie but the same was true of heroin in the early eighties and he soon figured out what made that world go round. Will had spent the greater part of the previous two days on the internet trying to find out what had motivated Williamson, Cullen and now McNeil to stick their noses in where it was not wanted. Geordie, without any research, concluded it was money in the case of the producer guy, glory for the reporter and jealousy for the songwriter. When the phone rang it was picked up with enthusiasm. 'What's happening?'

'McNeil and the reporter went on to Maggie Mays and met this old bloke. The reporter talked to him on his own. The old bloke said it was about an article on Dan Quick. I've got the guy inside now.'

'Where are the other two?'

'Went away in two different taxis, probably gone home. Mick is following the reporter.'

'Good boy. What's this old bloke saying?'

Gaz selected the relevant facts from Jimmy's fantasy account, which were that Dan Quick performed at the Ship Inn on Sauchihall Street, two nights before his death and that there was a chance someone recorded it.

'The two fucking pages. Ah bloody knew it'

'What Boss?'

'Never mind. Get back in and find out if he can tell you anything else, and make sure we know where to find him. One more thing, how long since McNeil left in the taxi?'

'Fifteen minutes Boss'

'I'll get back to you.' Geordie ended the call and picked up another phone. Cathy had supplied Donny's address along with his mobile and land-line numbers. That information was in his pocket. The land-line number was tapped in. After three rings, it was answered. Geordie broke the connection immediately, the songwriter was at home, that was all he needed to know.

Geordie slumped into an armchair to think. Someone going to the trouble of recording the boy, meant there was every possibility that he had changed his mind and had decided his songs were after all 'perfect' and ready to be shared with the world. It was not a good time for that information to come out. The two deals already signed had yet to yield any money and there was no telling how the public might react. At least the copyright deal was watertight, which was something, but the publicity would be bad. It could finish Kate Rydelle and he had gambled too much already on that project. Any story in the papers would also bring the sister out of the woodwork and if the original story didn't finish things, her story would. Geordie smiled to himself. He could always send Gaz on a winters break to Blackpool.

The Glaswegian rose and once more stared out of the window onto the deserted Edinburgh street. Will would be back with Cathy in an hour or so. The son had strict instructions not to let on why she had been summoned to Edinburgh. Keep them in the dark, that's how Geordie liked it when he had a question that needed answering. 'Hello Cathy. Come in, come in. Sorry I had to drag you here at this time of night. Can I get you anything, something to drink?' Big smiles then look her straight in the eye. 'Where's the missing pages?' Geordie had employed that particular ruse many times, if they tried to lie, he always knew. Cathy would be easy meat.

Selecting the first phone, Geordie tapped the last number from the history.

'Boss. Give me a minute I'll need to go outside.' Geordie moved the phone away from his ear. At arms length he could still make out Bowie's 'Suffragette City' before the din suddenly disappeared.

'That's me, Boss.'

'I need you to go up to Bearsden. The place will be empty, you'll need to break in.'

'Right Boss.'

'Do you remember the notebooks?'

'Aye Boss."

'I'm looking for two torn out pages. Cathy might have hidden them somewhere.'

'Right Boss.' Geordie ended the call without any further instructions.

# Chapter 37

Pat waited till half past nine before calling the waitress. He had arranged to call at ten but he could wait no longer. 'Hello, it's Pat Cullen here, you said to phone back this morning.'

'You're too early, I've no' spoke to her yet.'

'Sorry, but there is something else you might be able to help me with.'

'What is it?'

'I have been talking to a former roadie and he said there was a boy that came into the Ship that would record the bands. I think he was blind.'

'Peter Wilson. I forgot about Peter.'

'You remember him?'

'Oh aye he came in with his sister June, she was a friend of mine. They lived round the corner from me.'

'Do you think he might have recorded that night?'

'Oh if he was in, he probably did.'

'Is Peter still around?'

'Aye, he is married now. They live out past Cambuslang.'

'Do you have an address for them?'

'I send a Christmas card but I don't like giving out someone's address.'

'What about a telephone number?'

'I'll phone and see if there is anyone in. I don't know though, Peter still works. I'll pass on your number. It will be up to him if he wants to talk.'

Pat accepted the offer, there was no choice, and waited for the return call. It only took ten minutes for the phone to ring and it was Peter himself on the line.

'Thanks for calling Peter. Do you have time to talk?'

'Yes I'm not working today. Winding down they call it. Angela said you're from the paper, interested in my recordings?'

'Who?'

'Angela that worked in the Ship Inn.'

'Of course. I'm a freelance journalist Peter, I'm interested in one particular recording at the moment.'

'Dan Quick.1978. I've got it.'

'The recording? You've checked already?'

'Everything is in chronological order, it only took a minute.'

'What did you think of it?'

'I don't remember. I probably never listened to the tape. Acoustic was not my cup of tea. Rock was always my thing. I can make you a copy.' Pat asked if they could borrow the original cassette and Peter agreed.

Donny got the call at nine fifty.

'Bingo!'

'Don't tell me you found the blind boy?'

'I have and I've just been talking to him'

'And he has a recording?'

'Yes. He still has it and he is willing to lend it to us.'

'I can't believe it. When are you meeting him?'

'Not me. This is your show Donny. You did all the spade work.'

'And Colette.'

'And Colette. It's got to be one of you that picks up the cassette. He's expecting you this morning.'

Donny came off the phone in something approaching a trance. They had done it. He and Colette had actually done it. He called his friend immediately, knowing there would be no answer. He left the message, 'found the blind boy, picking up cassette this morning'. Donny had briefed her about the meeting with Jimmy via text on the way home the night before, receiving an acknowledgement in a text timed at 07.33.

Donny thought about breakfast but decided against it. He tapped the postcode that Pat provided into google to find out where he was going, discovering it was a new estate in Newton only five stops from Mount Florida station and a place he was familiar with. One of the function band's rare pub gigs had been in the Newton Arms for their Christmas Jumper night, the week before Christmas.

Donny quickly grabbed his coat and keys and left the flat.

Doubting the wisdom of forgoing breakfast, Donny bought a cheese and ham baguette and a bottle of water from Greggs on the way to the station. He did not notice the young man lingering in the doorway of the Tesco Local next door.

Gaz had been busy in the past twenty-four hours. For payment upfront and the promise of more to come, he had recruited enough bodies to protect the garage and the three pubs. All would now reopen. Tam had been persuaded to come back and Geordie had the prodigal son watching the Radisson Hotel. Watching Pat Cullen would have been the preferred choice but the reporter may have recognized Tam from their first encounter outside the newspaper office on Sunday night. Gaz's best work however had been done in Bearsden in the early hours. After twenty minutes of searching, he returned to the guitar case, one of the first places he had looked. This time however he looked inside the instrument itself. The folded up piece of paper was removed, laid out flat on the floor, photographed and sent to his boss.

From the top of the station steps, Gaz observed Donny waiting on platform 2. There were two trains due on that platform, Gaz bought a return ticket to the terminus on each line, his bearing being enough to deter any questions from the ticket clerk. He then waited, out of sight, on platform 1. The first train to arrive was for Neilston and Gaz moved just enough to see that Donny was not boarding. When the Newton train arrived, Gaz got on the carriage behind his mark.

The train out of the city centre had few passengers at that time of day. When it terminated at Newton, there were only three people left. Gaz remained on the train till Donny and the third passenger, a middle aged woman with two heavy looking bags, had passed, then followed them out of the station. Donny turned right, walked fifty metres to a roundabout, then turned right again. Gaz waited inside the station entrance till Donny was out of sight, then walked briskly to the corner.

There was a long stretch of empty road, the railway line

on one side and back gardens on the other.

Gaz approached the woman. 'You're struggling there, do you want a hand with the bags?'

'Ah widnae mind son. You're a gent.' Gaz took charge of the bags, it would look better, should Donny turn round.

'It's mostly tins, I go to the supermarket in Burnside. That's why it's so heavy.'

'It's nae bother.'

Gaz needn't have worried, Donny was oblivious to the couple, forty metres behind him. It had started to rain and he had pulled up his collar, as well as tilting his head down. When Donny passed the Newton Arms, he promised himself a lunch on the way back. It would also be an opportunity to line up another gig.

At the junction past the pub, Donny turned left. Gaz made an excuse and abruptly handed the woman her bags, then sprinted to the corner. Donny had crossed the road and was about to turn right. Gaz reached the intersection in time to see Donny standing at the front door of the third house.

It was Peter's wife who answered. 'You must be Donny?'

'Yes. I think Peter is expecting me.'

'He is. Come in, my name's Louise. Let me take your coat, you're soaking wet.' Donny handed over his duffel coat before being led upstairs.

Peter heard him coming. 'Come in. I've just finished recording the cassette on to the computer.' Peter had risen from his seat and met Donny at the door. There were no obvious signs that the man was blind. Louise retreated back downstairs, promising to put the kettle on.

'This is some set up you have here.' The room had been

kitted out with all manner of recording equipment, a reel to reel tape recorder, cassette recorder, mini disc plus a mixing desk and a pc that seemed to be operated by some kind of braille keyboard, all connected to an impressive amplifier and speaker combination. The walls of the room were shelved floor to ceiling, housing recordings in all the different formats.

'It keeps me out of mischief. Do you want to hear?'

'Are you kidding?'

'I'm burning a CD for you, we can listen to that downstairs.' Donny's heart was pounding. He could not have been more excited had he been offered the holy grail.

'I brought something for you. It's the first song that Dan wrote, thought you might be interested.' Donny handed over the reel of tape.

'Thanks. I'll stick it on to record while we have our tea.'

On cue, Louise shouted that tea was ready. Peter ejected the CD from the computer then handed it and the original cassette to Donny.

'You go on down, I'll set up your tape to record, I'll be down in a minute.'

Once tea was poured and biscuits offered, the play button on the CD player was at last pressed and Dan Quick's voice filled the room. With the knowledge that this was Dan's first public appearance and that it was performed under the influence of four or five pints, Peter listened with renewed interest. While Peter struggled to ignore the under par performance, Donny heard pure genius, even if the timing was a little shaky and the lyrics slurred. The third song was 'The Die is Cast' and it was way better than the versions from nineteen seventy-five.

Donny really wanted to listen all the way to the end but felt he was imposing on Peter and Louise. There were also lessons in the afternoon that he had yet to prepare for.

'Thanks for the tea Louise, I better be going. I've taken up enough of your time.' Turning to Peter, 'I can't thank you enough, this is exactly what we have been looking for.'

'You can listen a bit longer, I'm in no hurry.'

'I'd love to but I've got lessons planned and people to talk to. I better get on with it.'

Peter stopped the CD, ejected it from the machine and handed it to Donny

Louise said, 'I'll see you to the door.' She walked her visitor all the way to the pavement.

'Don't forget this.' Peter was at the door holding aloft the old reel of tape. With his other hand he was clutching the door frame. For the first time it was obvious that he was blind. Donny walked back to collect the tape, placing it back in the inside pocket of his coat.

'Did you get it all recorded?'

'All done.'

Donny headed back in the direction of the station deciding to skip the visit to the pub. He wanted to get home and play the remainder of the CD.

At the first corner, on the opposite side of the road, someone was standing beside a car talking on a phone. Donny paid him no attention but when he glanced to the right before crossing, something clicked. Gaz was wearing a short black coat, white shirt and dark trousers. From a short distance away, it looked like a suit and that was what nudged Donny's memory. He was one of the two minders who kept Kate Rydelle away from the press at the Concert Hall.

Donny tried to quicken his pace, without his watcher noticing. At the next junction, he made a show of checking all around for traffic. The man had not got into the car but was walking in his direction, some fifty metres behind.

The Newton Arms was only a minute away, beyond that was two hundred metres of empty road. Donny remained on the opposite side from the pub maintaining a steady pace. When he drew level with the hostelry, he quickly crossed over and entered. Donny chose the bar to the right, remembering that it had a door to the beer garden, He had no plan but thought the room with an escape route would be the better choice. The bar was not in use. Donny sprinted to the door leading to the garden. It was locked. He turned back the way he had come, his only option now was safety in numbers within the main bar. A creek from a door indicated someone had entered or left the pub. If it was someone coming in, it could only be his pursuer.

Donny pulled up part of the bench seating and deposited the cassette and CD in the void before securing the seat back into position.

Gaz had chosen the door on the left. He scanned the room, the songwriter guy was not present, that left the toilets and the other bar. Gaz turned towards the connecting door.

'The garden bar's closed mate.' Gaz ignored the bar man.

It was all over in a matter of seconds, none of the lunch time clientèle saw a thing and the barman who did witness it was not at all sure what he had seen.

When Gaz pulled the door open he came face to face

with Donny. One swift blow to the solar plexus with the right hand before the left hand snatched the five inch reel from inside Donny's coat. The assailant then walked casually out of the pub, before the barman had time to react.

'Did he just punch you?'

It was a minute before Donny could speak. When he did speak he played down the incident. 'It's nothing, don't worry.'

'It doesn't look like nothing mate.'

'Please, I'll be all right in a minute.'

The owner's wife insisted on making Donny a cup of tea which he gratefully accepted. He was now remembering that a man boarded the train at Mount Florida, same dark clothing, same build. That meant he had been followed from the flat, they knew where he lived. If they were following him, who else were they following? Donny took his tea to a quiet spot saying he had to call someone.

The first call was to Colette and surprisingly she answered.

'I was about to call you. I've stopped for lunch. Did you get it?'

'Yeah I got it but one of McSwiggen's boys has just tried to grab it'.

'What! Are you all right?'

'I'm fine. He took the old reel, I had it with me. He must have seen Peter hand it back to me. Peter's the man that recorded Dan at the Ship Inn.'

'And what about that tape?'

'I hid it before he hit me.'

'How did they find out what you were doing?'

'I think he followed me from the flat. Goodness knows how long they have been watching.'

Colette said she would get away and come to pick him up. Donny accepted, it would be best to wait for reinforcements before retrieving the cassette from its hiding place.

The next call was to Pat.

'It's got to be Jimmy,' Pat asserted. 'If you were followed to Maggie Mays, they could have talked to Jimmy after we left. I'll call him and find out.'

Donny sipped his tea and did some thinking. Cathy had a machine that could play old tape reels, the McSwiggens would soon find out they had the wrong tape. The cassette would need to be put out of their reach, and fast.

Stuart Williamson was called next. Pat had already told him about the recording at the Ship, Donny brought him up to speed with subsequent events.

'If you can get the cassette to me I can get it out of the country. Once that's done everyone should be safe. I can get straight on to the airline. I could be on my way within the hour. I've got Will McSwiggen's number. I'll call him from the departure lounge and tell him I have the recording from 1978.'

There was certainly logic in what Stuart was saying. With the tape beyond reach, there would be no point in coming after anybody.

'OK, you arrange a flight and call me back.'

Pat called to confirm the information had indeed come from Jimmy. 'They either followed you from Blackfriars or they were following me from the radio station, either way they will know Colette's Land Rover.'

Donny relayed Stuart's offer to get the cassette out of the country. Pat was relieved to hear it. Donny then called Colette to warn her about the car.

# Chapter 38

Content of missing pages

19 May

Bombshell!!!!! Brenda told me she's pregnant.

She wants us to get a house and is at me again to stop trying to form another band.

Thought about telling her about my songs but decided that would not be a good idea. She still thinks it is all a waste of time.

Will tell her when I get a record contract. Some hope?

Making up a tape to give to Willie, if I get the chance to see him while he is up.

DESPERATE TIMES? Can't keep them to myself for ever. I'd like Willie to be the first to hear them.

22 May

Willie phoned.

Still calling himself Stuart Williamson down there. What a guy.

He has gone all Punk. He said he has cut his hair short and got rid of all his old clothes. Looking forward to seeing him though, if only so I can take the piss out of his new style.

Meeting him in the Ship tomorrow night before he gets the overnight bus back to London. He has been up talking to the Alert, thinks he can get them a deal but only if they start playing Punk. Thinks I should do the same. Fat chance!

Told him that shite isn't music, but Willie says the record companies and the music press are interested in nothing else at the moment. They have all gone mad!

Don't know if there is any point now in

giving him the cassette I made up. It would
be funny though to see if he recognises
that Cut And Run is all about him. I'll see
how it goes.

Maybe some of the faster tunes could be
made into Punk. Scrub that last idea.
Nooooooo way

Going to take the acoustic along, could
be the chance of a wee jam in the dressing
room before the boys go on.

Will bumped the Golf over the pavement and into the guest car park. There were only three spaces. The other two were taken up by a Toyota pick-up truck with a flat tyre and a double wardrobe missing both its doors. At twenty minutes past midday, the curtains on the dirty windows were all still drawn. Will and Geordie had been on the road for five hours. Will could have made productive use of those hours, there was so much to do, but Geordie 'didnae like driving on the motorway.'

Gaz's photographs of the torn out pages had arrived at Nicolson Square before Cathy did, which was just as well for her. Geordie's instinctive reaction would have been to hurt her. Instead of a sore face, Cathy got a superior room at the Carlton Hotel on North Bridge, five minutes from Geordie's bolt hole. Will had dumped her there saying only, 'change of plan. Geordie can't see you tonight.' Cathy did not seek further explanation. A night in a smart hotel was an unexpected surprise and the longer Geordie McSwiggen was unable to see her the better.

News that the songwriter and the reporter were on the trail of a possible recording of Dan Quick from 1978 could only mean he played his own songs that night in the Ship Inn, which would explain the radio show. Williamson was clearly orchestrating everything and he was looking for anyone who witnessed that performance. It would be impossible to stop that information coming out one way or another. This revelation and the likely existence of a living heir, other than Dan's sister, were received calmly by the younger McSwiggen who had done all his panicking on

Sunday night. Now that the worst had happened, he would have to deal with it. Geordie on the other hand was close to exploding.

While the father detailed what he would do to that bitch, the son considered only what needed to be done to keep the Kate Rydelle bandwagon on the road. It would mean repositioning his artist in the marketplace of course, and an artist that did not write their own material did not garner the same respect in the music world as one who did, but there were ways to mitigate such an impediment. Expensive ways, but needs must. Expectations on earning would need to be downgraded and the record company and publishers will not be happy but on the other hand Kate's popularity was increasing faster than he had expected. It might just be possible to make this work.

While Geordie cursed and drank lager from cans, Will had been on the phone getting people out of bed.

Geordie opened the passenger door of the Golf. 'I'll deal with this.'

'Remember what Johnston said.'

'The lawyer works for me, no' the other way round. You get yourself a cappuccino.' Geordie said it in a dismissive tone, then more menacingly. 'It might take me time to explain things here.'

It was not an area of Blackpool that did cappuccino but Will felt like stretching his legs anyway. He walked in the direction of the prom while at the same time checking texts and emails. Will had the publicist and two helpers up all night adjusting the Kate Rydelle back story, to accommodate the new realities. Contacts in the media had also been asked for favours.

Geordie had grudgingly accepted Will's assessment of the situation. If Dan had played his songs to an audience in 1978, it would eventually get out that Kate Rydelle was no songwriter. There were at least three people determined to prove that fact.

Will knew the longer they kept up the pretence, the greater the backlash.

The one thing Geordie was not prepared to concede though, was copyright ownership.

# Chapter 39

Crawford Cunningham pulled up on Carmunnock Road, the opposite side of the block from Donny's flat. Colette was in the passenger seat, Donny was in the back. The Land Rover had been left at the Royal Infirmary should anyone be watching. Earlier in the day, Colette had left by the Alexandra Parade entrance, far away from the Coronary Unit and the car park, before dashing into her friend's Corsa.

'Are you sure about this?' said Colette as Donny opened the back door, 'You could get yourself badly hurt, or worse.'

'Don't exaggerate. I'll be fine. If they are watching the flat all they are going to see is me returning home. When people start arriving with guitar cases, they will know that I'm working and remember that Pat will be over soon, so we can look after each other.'

'You won't do anything stupid, like go out to the pub.'

'We won't cross the door before midday tomorrow.'

'Make sure you stick to that.'

'And you make sure you stay at your parents tonight.'

'I will.'

'I'll make sure she does,' said Crawford. 'I'll drive her there straight from the airport.'

It had been agreed that Crawford would deliver the cassette to Stuart, handing it to him immediately before he goes through security. It had to be assumed Colette would be recognized if McSwiggen's men were watching.

'Text me when you have passed over the cassette.' Donny pushed the car door shut and started to walk in the direction of his flat.

Pat arrived at Kingspark Road as Donny's first pupil of the day was leaving. They passed each other on the stairs. Pat had travelled by taxi and though he tried to check, he was not sure if he was followed or not. There had been one stop on the way, to buy a copy of the evening paper.

When Donny opened the door, Pat had his phone pressed to his ear and he was evidently involved in an argument. He thrust the newspaper into Donny's hand breaking from his conversation only to say, "read that."

Donny looked at the headline.

# Over The Castle Wall creator pours his heart out over old friend

Pat remained in the hall shouting angrily into his phone while Donny went to the living room to read the article.

Last night legendary record producer and the man behind classic Punk anthem 'Over The Castle Wall' was in tears on the Tom Martin show as they remembered his former band mate, the revered Glasgow songwriter and guitarist Dan Quick. Dan's life was tragically cut short, just as he was on the verge of stardom. He was killed in a horrific road accident in the city's East End. Tragedy struck only two days after Williamson had travelled up from London to attend Dan's first gig as a solo artist at one of Glasgow's premier music venues of the seventies, The Ship Inn on Sauchiehall Street. Williamson would not be drawn on whether he had travelled to Glasgow that fateful night to sign Dan to his record label, though sources close to the star revealed this was very likely. The station's switchboard was jammed as fans reminisced on the young musician's talent. All lamented his early passing. A spokesperson for Glasgow Fm confirmed that it was the most calls they had ever taken for a phone-in program.

Dan's music could have been lost forever were it not for the the determination of our very own Kate Rydelle, winner of the Newcomers Award at this years Celtic Connections festival. She has single-handedly fought the music establishment to make sure people get to hear Dan's great songs.

It was Kate that sent a demo of one of Dan's songs to the producer. He was so knocked out by its quality he offered her the chance to record with him.

An industry insider said 'If it were not for Kate Rydelle, nobody would have heard of Dan's music. It was her that had faith. We can't thank her enough.' A spokesperson for Kate Rydelle said it was the singer's mission to bring the music of Daniel Quick to the public's attention. Such is the singer/songwriters faith in Dan's music she will forsake her own songs in order to dedicate her entire debut album to the music of Daniel Quick.

**Even before the Tom Martin show had ended, a facebook page had been opened in Dan's memory. One fan who had been on the phones last night said, "As soon as I heard his name it all came flooding back. If Stuart and Dan had made records together, they could have been bigger than the Beatles.' Many praised Kate Rydelle for her tireless efforts in promoting Dan's music.**

The accompanying picture showed a band on a dimly-lit stage. The hair was long and the jeans were flared indicating the seventies, pre-punk. There was no caption saying it was Daniel Quick and Stuart Williamson.

When Donny had finished reading he could not decide if it was good news or bad. The real writer had been given full credit for his labour. Was that not what he had wanted? Also it would appear to pave the way for Brenda and Daniela to pursue their claim. A result! Or was it?

Pat ended his call in frustration, cutting off the other person in mid-sentence.

'What did you make of that then?'

'I'm not sure what to think.'

'It's total bullshit that's what.'

'But it's out there. Daniel Quick is the writer, not Kate Rydelle. Isn't that what we have been trying to prove?'

'I suppose so.' Pat's chance of landing that big story had

gone. He would just have to let it go.

'How did they find out?'

'Who?'

'The paper. How did they find out about Dan and the songs?'

'Don't you get it.'

'Get what?'

'There is no byline. That's what I have been on the phone about.'

'What do you mean?'

Pat pointed to the foot of the article. 'There is no name. It was emailed this morning at 5am, the whole thing complete, and some stupid bastard put it straight in today's edition. They never checked the facts and of course they never asked the freelancer, who had done the last piece on Kate Rydelle.'

'Do you mean Will McSwiggen got that article in the paper?'

'That's exactly what I mean. You have got to hand it to him, he can work fast. Jimmy only spilled the beans at half twelve last night and he manages to beat the deadline for printing today.'

Donny and Pat checked the Kate Rydelle website and her social media. All had been subtly altered to acknowledge Daniel Quick.

Donny took out his phone. As soon as Brenda answered, he knew she had already seen the paper. There was noise in the background, happy noise.

'Daniela and the family are here, and a few neighbours and friends.'

Donny did his best to warn her that Geordie McSwiggen

was still out there but it fell on deaf ears. He did not get the chance to explain the background to the story in the newspaper, Brenda was too keen to get on with the party and he only managed to squeeze in that she should say nothing till she had heard from Stuart.

Donny slumped in a chair feeling a little deflated. He was not angry with Brenda, how could he be. That article had probably righted a thousand wrongs for her and her daughter, especially Daniela. She had to grow up without her father and had to watch her mother struggle. They were happy tonight and he was glad.


Stuart had managed to get a flight via Paris. It would mean a fifteen hour wait at Charles de Gaulle but it was the best he could get. As he wheeled his large case to the waiting taxis, there would be little doubt as to where he was heading.

If anyone was watching, Stuart could not see them. 'The airport, driver.'

The cabbie knew a big tipper when he saw one and was out of his seat in a flash to help with the case. Once the cab was out in the traffic and had turned two corners, Stuart leaned forward and said, 'Sorry driver. It's Edinburgh airport. Is that all right?'

'Certainly sir. It will take about an hour.' The driver did not think it necessary to indicate the cost.

Crawford was already in position when Stuart approached. The package was passed without fuss, before Stuart scanned his boarding pass and passed through the barrier.

Once Stuart had cleared security and had passed through

Duty Free, he asked for directions to the Fringe Bar. There were only a few customers inside. It was easy to spot the one he had arranged to meet.

'Hello Kate.'

# Chapter 40

Two weeks later.

**'For your safety and comfort please remain seated with your seatbelt fastened until the Captain turns off the Fasten Seat Belt sign.'**

Gillian Carswell was happy to follow the instruction. Seated in the second row, she did not need to rush, she would be one of the first passengers off the plane. The lawyer had paid for that advantage.

The trip to Glasgow was inconvenient but necessary. With emails going unanswered and phone calls not being returned, she had no alternative but to seek a face to face meeting with Kate Rydelle's former management. Instead she was told to speak to their lawyer.

Gillian Carswell had contacted the publisher and record company and informed them that copyright ownership was being claimed by her client. Royalties collection agencies worldwide had also been alerted. All that remained was to secure the release of Kate Rydelle from her management contract with the McSwiggens. Ms Carswell hoped to be back in central London by mid-afternoon.

Despite the hassle of coming up to Scotland on a Monday morning, she had resolved to remain magnanimous. Mr McSwiggen's lawyer had agreed to meet her and she would be gracious, despite the discourtesies shown to her, and afford the man the satisfaction of playing his only remaining card. Her briefcase already contained a generous written offer for the purchase of Kate Rydelle's contract. The sum, in her opinion, represented more than adequate compensation for any investment George and William McSwiggen had made in the singer's career. There would be no mention of all that had been printed in the papers these past few days, just make the deal and get away.

Stuart Williamson had engaged the lawyer on behalf of himself, Brenda and Daniela with the agreement that fees would be paid out of future royalties. Gillian Carswell was expensive but worth it, she was efficient and got things right first time. That's why clients like Stuart kept coming back.

The taxi dropped the lawyer on West George Street in the city centre. She recognized the premises of McQuarry and Johnston from a street view search of the address. The internet had revealed little other information about the firm. Inside the building was all dark wood and leather, and unsettlingly quiet. She was fifteen minutes early for her eleven o'clock appointment.

It was not until eleven on the dot that the visitor was shown into the office of Angus Johnston. What had kept the lawyer occupied the previous quarter of an hour she did not know, for no client had left and his large desk was completely clear.

'Good morning, Ms Carswell. Please take a seat.'

'Thank you.'

'You wish to discuss Kate Rydelle's contract, I

understand.'

'Yes and some other things. Can I come straight to the point?'

'Please do.'

'I represent someone who is prepared to buy out Ms Rydelles's contract.'

'Mr Williamson, I presume.'

'I can't say.'

'My client is willing to release Ms Rydelle from her contract. Once suitable compensation is paid.'

'Of course. I am sure we can reach an agreement. Do you have a figure in mind?'

'I do. Do you have an offer prepared?'

'I do. There are one or two loose ends I'd like to clear up first if that's all right. It is in relation to my other clients who are now the copyright holders. I think it will be quite straight forward. '

'Oh, things are often less straight forward than one might wish when it comes to copyright.' There was a flatness to the man's speech that made him difficult to read. Was it simply the voice of experience or was it a veiled threat? Gillian Carswell could not decide but thought she better find out.

'Surely you are not disputing ownership?'

'No Ms Carswell, that is what you are doing.'

'You can't be serious. There is physical proof that Daniel Quick performed in nineteen seventy-eight, the songs later credited to K. Rydelle and W. McSwiggen. There are also a growing number of witnesses coming forward.' Ms Carswell could have added, 'thanks to the publicity your client generated,' but thought better of it.

'Yes.'

'Brenda McGuire was the long term girlfriend of Daniel Quick and she was pregnant when he died. There are any number of people who can confirm these facts. I am assuming you don't dispute any of the facts.'

'It is not for me to accept or dispute facts, that would be for others.'

'If your client is still claiming ownership he will be laughed out of court and substantial costs will be awarded against him.'

'Thank you for the advice on costs, I will bear that in mind. I must inform you that George and William McSwiggen purchased from Marie Blackman, formerly Quick, the rights to all the works of her late brother. He did so in good faith'

Gillian Carswell did not see that one coming. She had been briefed on the existence of such a contract but was astonished to hear McSwiggen was standing by it.

'They were not hers to sell.'

'That is not what my clients believe. Also, are you aware of Elizabeth Anderson? She has been in the papers this week. Her mother has come forward to claim that Elizabeth, born in May nineteen seventy-eight, is also the daughter of Daniel Quick. I have heard though the grapevine that her solicitor is preparing to go to court at the earliest opportunity.'

Gillian Carswell had acquainted herself with all Kate Rydelle related publicity. She viewed that particular article as just another way of keeping the story going and doubted if such a person even existed. Brenda had been furious, dismissing the claim as rubbish. It took a great deal of persuading to stop her contacting the press herself.

Ms Carswell's face gave nothing away. 'I am aware of that ridiculous claim. Do they have any proof that would stand up in court?'

'As much as you do Ms Carswell.' There was more than a degree of smugness in Angus Johnston's demeanour.

'This could all be settled with a DNA test of course.'

'I agree. Perhaps Elizabeth Anderson intends to present such evidence.'

'Has Marie Blackman agreed to a test?'

'I have no idea, she is not a client of mine.'

Gillian Carswell did make it back to central London for a little after three as planned, but without any agreement being reached. On leaving the premises of McQuarry and Johnston, she noted the accuracy of the description 'Criminal Lawyers' on the brass plate. Angus Johnston had savoured her discomfort as she was shown a copy of the contract between George McSwiggen and Marie Blackman. It was a very thorough piece of work. All relevant checks regarding identity and eligibility had been taken. Angus Johnston maintained his flat expression as he handed over a copy of Mrs Blackman's address in Blackpool. A private investigator would be sent to find her, but Gillian Carswell already knew it would be a waste of time.

Stuart Williamson received the email containing a five page attachment while he was eating breakfast. He went straight to his den and printed out the document, before reading it. The report was not what he had expected or hoped for. The McSwiggens were asking for four million pounds to release Kate Rydelle from her contract, more than five times his offer and way above what he could afford. For Brenda and Daniela it was no longer a straight forward case of establishing ownership of copyright. It was now a case of disproving someone else's claim, something entirely different. Stuart had some experience of this particular scenario. Lawyers could muddy the waters and tie you up in knots for years. It was more often than not, the person with the deepest pockets that won in the end. Gillian Carswell had laid out a strategy if she were to keep going but pointed out that the present arrangement on fees could not continue.

This was not good news. Stuart had no funds to fight a legal case on behalf of Brenda and Daniela. The money to buy out Kate Rydelle's management contract had been a loan, conditional on getting the singer's signature on a recording contract. That was a conversation he was not looking forward to.

Kate had contacted him in desperation, fearing for her life after Geordie had found out that she had kept from him the knowledge that Dan most likely had a child. She had to take a huge risk returning to Bearsden in order to pick up her passport. Stuart had promised to look after her and that she could continue her career in Los Angeles. That would now be on hold, until she was released from her contract. It could be done through the courts but that would take time and money. Stuart and Kate had neither.

Stuart looked at the clock. He would give himself a few hours to digest the information before making calls to Glasgow.

It was four hours later, before Donny got the call.

'Stuart. How're you doing?'

'Not good Donny, not good at all.' Stuart explained all that had been happening and relayed his lawyer's gloomy assessment.

'There's no way Brenda and Daniela are going to walk away.'

'I know what you're saying Donny but there could be no choice. Without the sister agreeing to a DNA test, there will be no absolute proof.'

'Surely the courts could force her to give a sample.'

'I don't know Donny but if she can't be found, does it matter? I phoned you first, I'm not looking forward to telling Brenda.'

'Don't phone Brenda, not yet.'

'She'll need to know. Probably the sooner the better.'

'It's half nine here. Give me a couple of hours. Promise you won't call Brenda till you hear from me. Two hours and I'll call you back.'

'What's this about Donny?'

'Two hours and I'll explain.'

'OK, two hours.'

Donny ended the call then called Colette. 'Hi. I know it's late but can you meet me in the Scotia, say in half an hour.'

'I take it something's happened.'

'Oh yes.'

'Problems?'

'Big problems, but I might have the solution. I'll explain when I see you.'

Donny and Colette took seats at the same table where they had sat exactly three weeks earlier. Donny was still relaying his conversation with Stuart when the Briggait

Blues Band arrived, he had been banking on them rehearsing every Monday.'

'Mikey,' shouted Donny. The guitarist turned round and smiled.

'Still looking then?'

'One last piece of the jigsaw and that's me done.'

'What's that then?'

'The guy that sold you the guitar. I need to talk to him.'

'I told you he's a shifty wee prick. There's no point in talking to him you can't believe a word he says'

'That doesn't matter, he's the only person that's got what I need. Do you still have a number for him.?'

Mikey shrugged his shoulders and scrolled through his contacts. 'You're in luck.'

# Chapter 41

One month later.

'Let me help with the bag, it looks heavy.'

Brenda stopped and looked at the man. He was her age and better dressed than the other men on Duke Street at ten in the morning, but he did not look as friendly. 'I can manage fine, thanks.'

'Ah insist.' The plastic bag was yanked from Brenda's hand. She did not resist. Brenda somehow knew who the man was. She did not know how she knew, she just did.

'Let me introduce myself.'

'Don't bother. I know who you are.'

'Me and you Brenda, have things to discuss .'

'Well I'm busy if you don't mind.' Brenda spoke with a courage she did not know she had.

'It'll no' take long. I brought you a present.' Geordie offered Brenda the battered notebook he held in his hand. 'It's your auld boyfriend's.' Brenda hesitated then accepted the gift, tears welling up in her eyes. 'There's another two you can have and a pile o' papers. Do you want the tapes and the recorder? They're nae use tae me.'

'I've heard everything that was on the tapes.'

'Thought it would be a nice for you to have the originals but suit yersel'. Let's walk. It's this way you stay, is it no'.'

Geordie started to walk swinging the plastic bag as he went. Brenda followed.

'If it's about Dan's songs, you'll need to talk to my lawyer.'

'London lawyers don't understand Glasgow. Better we sort it out ourselves. We're both victims Brenda, victims of a fraud. I bought the rights in good faith.' Geordie removed an envelope from his inside pocket. 'Here, it's the contract Marie signed. Ye can read it at your leisure but you'll see, she states clearly that Dan had nae children.'

'She was lying.' Geordie and Brenda had turned into Whitevale Street. They were only two minutes from her house.

'She did lie, Brenda. Now if she had told me about Daniela and yourself I would have bought the rights from you.'

'And what makes you think I would have sold?'

'In October Brenda?' Geordie had stopped and was blocking Brenda's path. He looked her straight in the eye. 'Back in October, what would you have done? Honestly Brenda, what would you have done?'

'Ah don't know.' Brenda's voice was weak, Geordie had made his point.

'You can see how it is from my point of view. Ah'm a business man, Ah don't like losing money.'

'I'm sorry if you have lost money but that's not my fault, is it?'

'Ah don't blame you Brenda, or your daughter. Daniela's her name, that's right is it no'. Ah hear she has a lovely wee family out in East Kilbride.' Brenda's legs were instantly weak as she thought of her grandchildren and she had to

348

stop walking. It was the effect Geordie had intended. 'Some would say it's the guitar teacher and his pretty wee side-kick that are to blame.' Geordie paused to let the implication sink in. Brenda got the message. 'In ten minutes Brenda my lawyer Angus Johnston will phone you. He will make you an offer to get this all sorted out. I really hope you accept it.'

They had reached the entrance to Brenda's flat. Geordie handed back the bag of shopping, then continued down the street in the direction of Gallowgate, where a car was waiting.

# Chapter 42

Six months later.

Donny's last lesson of the day had ended, leaving just enough time for a shower and something to eat before heading into town for The Songwriters Club annual Covers Night. He had persuaded Colette to join forces with him and perform as a duo. They would be covering the songs of Dan Quick.

Out on Kingspark Road, Donny glanced at the bus stop opposite, there was no-one waiting. He decided to walk to the Battlefield Rest and catch a bus there. He did not want to be late, not with Dan's partner and daughter in attendance.

At eight thirty in the evening, diners were still sitting at tables outside the restaurant, it had been the warmest day of the year so far. Doors and windows were all fully open. Those waiting at the bus stop were also soaking up the last of the evening sun. Donny remembered how different the scene had looked the night Dan Quick's songs were first performed at the Songwriters Club.

Donny's career as a songwriter and musician was picking up. While he had been immersed in the Kate Rydelle mystery, the submission he had made to the film production company was passing though the numerous stages of the selection process. It was chosen to play over the opening credits. It was a low budget Scottish film, but a film nevertheless, and Donny's first proper success as a songwriter. Colette too was finding success with her writing. She gave up the tribute band and started to record her own songs with a new band. The band were also doing regular gigs and hoped to soon release their debut E.P. Brenda had passed on all of Dan's notes and recordings for Donny and Colette to study and they both now had a mentor in the shape of Stuart Williamson.

Daniel Blackman, nephew of Dan Quick eagerly agreed to supply a sample for DNA testing, but only after a payment of five hundred pounds was promised. The results confirmed he was a close relative of Daniela and pointed to high probability that Daniela was the daughter of his uncle. The information however, did not deliver the knockout blow hoped for.

Brenda and Daniela reluctantly accepted Geordie's offer. It was preferable to the long, drawn-out legal battle threatened by Angus Johnston. A legal battle was something they could ill afford, a point the lawyer had alluded to. It was also better than the prospect of looking over their shoulders for the rest of their lives. More importantly it meant that everyone who had helped would be safe.

On Gillian Carswell's second visit to the premises of McQuarry and Johnston on West George Street, she expected to find Mr Johnston in a more conciliatory frame of mind. She was wrong. An improved offer of one and a half million dollars from Stuart Williamson to buy out Kate Rydelle's contract was turned down flat. Mr Johnston also pointed out that the name Kate Rydelle was a registered trademark owned by his client and insisted that the singer stop using that name. It was further made clear that as fifty percent owner of the copyright to Daniel Quick's songs, George McSwiggen would not allow Cathy Riddle first recording of any of the writer's works.

What was agreed was that Will McSwiggen and Gillian Carswell would jointly control and manage the copyright. Their first task was to sort out the publishing deal with Mi.P. When a Glasgow daily ran an article on businessman George McSwiggen relocating to Florida, everyone connected with exposing the truth, slept easier in their beds.

'Main Street' was released as a single on the 28th of May sung by America's rising star, Tom Gill. It reached number one in both the UK and US charts and in eight other countries around the world. 'Now That I Found You' was recently released as a single by country band South Ridge and is well on its way to emulating the success of 'Main Street'. To date another five Daniel Quick songs have been recorded by some of the biggest names in the industry. A request by Stuart Williamson to produce 'Cut and Run' had been granted by Gillian Carswell and Will McSwiggen, only to be blocked by Geordie.

Blackfriars basement was close to capacity by the time Donny arrived. Billy Bongo was on stage conducting a sound check. Colette was seated with Pat Cullen and they had saved three other seats.

'I didn't think the press would be covering the event.'

'It's worth a paragraph or two in the blog.' Pat did get his big story into print and it landed him a contract with the paper. An uplifting account of how two Glasgow musicians solved the mystery of the genius songwriter whose work lay undiscovered under a bed in Bridgeton for forty years.

'Donny! You got a minute?' It was Billy Bongo calling from the stage. Donny went over and Billy guided him to the back. 'Have you heard anything more about Cathy?'

'Still planning to play some dates in America according to Stuart Williamson, but it will have to be under her own name. Without the stage name and Daniel Quick's songs I don't fancy her chances.'

'So that's it then. Her career, finished just like that.' Billy raised his arm and clicked his fingers.

'Looks like it.' Donny tried to show sympathy for Billy's sake. He wondered how things might have turned out for Cathy if only she had played it straight. It was her after all that first recognised the quality of Dan's songs. If it was not for Cathy, the songs would probably have been lost forever. Now, thanks to Geordie's block on using the name Kate Rydelle or recording any of the songs that she had made her own, her career was effectively over. 'She'll probably end up back back in Oban with her mother. Maybe she will turn up here some night.'

'And sing what?' Billy had a smile on his face.

'Well, let's hope it's Covers Night if she does turn up.'

Brenda and Daniela turned up ten minutes before Donny and Colette took to the stage. They had been looking at houses, the first royalty cheques would be arriving soon. A large house where Brenda could live with Daniela and her family was the only purchase considered so far. The publishing company had offered an advance but it had been declined. It was not the way Brenda or Daniela did things. They had waited forty years, another few months would not hurt them.

# EPILOGUE

Cathy had split her time between watching the boats come and go from the harbour and watching the house. Each time she checked, there were still two cars outside. Cathy wanted only one person to be at home when she rang the doorbell.

It was a quarter to five before one of the cars pulled out of the driveway. Cathy watched as it turned right and headed up the coast road. It was what she had been waiting for. Walking up to the house her heart began to beat faster. Cathy had rehearsed all afternoon what she would say but now she couldn't remember any of it. 'Come on, you can do this,' she told herself.

Cathy took in a deep breath and pressed the bell. It seemed like an age before footsteps could be heard on the other side of the door. Would she be recognised with her dyed black hair? The shutters on the adjacent window moved an inch, then the door was opened.

'Can I help you?'

'Don't you recognise me?'

'Oh it's you. Did your American fancy man throw you out?' Cathy did not show any emotion. 'If you're thinking you can come back, forget it.'

'I'm not asking to come back.'

'So what is it you want then?'

'Nothing.'

'Then why are you here?'

Cathy removed her right hand from the jacket she was wearing and quickly raised it up, then pulled the trigger three times in rapid succession.

Glasgow's former crime boss lay dying on the floor of his Florida home.

The End

Cathy Riddle is as far away from Florida and Glasgow as she can get. The one thing she can't escape though, is her conscience. The story continues in,

# The Busker of Buenos Aires.

**Frank Chambers**

Printed in Great Britain
by Amazon

72210627R00218